Previously published Worldwide Mystery titles by
SHELDON RUSSELL

THE YARD DOG
THE INSANE TRAIN

DEAD MAN'S TUNNEL

Sheldon Russell

W🌐RLDWIDE®

TORONTO • NEW YORK • LONDON
AMSTERDAM • PARIS • SYDNEY • HAMBURG
STOCKHOLM • ATHENS • TOKYO • MILAN
MADRID • WARSAW • BUDAPEST • AUCKLAND

Dedicated to Felicia, Ayden and Ava

Recycling programs
for this product may
not exist in your area.

Dead Man's Tunnel

A Worldwide Mystery/April 2015

First published by Minotaur Books, an imprint of
St. Martin's Press

ISBN-13: 978-0-373-26941-9

Copyright © 2012 by Sheldon Russell

Printed in U.S.A.

Acknowledgments

Thank you to my editor, Daniela Rapp, to my agents, Michael and Susan Morgan Farris, and to the other professionals at Minotaur Books, dream makers all.

PROLOGUE

HE TOUCHED HIS eyelids to make certain they were open. Blackness spilled into his lungs and rose into the cavities of his body. He gasped and reached out for the boundaries, but only emptiness reached back. A draft swept over him from somewhere, and he shivered.

Such cold had been with him always, and he struggled to remember where. His name came first: Joseph. It came clear and true and in his own voice. His breath hung in the morning like frozen puffs of smoke, and his sister, sucking on icy fingers, whined and wiped her nose on her sleeve. And he heard his father cutting wood down by the boat dock. Chips flew up from his ax and spun out onto the ice. The smell of pine filled the air.

But that was then. He was not that boy now but Sergeant Joseph Erikson, U.S. Army, assigned to guard the Johnson Canyon rail tunnel in Arizona. Even though the war had ended with the dropping of the atomic bomb, Joseph was lost now in the universe.

He held his hands in front of him and stared into the blackness. For an instant he saw them, it seemed so, but then they were gone. Looking up, he searched for the stars, those points of light that placed him in the cosmos, but they, too, were gone.

He touched the wound behind his ear, and something hot settled into his stomach. He shivered again, not from the cold but from the memory that crept in from the darkness like a troll.

The sound behind him on the trestle had been someone breathing, that much he remembered, and the blow had exploded in his skull with a flash.

Had he pitched over the side of the trestle and into the abyss below? Often in the lonely hours of the guardhouse he'd thought about the falling, the certain death that awaited in the rocks, the terror, the monstrous seconds between life and death.

He smelled creosote and oil, smells of the tracks and the trestle. But where were the stars, the desert night? Suddenly his mouth went dry. Out here only one place obliterated the sky and the sounds of life. Only the tunnel could plunge a man into blackness as suffocating as death.

He'd double-checked the schedule of the westbound before making his rounds. There were three hours to spare, if she came on time. The old steamers were often late, but the diesels sometimes were even early; a man could just never be certain. But then how long had he been here? How long had he lain unconscious in the darkness?

The tension in his neck crawled up into his scalp. The railroad had chiseled the Johnson Canyon Tunnel through solid basalt, only a few hundred feet in length, but with a curve at its center. They built a trestle as wobbly as an orange crate to its entrance. Trains raced from the mountains, the trestle quivering and creaking and clouds of dirt sifting into the canyon below as the trains shot into the tunnel at breakneck speeds. They plunged down a three-degree grade, their wheels screeching and smoking against the weight. The tracks shuddered beneath them, and rail spikes shot into the air like popcorn.

The ones climbing, however, groaned up the steepest ascent in North America, at times moving no faster than a man could walk. They came with pushers at their backs, their engines hauling against the tons of rolling stock.

Section men hated the tunnel for obvious reasons, and the track foreman cussed her and the sons of bitches who built her every chance he got.

Sergeant Erikson knew the tunnel better than anyone alive. He'd walked it every day from end to end. At midpoint, all light blinked away, and the world went silent. The air fell still as death, and panic welled up in even the bravest of souls.

Even so, a man caught between the wall of the tunnel and an oncoming train had no chance. Once, a section hand, who had fallen asleep in the tunnel, awoke to a westbound making the curve. He'd lost his rib cage on a ladder rung.

Either way, Sergeant Joseph Erikson had no intentions of sticking around for a freighter plunging down the mountain like the end of the world. Dark or not, there were two ways out of a tunnel, and he figured to take one of them.

As he turned, he spilled forward into the railbedding. Pain pooled in his groin. Groping in the darkness, he found the chains threaded beneath the tracks and wrapped about his ankles.

"My God," he said, and his voice echoed back.

He'd been trussed between the rails like a butchering hog. He took a deep breath. The railroaders were forever pulling shit. Once, they nailed the guardhouse door shut, and another time they put a porcupine in the outhouse. But this had gone too far. This time he intended to settle with the foreman.

"Hey," he shouted, and his voice pinged away.

A tingle buzzed against his ankles, like a fly in a windowpane. He knelt and put his ear against the track. It smelled of grease and metal, and a rumble traveled in from somewhere far away. Fear rushed through his veins, and his ears rang.

"No," he said.

The wail of the engine drifted down from the mountain. Her rumble gathered up in the sky, and her brakes smoked against the plunging grade. And when her lights dropped over the precipice, shadows leapt up the canyon wall. The earth trembled, and the roar of engines filled the desert as the train shot into the darkness of the Johnson Canyon Tunnel.

ONE

THE QUARTER FELL out of Hook Runyon's britches and rolled the length of the caboose, clattering against the wall. The bastards hadn't bothered to park the caboose on level ground when they'd sided it at West's Salvage Yard in Ash Fork, Arizona.

He searched for his arm prosthesis, finding it under his bunk. "Goddang it, Mixer," he said. "Leave my arm the hell alone." Mixer, his dog, peeked up through his brows and clopped his tail against the floor. He'd been known to steal things, given the opportunity, and had recently taken a liking to Hook's prosthesis. Just last week Hook had found it buried in the right-of-way alongside a porkchop bone. Had he not seen the hook peeking out of the sand, it would have been gone forever.

A meager salary, a passion for rare books, and an occasional drink or two had not lent itself to buying a new prosthetic. He'd managed his own repairs on the thing over the years, though it suffered from the lack of proper maintenance.

Scrap West, the owner of the salvage yard, told him the prosthetic looked like a bent crankshaft, and why didn't he just throw it in the shredder along with the rest of the junk? When Hook suggested that he might just throw him in with it, Scrap grinned and walked away.

Hook strapped on the arm before lighting a cigarette.

He put on coffee and sat down at the table to watch the sunrise over the mountain of squashed cars. Beams of sunlight skittered about in the broken windshields and off a thousand shattered mirrors. By midmorning, the yard would swelter under the sun. By noon, heat would quiver up from the piles of junk. And by day's end, gasoline fumes would hang over the yard in a blue pall.

Hook poured his coffee and sipped at the lip of his cup. He set it aside to cool. Opening his latest acquisition, a mint copy of Steinbeck's *Cannery Row,* he thumbed through the pages. He liked Steinbeck's stuff, the dialogue was like listening to secrets through an open window. Someday Steinbeck's writings would go for a fortune. But then what true collector sold his books? He'd rather sell his soul, or his children's souls. In any event, finding such a book in such condition had been lucky, given his exile in the desert.

Scrap West had complained to the railroad about thieves stealing copper off loaded cars. So Eddic Preston, the divisional supervisor, being an intemperate sort, and still hot over a little incident Hook had been involved in back in Amarillo, had taken the opportunity to even things up by putting him on the salvage detail.

The night of the Amarillo incident, Hook had found the door seal broken on a sided car. Concerned that she'd be emptied out by morning, he'd asked the switchman to side her closer in to the yard office. In the process, the switchman stuck his thumb in the coupler and pulled back a stub. He commenced screaming and cussing, his stump spewing blood the whole time.

Hook rushed in to help stop the bleeding. But when the sided car rumbled by, he realized he'd failed to set the brakes. The car rolled out onto the main line, gathering up speed as she went. She passed the yard office and then the depot, and by the time she hit the stockyard switch, she sped along at twenty miles an hour. Hook watched in disbelief as she teetered and then heaved over onto her side like a shot elephant.

Half her contents, army surplus items, mostly cots, boots, and mess hall equipment, spilled across the tracks, shutting down the main line. About the time they'd loaded the switchman into an ambulance, a thunderstorm blew in from the southwest and soaked the spilled freight.

St. John's Orphanage offered to bring out their truck and load up the supplies if they could have them, so Hook had agreed, finding it prudent to not close the main line.

In the end, no one ever located the switchman's thumb, and Eddie Preston had been less than understanding about the whole situation. In short, that's why Hook now stood guard over a mile-long line of scrap cars in Arizona.

Having seniority over every other cinder dick on the force, Hook had threatened to file a complaint with the big boys. But Eddie suggested that an investigation might turn up more than Hook could explain and that if he was smart, which he doubted, he'd keep his mouth shut.

The result had been three of the longest months in Hook's life. In all that time he'd nabbed only a couple boys stealing spike kegs and a drunk sleeping under one of the cars.

Pusher engines, old steamers for the most part, idled day and night on the siding across from his caboose. Used for boosting hotshots up the grade, they sometimes doubled as switch engines for moving cars in and out of the salvage yard. The chug and thump of their engines never ceased, and Hook had not had a good night's sleep since his arrival.

Hook sought out the engineers for news, brief encounters with civilization, inasmuch as engineers could be considered civil. Beyond that, he passed his days alone or in the company of Scrap West, which came mostly to the same thing.

Even Mixer, who loved a good fight more than life itself, had succumbed to the isolation, resorting to extended naps, sometimes spiraling into deep unconsciousness. Several times Hook had checked his breathing to make certain he hadn't died.

Hook poured himself another cup of coffee and lit a cigarette. As soon as the sun was fully up, he'd make his rounds. He'd noticed footprints in the sand down by the switch and again where a load of copper had been sided.

As he sat back down at the table, the engine on Scrap's twenty-five-ton crane roared into life. The noise rode down the tracks and set up miniature tidal waves in Hook's coffee.

Scrap had purchased the crane from the army and took pride in what he considered to be the bargain of the century. He maintained that the crane had increased his output by 25 percent and could not have been purchased anywhere else at twice the price.

Scrap never passed up a chance to make a dime, even keeping chickens in the back of the salvage yard. He claimed eggs big as basketballs and that he'd made enough from selling them to pay his monthly water bill.

Mixer, who hated the crane even more than Hook did, rolled onto his back and groaned. Once started, the roar of the engine stopped only for lunch and then again at quitting time. Now and again, a car body would plummet from the crane and crash onto the growing heap of metal.

When the crane suddenly stopped, Mixer glanced up at Hook. Within moments, a knock rattled the caboose door. Hook tucked his shirt in and opened it to find Scrap West standing with his arms folded over his chest. Scrap had been named Reginald by his mother, but hardly anybody in the world knew it. Hook knew it only because Scrap had gotten drunk one night and spilled the secret.

"Eddie Preston's on my phone," Scrap said.

"What does he want?" Hook asked.

Scrap pinched up his face, which looked a good deal like one of his wrecked cars. His nose spread out on the end like a spade and was the exact color of a radish. A scar ran through his eyebrow where a leaf spring had hit him, and his thumbnails were permanently blue from having been squashed over the years. His eyes were hard as ball bearings. He had a missing front tooth, which he covered with his hand when he grinned. Scrap claimed he'd been born with a full set of teeth, except for that particular one, and it had refused to grow even after fifty years of trying.

Scrap looked for the world like the bums Hook had run into his whole career, except beneath that beat-up mug was a brain that chugged away like a perpetual motion machine. It concocted one scheme after another in an attempt to screw the world out of yet one more dollar. Most of his schemes failed, but some didn't. Either way, it didn't matter because Scrap had already moved on to the next one.

"I ain't no goddang messenger for Division," Scrap said. "For all I know there's a call coming in on copper prices this very minute. She goes up a penny, and I lose a day's wages. On top of that, my crane's down there drinking diesel like a drunk sailor, and I'm up here talking to you."

"Hell, Scrap, you're getting free security, aren't you, not to mention all that track you pilfered off the right-of-way. I figure you owe the railroad a minute of your time."

Scrap worked the slug out of his pipe without looking up. He blew through the stem and then fished through his pockets for his tobacco.

"I did the railroad a favor moving that rail," he said, torching up his pipe. "I went in the hole on that one, I tell you. Anyway, it would have cost the railroad plenty to bring in equipment all the way from Flagstaff just to haul away that old track."

Blue smoke enveloped Scrap's head. "And you can just tell Eddie Preston these bastards are still walking off with my copper and in broad daylight, too. Maybe he should send a yard dog out here that does something other than read books and take naps."

"Maybe you could hire some extra hands, Scrap. I never knew a man any tighter in my life."

Scrap poked his finger into the bowl of his pipe before firing it up again.

"Just 'cause I wasn't raised up rotten like some I know, and just 'cause I eked out a living on what others threw away, doesn't make me tight. Makes me economical."

"Makes you tight," Hook said. "You probably got money stashed all over this junkyard."

"Maybe you ought try saving a dime yourself once in a while," he said, "instead of squandering it on old books and raw whiskey."

"One day the government's coming after their taxes, Scrap. What you going to do then?"

"What's the government got to find but my good word?"

"Not paying taxes is illegal. And what about those switch brackets down by the south entrance? Where did those come from, I wonder?"

"You just quit nosing around my stuff and spend a little more time guarding my cars."

Hook slipped on his shoes and lit a cigarette. "Come on, Mixer," he said. "We better lock up, or the silver will be missing when we get back."

Hook pushed the office door shut just as Scrap's crane fired up again. He took a deep breath and picked up the phone.

"How's it hanging, Eddie?" he said.

"Runyon, I been sitting on this phone for half an hour. You think all I have to do is to wait on you?"

"Sorry, Eddie, but my secretary couldn't make it in today."

"Cut the wisecracks, Runyon. There's been a death out at the Johnson Canyon Tunnel."

A chill ran through Hook. He hated that damn tunnel. "A death?"

"You know, when someone stops breathing, forever."

"Yeah, I know what death is, Eddie. It's working security in a junkyard."

"I want you to go check it out."

Hook lit a cigarette and watched the crane lift a wrecked Cadillac into the sky.

"And leave Scrap's copper unprotected? Jesus, Eddie, do you think that's a good idea?"

"Believe me, Runyon, I'd send someone else if I could, but that line has to be kept open. If that tunnel shuts down, the whole system goes with it."

"What do they think happened?"

"Accident, one of the military guards that's been stationed out there."

"Accident?" Hook flipped his ashes into the waste-basket and looked out the window, which was gray with smoke and dust. "How do they know?"

"A man don't stand in the middle of the tunnel in the middle of the night with a hotshot charging down-grade on purpose."

"Jesus," Hook said.

"The engineer called it in. Took him half a mile to get shut down," Eddie said. "He near fainted when he saw the guard's boot stuck on the catwalk."

"All right, Eddie. I'll take the popcar out."

The popcar, sometimes called the popper, was a small gasoline-powered trolley used mostly for track in-spections. It could be an uncomfortable ride in the des-ert but was Hook's only transportation at the moment.

"I released the engineer on to the next stop. He'll catch a hotshot back. You can talk to him then."

"Damn it, Eddie, I should take a look at things be-fore the engine's released."

"There's still another army guard assigned to duty out there. He might have some idea what's going on."

"I'll check it out, Eddie."

"This thing has to be wrapped up fast, Runyon. That line can't be tied up. It ain't the first tunnel accident out there, you know. They killed off half of Arizona building that damn thing."

"What's the rush, Eddie? The war's over, hadn't you heard? Japan has been bombed into oblivion."

"I want this thing resolved, see. On top of everything else, that line is being upgraded, and there's equipment and people. We can't shut the railroad down while you play detective."

"I *am* a detective, Eddie."

"And there's that other little problem, too," Eddie said.

Hook's pulse ticked up. Eddie had been looking to nail him for years.

"They give me a promotion over your head, Eddie?"

"In your dreams, Runyon. You might just recall dumping a boxcar back in Amarillo."

Hook lit another cigarette and watched Mixer dig through Scrap's trash.

"That switchman cut off his thumb, Eddie. What the hell was I supposed to do, let him bleed to death?"

"And deprive the railroad of paying his medical pension for the next thirty years?" Eddie said. "I should hope not."

"I'm missing an arm, Eddie. No one pays me a pension."

"That's not your biggest problem, Runyon. For example, there's that little donation of Santa Fe property you made to the St. John's Orphanage."

"They had a truck and volunteered to clean up the wreckage if they could have the goods. I had to get that line open, didn't I?"

"Oh, St. John's was real glad to get the army cots," he said.

"And the other things, too."

Mixer found Scrap's old lunch sack in the trash and proceeded to tear it open.

"What other things?" Hook asked.

"That box of army condoms the kids opened back at the orphanage. They thought they were goddang balloons. The priest said it looked like New Year's Eve.

"So the diocese calls Chicago, and Chicago calls me. Turns out everyone is unhappy."

"Jesus," Hook said.

"You've bagged your limit of Brownies for the year, Runyon. I don't know if I can head this thing off. Maybe you ought to learn the salvage business just in case you have a career change."

"I'd like to visit, Eddie, but there's a corpse waiting."

"Open and shut like they say," Eddie said.

"Yeah," Hook said. "Like they say."

TWO

BEFORE LEAVING SCRAP'S OFFICE, Hook called the operator at Ash Fork to check the board. The line was clear until two, which would give him ample time to get out to Johnson Canyon Tunnel. Maybe it wouldn't take that long to wrap things up.

Mixer, who had a gob of meringue stuck to his nose, waited for him at the door.

"All right, all right," Hook said, ruffling his head. "But you'll have to stay with the popcar."

Mixer fell in at his heels as they made their way through the yard. West's Salvage sat on the outskirts of town right next to the main line. The only way a salvage business could exist without the muscle of the railroad was if it had access to river barges, and Ash Fork was a hell of a long ways from the nearest barge.

A fence encircled the yard proper but with little effect. A side gate leading to the tracks was left open a good deal of the time. The office sat within a few yards of the main gate. In a way, it reminded Hook of the prisoner of war camps that had been built in America's interior for retaining German soldiers.

A mile-long siding ran parallel to the yard and was used for making up smelter runs. A series of shorter sidings switched off at various points for maneuvering empties and accommodating pusher engines.

The yard itself covered as much as fifteen to twenty

acres of desert scrubland. Piles of salvage in stages of disassembly covered nearly all of it. Hook's caboose had been parked in such a fashion as to expose him to the comings and goings of both the yard and the main line. The noise never ceased, and the smell of torches, gasoline, and oil permeated everything, including his clothes.

Hook stopped at the crane and signaled for Scrap to idle her down. Scrap leaned out of the cab and put his hand to his ear.

"Got an emergency," Hook hollered over the engine. "Be back before dark."

"What happened?"

"Accident. Guard out at the tunnel."

Scrap knocked out his pipe. "Been figuring it would happen sooner or later," he said.

"Keep an eye on my caboose," Hook said.

"Oh, sure, sure," he said, waving Hook off.

Hook cranked up the popcar before rolling her out onto the main line. She snuffed and coughed like an old man. The popcar was worn-out and slow, and his ears would ring like church bells by the time he got back. He'd requested a company truck, but Eddie had not been able to locate one. Scrap kept an old army jeep in the yard, but he'd sold the transmission out of it last time Hook had checked.

A one-lane road paralleled the tracks for about three miles out before curving off to skirt the roughest terrain. Even though it took a little longer by road, at least there weren't trains to worry about. No matter how many times he checked the board, uncertainty lingered. He'd worked the railroad long enough to know that people made mistakes, and meeting an oncoming train on a popcar qualified as one hell of a mistake.

Mixer jumped onto the seat. Hook throttled up and rolled off down the tracks. He dried the palm of his hand on his knee against the prospects of what awaited. The human body did not fare well against a train. The first time he'd investigated such an accident he hadn't slept for days. When he finally did, the nightmares left him shaken and sad.

Since then there had been many such investigations, but all were disturbing in their way. At least he'd learned how to keep his meal down through the process, though the nightmares still visited from time to time. Why anyone would take a chance against a train escaped him. The brutality of such a death touched everyone involved, but especially engineers. He k new hardly a single one who had not been traumatized by a fatality.

The wind blew clean and crisp as the popcar climbed the grade. She slowed to walking speed up the ascent and clattered along like an old roller skate. Mixer, asleep at the first sound of the motor, lay sprawled out on the seat next to him.

A few miles out, they passed a survey crew that had been contracted by the railroad. Hook had seen them at work for a couple of weeks now. While he hadn't been informed, a line upgrade had obviously begun in earnest.

Mixer came alive when he saw the men, and he leaned out over the popcar, barking and growling as they chugged by. One of the men shot Mixer the finger, which only increased his frenzy. When Hook scolded him, Mixer dropped back down on the seat to finish his nap.

Hook lit a cigarette and propped his foot up. The guards had been placed at the tunnel at the onset of the war with Germany.

Sabotage had been the main concern, since the closing of the tunnel would have shut down the entire northern corridor. But the scenario had always struck Hook as unlikely, even at the height of the war. But now with the bombing of Japan, it surely made no sense. But then as far as he could tell, making sense had never been a prerequisite for decisions in the army.

The tunnel, short by most standards, had been cut through solid rock at great expense in lives and money. A siding had been built on the approach to the trestle. As a train crossed over the canyon, the mountain rose up into a rock face ahead, and within moments the engineer was faced with the dangerous midtunnel curve. Add in the steepest grade in North America, and trouble of one sort or another rode through that tunnel nearly every day.

A guardhouse had been built high up on the grade near the tunnel entrance so as to oversee the canyon and trestle. On occasion, Hook would spot a guard walking the line or sitting and smoking on the guardhouse porch. One time, he sided the popcar and climbed the hill to introduce himself, but the guard had fallen asleep in his chair. Hook decided not to awaken him. Any poor bastard assigned to Johnson Canyon for the duration deserved an undisturbed nap.

As Hook reached the top of the grade, he pinched off his cigarette and dropped it onto the floor. For a brief moment, the trestle would disappear from sight below a small rise, and nothing but blue sky and open space could be seen ahead. But once over, the popcar would plunge down like a roller coaster.

The popcar groaned as she climbed the rise. Only the sheer wall of the canyon and the singular black hole of the tunnel could be seen. In that brief moment, it was as if the popcar had flown into the yawning abyss of Johnson Canyon. He'd made the trip many times now, but the sensation never diminished.

The popcar clattered and clanged as Hook brought her into the siding just short of the trestle. The siding had been built to accommodate maintenance equipment and the occasional breakdown.

Hook shut off the engine, and his ears rang in the morning stillness. The sun cut hot through the thin sky as it only could in the high desert. Mixer bailed off and commenced a search of the rocks that had slid down the canyon wall.

"Don't you run away," Hook said, checking his flashlight. Mixer stopped and looked at him for a moment before scrambling off. Mixer loved finding something obscene and smelly to retrieve for Hook's approval. It didn't matter what, whether alive or dead, or how long it may have been ripening in the sun. He preferred skunks to nearly all other prey.

Hook walked to the mouth of the tunnel and looked into the darkness. He took a moment to gather up his courage. Wiping the sweat from his forehead, he checked his watch.

At some point he'd talk to the other guard, but he wanted a look at the scene first. Clicking on his light, he stepped into the darkness. The air bled cool from out of the tunnel, and his footsteps crunched in the gravel.

Hook panned the area as he made his way down

the tracks and into the heart of the mountain. Wooden beams, so large as to leave little room between track and wall, supported the enormous weight of the overburden.

Nearly to the curve, he spotted the first signs of carnage, body fluids and flesh atomized by the collision. Experience had taught him that the point of impact, that moment when the speeding train and the body collided, often left only the smallest evidence behind. The actual remains might well have been dragged down line for miles.

Hook made a mental note of the location before kneeling to study the tracks. The rail had been gouged and scratched, and something shiny caught his eye. He took out his knife and dug it from the gravel, a metal ring of some sort, squashed and distorted by the weight of the engine.

He held it under his light. It might have been a washer or any number of things, since track crews sometimes sought the tunnel out to escape the heat during lunchtime and left behind all manner of trash.

Hook dropped the metal into his pocket and worked his way farther into the tunnel. A few yards more, and he found an army boot tossed against the wall. The toe of the boot had been severed, and part of a blood-splattered sock remained inside it.

Just to the right of the boot, he spotted a military dog tag and could just make out a JOSEPH ERIKSON and a serial number on it. Sitting back on his haunches, he considered the horror of what those last few seconds must have been like.

He rose and dabbed at his face with his handkerchief. The body could not be far away. Just then he saw a lump lying next to the wall.

He swallowed hard and turned his light on the torso, which had been rolled and crushed between the locomotive and the railbed. Hook cleared his throat and lit a cigarette. He listened to the silence of the tunnel. The local sheriff would have to be contacted, as well as the undertaker. The army would most likely notify the family. At least he'd be spared that.

Hook took note of the location of the body again and then looked at his watch. He had time yet before the next train came through. If he was going to shut the line down, he'd have to do it soon. There should be a phone at the guardhouse. But shut it down for what? Not that much of the body remained, and keeping the line open would lower Eddie's blood pressure.

In the meantime, he'd talk to the guard. No two men worked together in a place as isolated as this tunnel without knowing a good deal about each other.

He turned to go when he heard footsteps coming down line.

He clicked off his flashlight, stepped back against the tunnel wall, and unholstered his P.38. No one had business being in the tunnel, especially while an investigation was under way. Flipping off the safety, he leveled his sidearm in the darkness and waited.

THREE

A LIGHT IN the tunnel swept the area, stopped, and then moved forward once again. Hook pressed his back against the cool wall, and the smell of creosote hung in the dampness. He waited until the light rounded the turn before he spoke.

"I've a pistol aimed at your head," he said from the darkness. "Put your flashlight on the tracks, and place both hands in front of the light so that I can see them."

When Hook could see hands on the rail, he circled to the side.

"Now your weapon. Set it on the rail, but do it slowly."

"I'm unarmed," a woman's voice said.

Hook paused. "Now, put your hands behind your neck and turn toward me."

When she turned, he shined his light into her face. Her hair, cut short, was the color of copper, and her eyes lit green under the beam of his light. She wore an army uniform, and her hat sat squarely on her head.

"My name is Lieutenant Allison Capron," she said, "U.S. Army Department of Transportation. May I put my hands down?"

"What are you doing here?"

"I might ask you the same," she said. "Had I not a gun pointing at me."

Hook slid the weapon into its holster.

"You can drop your hands. I'll ask you again. What are you doing on railroad property?"

"I'm not sure it's your business," she said.

Hook took out a cigarette and lit it. Smoke curled in the beam of his flashlight.

"My name is Hook Runyon, and I'm the railroad bull. It *is* my business."

"I'm investigating the death of Sergeant Joseph Erikson," she said. "When one of our soldiers dies, it's the military's responsibility to investigate."

"A death on railroad property is of some concern to railroad security as well," he said.

"You don't strike me as a railroad detective," she said. "Perhaps you could show me identification?"

He took out his badge, showing it to her. "Don't let the missing arm fool you."

"It's not the arm so much as the lack of professionalism," she said.

"Professionalism is for those sitting behind desks," he said. "Out here it doesn't count for much."

"Do you intend to let me conduct my investigation or not?" she asked.

"Look, Lieutenant, there's a hotshot due through here any time now. My suggestion is that we leave the tunnel."

"Hotshot?"

"That would be a freighter in a damn big hurry," he said. "One that has no intentions of stopping for anyone, including army lieutenants."

"Really," she said.

"Next time you decide to trespass in a railroad tunnel you might want to check the train schedule first."

"I'm not easily intimidated, Mr. Hook. If a train were coming, you wouldn't be in here, now would you?"

"It's Runyon," he said, "Hook Runyon, and I don't kid around about train schedules."

"And I don't intend to leave without completing my investigation. I'm searching for Sergeant Erikson's body," she said.

Hook dropped his light beam onto the bundle lying against the wall.

"I think your search is over," he said.

Lieutenant Capron walked over to the bundle and paused. Clutching her stomach, she then bent forward into the darkness.

"I wasn't prepared," she said, taking out her handkerchief.

"It's not something you can prepare for."

"How do you know it's him?" she asked, dabbing at her mouth.

Hook took the dog tag out of his pocket and handed it to her. "It's a horrible way to die," she said.

He checked his watch. "Come on," he said, taking her by the arm. "Time is up."

They'd no sooner stepped into the daylight when the hotshot blew her whistle at the other end of the tunnel. Within moments, she thundered by, her engine blasting heat as she charged full bore up the grade. Two old steamer pushers nipped at her heels. The ground trembled, and the smell of oil hung in the air as they roared away.

Lieutenant Capron pulled her arm from his grip and straightened her hat. She searched her handbag for a handkerchief, dropping it onto her throat. Hook could see the red flush on her face and the snap of her green eyes.

"I don't appreciate being manhandled," she said.

"One body a day is sufficient for me, Lieutenant," he said. "There's no room between a train and that tunnel wall. It's not a place you want to be when a hotshot comes through."

"As the railroad security agent, you should have shut this tunnel down until the investigation was complete," she said, hooking her purse over her shoulder.

"It *was* complete," he said. "Until you showed up."

"You put our lives at risk."

"Shutting down this line sends a ripple from one coast to the other. I'm figuring that's why the army saw fit to place a guard out here in the first place. Course, if I'd known you were coming, I'd sure enough shut down the entire system for your convenience.

"Now, there's not another train scheduled until nine this evening, keeping in mind, of course, that trains don't always run on schedule. In the meantime, I'm going up there to talk to that other guard."

Lieutenant Capron shifted her purse to her other arm.

"This is a military matter. No one talks to that soldier but me."

"And no one touches the evidence in that tunnel but me," he said. "That soldier died on railroad property. What's more, he was killed by one of our trains. And as long as it's under my jurisdiction, I don't intend to have the evidence contaminated. Furthermore, I'll not have some upstart lieutenant telling me how to proceed with my case."

Lieutenant Capron's jaw tightened, and she pushed her purse back onto her shoulder.

"You mean female lieutenant, don't you?"

"I hadn't noticed," he said.

"Look, this tunnel is critical to the war effort and has been under guard for the duration of the war. There are reasons for that for which you might not be aware. If I have to, I'll go over your head."

Hook looked down the line. Riding that popcar after dark could freeze a man solid, and he'd left his coat back at Ash Fork. "Never let it be said that I'm not a patriot. I'll cut you a deal, Lieutenant. You let me talk to that guard up there, and I'll give you access to the tunnel."

She looked at her watch and then up at the guardhouse. "I'll have to be there," she said. "He's not to be questioned without me present."

"Fine," he said. "That way everything will be professional, won't it?"

FOUR

THE GUARDHOUSE WALLS were native rock, as were the steps leading up to it. Though small and otherwise primitive, the guardhouse had a telephone line. Out front, an army staff car had been parked in such a fashion as to catch the shade of a single juniper.

The lieutenant led the way. A cobweb still clung to her hat. One of her heels had broken loose in the process of getting out of the tunnel, and she limped now as she climbed the steps.

He'd lied when he said he hadn't noticed that she was a woman, the curve of her hips beneath the uniform. He'd also noticed the way she held her head as if to dare the world to take a shot. But he didn't take to being pushed by anyone, including Lieutenant Capron.

She moved aside to let him get to the door and glanced at his prosthesis when he knocked. He'd seen that moment often since the loss of his arm, that point at which curiosity prevailed over propriety.

There had been a time he would have challenged such a moment, would have pulled his sleeve high and demonstrated the contraption for her satisfaction, but the years had changed things, not so much for others as for himself.

He'd learned that curiosity was as much about human nature as love and anger. It resided in him no less than in everyone else. So, more often than not, he let such moments pass now, and his life had become less difficult for it.

The door opened to reveal a man in his late twenties. A shock of straight black hair fell over an eye, and he pushed it back with his hand. He snapped to attention when he spotted Lieutenant Capron's bars.

"At ease, Corporal," she said. "We're here about Sergeant Erikson."

"Yes, ma'am," he said. "I'm Corporal William Thibodeaux, the one who called about the sergeant. I've been expecting someone."

"This is Hook Runyon, railroad detective," she said. "We need to ask a few questions."

"Come on in," he said, tucking in his shirt. "I haven't had time to straighten up just yet."

An invisible wall divided the one-room guardhouse down the middle, a bunk on each side of the room with footlockers at the ends. On the sergeant's side of the room, all items were grouped by function, and his bunk covers were stretched tight and wrinkle-free. In contrast, Thibodeaux's bed lay rumpled, and his boots were tossed on their sides at the door. Magazines were strewn about his bunk. A kerosene lantern sat in the window.

Thibodeaux pointed at a small table with chairs. "Would you like to sit?"

"Mind if I smoke?" Hook asked.

"No, sir," he said. "Love a good cigar myself."

Hook lit a cigarette and leaned back in his chair. "Now, perhaps you could tell us what you know, what you saw."

Thibodeaux walked over to the window and looked down on the tunnel.

"Joe and me," he said, "that would be Sergeant

Erikson, have been guarding that tunnel out there for a good long while now, walking the trestle, checking support beams for signs of sabotage."

"What about your patrol schedule?" Hook asked.

"That's classified," Lieutenant Capron said.

"I assume you'll be changing it anyway, Lieutenant," Hook said.

Thibodeaux looked over at the lieutenant. "Well," she said. "I suppose. Go ahead. We'll reset the schedule."

"Yes, ma'am. To start off we took twelve-hour shifts, you know, rotating days and nights, but then later we changed to twenty-four-hour shifts because of the back-and-forth on the road all the time. A man had hardly an hour to call his own."

"Go on," Hook said.

"Once on duty, we patrolled just before a scheduled run. Those were pretty regular, but sometimes they'd send through a hotshot or a troop train at odd hours. So we never patrolled without checking the board first. Even then the time varied too much for comfort. It's a rare railroad that runs on time and getting caught in the tunnel… Well, it had its worries."

"Did you sleep during your shift?" Hook asked. "Twenty-four hours is a long haul."

Thibodeaux glanced over at the lieutenant. "Tell us everything, Corporal," she said.

"Once in a while there'd be a good bit of time between trains, and we'd catch a nap. The sergeant said it didn't matter so long as the scheduled runs were made. Being just the two of us, it got mighty tiresome, and then after the bomb ended things, it hardly seemed important anymore."

Hook squashed out his cigarette on the bottom of his

shoe and looked for a wastebasket. A picture of a girl sat on the stand next to Thibodeaux's bunk. An open letter lay next to it.

Pausing, Hook said, "How long have you been doing the twenty-four-hour shifts, Corporal?"

Thibodeaux thought about it for a moment. "I'd say about a year now. They're long shifts, a lifetime. There ain't no getting around that. Sometimes I thought I might go crazy out here by myself. But then it's mighty nice getting back to town with a whole twenty-four to rest up."

Lieutenant Capron set her purse on the table. "Did Command approve the shift change?" she asked.

"Sergeant Erikson did, being senior man. I never asked more."

Hook said, "So tell us how you discovered the sergeant."

The corporal looked out the window. "I'd been on rotation in town and had come back for my shift."

"What time?" Hook asked.

"About five in the morning, I'd say. My shift started at seven. Joe wasn't around, so I checked the log and saw where he'd signed out on patrol."

"Was the lantern lit when you arrived?" Hook asked.

"Yes. We always left it lit. Coming back to the guard-house on a dark night you can't see spit."

The lieutenant pushed her hair back with her fingers and looked at the corporal. "How long does a patrol take?" she asked.

"About an hour if the trestle supports in the canyon are checked; otherwise, it takes about fifteen minutes to walk the tunnel and the topside of the trestle. We usually don't go under the trestle at night. It's too dark to see anything, anyway."

"And then what happened?" Hook asked.

Corporal Thibodeaux fell silent for a moment.

"When Joe didn't come back, I thought maybe he'd fallen or something. Maneuvering that trestle in the dark can be kind of tricky. I near broke my leg out there one time when I stepped between the ties. My shin turned black as coal.

"Anyway, just as I opened the door to go find him, there stood this railroader, all sweating and breathing hard, and I could see the fear in his face."

"And what did he say?" the lieutenant asked.

"He said he was an engineer, and he had hit a man in the tunnel. He said he couldn't get the hotshot shut down, what with the grade at his back. He said he'd gone a good half mile before getting her stopped. Said it had taken him a while to get back, given he wasn't in such great shape anymore."

"Go on," Hook said.

"He used the phone to call railroad security. They told him to go ahead and clear the track, and they'd send a bull out to investigate. I guess that must be you.

"After that, the engineer went on back to the train, and I called Command to tell them what had happened. I knew it had to be Joe. I mean, who else could it have been?"

"You didn't go look?" the lieutenant asked.

The corporal dabbed at the sweat on his upper lip with his sleeve.

"The engineer said looking couldn't help anyone at that point. I told Command, and they said I should just keep an eye out, you know, for any comings and go-ings, and they'd send someone. So that's what I did."

"And did you see anything in the meantime?" the lieutenant asked.

"Not until the popcar rolled in and I saw a one-armed fellow…"

Hook picked up the letter and looked at the address. "Do you carry weapons when you patrol?"

"Yes, sir, a rifle," he said.

"Every time you go out?"

"Truth is, it hardly seemed worth it after a while."

"And did the sergeant carry his rifle last night?"

"It's there by the window where he usually kept it."

"Anything else you'd like to add, Corporal?" Hook asked.

"No, sir. That's how it happened, best I can recall."

"If that's all, Mr. Runyon, I'll take it from here," the lieutenant said.

"Just one last thing: how did you and the sergeant get along? Did you socialize, that sort of thing?"

"Joe kept to himself, and that was fine with me. We saw plenty of each other out here. You can bet on that."

"Did Sergeant Erikson express any problems or con-cerns to you?" the lieutenant asked.

Thibodeaux paused. "Sometimes he talked about how he'd wound up guarding a worthless tunnel and how he hadn't gone to the front like other soldiers.

"Once, he said his father asked him what he did in the army, and why did he never talk about it. Joe told him that what he did was classified and that he wasn't allowed to talk about it to no one."

"He wanted to be in combat?" Hook asked.

"I guess we both worried about being stationed at

home. A man doesn't join the army to sit in the desert and guard a hole in the mountain."

"Did Sergeant Erikson have a girlfriend?" Hook asked.

"And what is the point in that, Mr. Runyon?" she asked.

"Just a question, Lieutenant."

Thibodeaux shrugged. "We never talked about stuff like that."

"Is there anything else you'd like to add?" Hook asked.

"No, sir. Only that there have been times I wondered how it would be, you know, getting caught up in that tunnel with a hotshot coming down line. A man can't help but wonder."

At the bottom of the steps, Lieutenant Capron turned to Hook. "I'm holding the railroad responsible for the death of that young sergeant," she said.

Hook looked up at the guardhouse. The evening shadows had swallowed the light, and Mixer barked somewhere far off. The first chill of the evening swept over them.

"That's an interesting conclusion, Lieutenant. How is it you came about it?"

"Sergeant Erikson didn't receive warning about that train."

"You heard the corporal say that they always called in and checked the board first, didn't you?"

She lifted her chin. "I also heard him say that arrival times were notoriously unpredictable. You said it yourself, as I recall."

Hook took out a cigarette and looked at her. "I'm a strong believer in sleeping on a problem before I start making decisions, particularly when it comes to life-and-death matters. I suggest you do the same," he said.

Lieutenant Capron started to turn, but the loose heel caused her ankle to slip sideways. Hook pulled her back onto the step.

She drew her arm free and adjusted her hat, which had nearly fallen off.

"I must say," she said, digging through her purse. "Letting a key witness leave before he's interrogated strikes me as sloppy detective work. In any case, I allowed you access to Corporal Thibodeaux for your investigation. I'll expect the same courtesy when your engineer arrives. Here's my number."

"Engineers aren't known for having much to say," Hook said.

"Nonetheless."

"I'll let you know," he said. "Now, I best be on my way. After dark, that popcar is like sitting on an iceberg."

As he walked away, Lieutenant Capron called after him.

"But what about Sergeant Erikson?"

Hook pulled his collar up against the cool. The sunset cast light in her eyes, and her arms were locked over her chest.

"What about him?" he asked.

"You can't leave him in there," she said. "People have to be called. Things need to be arranged."

Hook snapped a match against his hook and lit his cigarette. "Yes, ma'am," he said. "Normally I'd do just that, but then I'm not one to interfere in military matters any more than is necessary. The tunnel is yours now. It's only professional."

FIVE

As HOOK WALKED toward the popcar, the lieutenant's eyes burned into his back. She was nothing if not tough, the way she'd come back after seeing Erikson in the tunnel. He'd seen hardened men lose it in such moments. But he'd learned long ago that his best allies were time and thought, and having someone trail him around made neither possible.

At the trestle, he whistled for Mixer and then checked his watch. He had plenty of time before the next train came through. Walking out onto the trestle, he looked into the blackness of Johnson Canyon. He needed a closer look down there, but it would have to wait until another time. One slip in those rocks and a man could disappear forever.

Just then the moon broke on the horizon, and the trestle rails shot off into the darkness like beams of light. He could hear Mixer climbing up through the rocks, his nose puffing like a steam jenny.

Hook picked his way back to the popcar, trying to gauge the ties in the darkness. What kind of idiot had planned the spacing between them? One tie was too short for a single step, and two ties were too damn far. Whoever he was, he'd never had to walk the rails.

Hook found Mixer lying sprawled out in the seat of the popcar. Blood dripped from a cut in his nose.

Hook pushed him over and wiped off the seat. "Damn it," he said. "Don't you ever learn?"

Hook cranked up the popcar and rolled out on the line. As he coasted through the night, the wheels clacked steady as a clock. Soon the stars exploded into the sky and slid overhead like a million sparklers.

He hunkered down against the cold. He knew better than to get on a popcar without a coat, but he'd let Eddie stampede him. Eddie had a way of pushing too damn hard and fast on everything.

When the lights of Ash Fork winked in the distance, he idled back, coasting into the salvage yard. An old kettle waiting clearance huffed and sighed at the head of a line of scrap cars.

Since delivery times were more or less flexible for salvage, the old steamers were often assigned to the duty. The indignity of the assignment failed to diminish their willingness to haul and slug their way overland. Like old hands, they turned to their labor with experience and determination.

Scrap took care in separating out the high-quality copper, and it hadn't gone unnoticed by the local thieves. At some point, large amounts of copper were disappearing. So far Hook had been unable to catch them.

As the popcar approached the drainage ditch that ran under the tracks, Hook spotted a shadow slipping off into the darkness. He switched off the engine and rolled to a stop. Sometimes boes gathered up close to the track when they knew a slow freighter would be coming through.

All in all, Hook didn't mind so much. He'd been known to overlook a bo now and then, particularly when the weather turned bad. But the weather was fine, and he had no intentions of letting them pitch a jungle this close to the salvage yard.

He waited in the darkness for some time, deciding finally that they must have spotted his light and taken off.

"Those boys are pushing their luck," he said to Mixer. "I guess they don't know who's the yard dog around here."

Mixer thumped his tail against the seat. Hook cranked up the engine. "Maybe it's time I introduced myself."

Back at the yards, he sided the popcar and headed for the shower. Scrap had rigged it up special for his employees. He said he was sick and tired of them smelling up his office every time they came in, so he'd painted an old oil drum black, equipped it with a salvaged showerhead, and mounted it on a fuel-tank stand. The sun heated the water, and a bailer canvas spared the community from the shock of seeing naked men showering.

But the best part, according to Scrap, was that it didn't cost him hardly a cent. He particularly liked cloudy days, which he calculated cut water usage by as much as a third.

Hook pulled Mixer into the shower and scrubbed him with a bar of soap someone had left in the tray. On the way back, Mixer rolled in the dirt and didn't shake it off until they were back inside the caboose.

Hook threatened him with death and then fixed himself a shot of Beam and water. He tossed his prosthesis on the table and took his copy of Steinbeck to bed to read.

But what with the day's events still pressing, he couldn't concentrate. Shutting off the lantern, he lay in the darkness. He thought about Sergeant Erikson and his last moments in the tunnel. He thought about the lieutenant, all cocky and squared off for a fight, and he thought about the condom balloons floating about in an orphanage.

Rolling onto his back, he watched the moon slip over the cupola. Times like this he wondered why he had become a yard dog at all, but then, of course, he knew why. The line between lawmen and outlaws could be unclear. Only fate had landed him on the right side of the line.

WHEN HE AWOKE, the sun bore through the cupola. He checked his watch: nearly noon. He'd slept half the day away. Time was he'd have been up with the sunrise no matter how late the evening had been. He climbed out of bed and put on his prosthesis.

Mixer wagged his tail and begged to get out. Hook opened the door and watched as he bound off down the tracks.

By the time Hook headed for the office, the sun had heated the yards into a furnace. Sparrows, bent on out-chirping each other, lined up on the fence, and the smell of acetylene drifted in from the cutting torch out in the yard.

Hook opened the office door to find Scrap examining his face in a hand mirror. The remains of his lunch were still on his desk.

"Well?" Scrap said, looking at Hook through the mirror.

"Well what?" Hook said.

"Well, now what do you want?"

"I don't want a goddang thing," Hook said. "Except to be left alone."

Scrap put on his hat and took another look in the mirror. "You walked all the way down to my office to tell me to leave you alone?"

"I just figured to get a head start on it," Hook said.

Scrap stoked his pipe and snapped a match across his zipper. "I took a look at my figures," he said, puffing on his pipe. "I calculate they lifted a thousand pounds of copper this time. Looks to me like the railroad dick ought to be taking care of business around here instead of gallivanting up and down the track on a popcar."

Hook pulled Scrap's hand over with his prosthesis and lit his cigarette off his pipe.

"Consider the possibility that a man run over by a train just might be more important than your copper, Scrap."

Scrap tamped his pipe and sucked it back to red. "I've considered it," he said. "No one in the world's got fewer problems to worry about than a man run over by a train."

"You got the heart of a railroad official, Scrap. How about me using your phone?"

Scrap paused. "I put myself a plan together while the likes of you slept away the night. It's going to make me rich. The thing is, I've got to have start-up capital, operating money, which I can't gather up long as these bastards are stealing my profit."

"Yeah, but will it make you happy?"

"You goddang right," he said, walking to the door. "Just leave the money there on the table for the phone. And then you might give some thought about how to stop the thievery around here. This is a place of business, you know."

HOOK DIALED EDDIE PRESTON and watched through the window as Scrap headed for the crane. Eddie answered on the third ring. "Eddie, this is Hook."

A puff of black smoke shot out of the crane's exhaust. "Runyon," Eddie said, "I got a call from the army complaining that you weren't being cooperative with their investigator."

"You didn't tell me the military would be involved, Eddie."

"I thought you might have figured that out by yourself, Runyon, given it was an army sergeant who was killed."

"Some of us aren't as quick as you, Eddie."

"Pull your head out and look around once in a while," he said. "That's how a man gets to be supervisor."

"That's how I figure it, too," Hook said.

"Anyway, it's pretty obvious, isn't it?"

"What is?"

"That it was an accident."

"I haven't even talked to the engineer yet," Hook said.

"The engineer's deadheading in day after tomorrow. I told him to stop by the salvage yard and give a report."

"That's a little late, isn't it, Eddie?"

"There's others involved, here," he said.

"Exactly who's in charge of this sideshow, Eddie?"

"Relax, Runyon, the sideshows are all yours, but things have to be coordinated with the military."

Hook lit a cigarette and watched Scrap turn his hat around backward on his head. Scrap looked in the side mirror of the crane and adjusted it.

"Anyway, I'm not so sure," Hook said.

"Sure about what?"

"That it was an accident."

"I just told you it was, Runyon."

"It doesn't add up," Hook said.

"Look, this guy was standing on the tracks in the tunnel, wasn't he?"

"That's right."

"And a train hit him, didn't it?"

"Yes."

"And it killed him, didn't it?"

"Hell, yes, Eddie. I had trouble finding the pieces. What the hell you think?"

"So, you have this guy in a tunnel standing on the tracks, and he's run over by a hotshot. That's pretty straightforward, isn't it? For Christ's sake, Runyon."

"I've got this feeling, Eddie."

"It's your brain looking for a reason to live. The first thing a real detective learns at Baldwin Felts Detective School is that he's got to rely on facts, not feelings."

"He was standing in full view of the oncoming when it hit him. Another hundred yards, and he would have been out of there."

"What does that mean?"

"He had time to get out. He would've seen the train and had time to beat it."

"Look, Runyon, you got enough troubles with this orphanage fiasco."

"What troubles?"

"The diocese is upset about them rubbers."

"That wasn't my fault!"

"Who in their right mind gives rubbers to an orphanage, Runyon? And I can tell you the disciplinary board is not happy about those supplies.

"Now, I want you to wrap up this tunnel deal."

"Hello. Hello," Hook said. "Can't hear, Eddie. Will call back later."

SIX

HOOK SPENT THE remainder of the afternoon finishing his book. He slipped it on top of the growing stack and checked his watch. It would be dark soon, and he figured to take a hard look for Scrap's copper thieves.

If a thousand pounds had come up missing, and he figured it had since Scrap kept a tight rein on his copper, then it had to be a sizeable operation. A thousand pounds of copper would require considerable effort to steal and some form of transportation to haul off.

While it might be a bo, he doubted it. Most boes were on the move with little but drink and food on their minds. Hoboes had neither the means nor inclination to deal with a thousand pounds of copper.

Come dark, Hook planned to check out the yards yet again, even though to this point he'd found no breach of the security fence. One thing sure, Eddie Preston intended not to give him a new assignment until he'd taken care of Scrap West's copper thieves.

Outside, a switch engine bumped and groaned as she made up yet another line of salvage cars. The sounds of the old engines filled the salvage yard as they pushed and hauled and sorted cars. Smoke hung over the compound like fog, and the stacks of wrecked cars blocked away the horizon.

When dusk fell, Hook checked his sidearm and headed out the door. Mixer fell in behind him, his nose skimming the ground. Hook worked his way through the cars and to the fence. He paid special attention to ditches and low spots where someone might crawl under.

Even though Scrap West had cultivated a particular hatred for thieves, his need to save money often took precedence over good security procedure. Near the back of the yard, for instance, a drainage ditch had been cut. Instead of proper fencing, Scrap had used old tires strung over a cable to close in the gap, which made an attractive entry for aspiring thieves.

Hook crawled into the drainage ditch and shined his light around. Over the years, sand had gathered where the water slowed, and it was there that he spotted the footprints.

Someone had been in, but the footprints appeared to be old. The heel print had worn and indistinct edges, and water had seeped into the low parts of the impression.

He looked around for Mixer, who had tired of Hook's meandering and taken off on his own. Hook moved along the fence until he could see Scrap's chicken house, an old shack with a tin roof that had been set smack in the corner of the yard. A roll of chicken wire had been stretched from one corner to the other to imprison Scrap's collection of nesting hens.

When a noise issued from the chicken coop, Hook cut his light. He crouched in the darkness, uncertain as to the sound. And when it came again, he knew that someone was into Scrap's chickens. He pulled his P.38. Hoboes were survivors and as likely to kill a man over a chicken as over a thousand pounds of copper.

He worked his way forward, stopping now and again

to listen. At the pen, he hoisted a leg over the fence and into the yard. It smelled of old straw and manure. Melon rinds crackled under his feet. Scrap had traded a set of tire rims for a truckload of overly ripe melons, which he in turn fed to his chickens, the problem being that the Arizona sun had instantly dried the rinds to the consistency of an Egyptian mummy. The chickens, uncertain as to their function, carried them about in their beaks.

Hook pushed himself against the chicken coop wall. Inside, the chickens clucked in alarm from their roost. Hook, P.38 at the ready, kicked open the door and squared off.

"Come out of there now," he said.

Chickens, feathers, and dirt exploded out the door and over the top of him. Hook threw his arm up to ward off being pummeled to death by frantic chickens and, in so doing, tripped and fell backward into the yard. All about him chickens squawked and flew and darted about in terror. Some drove headlong into the fence as they tried to escape.

Hook sat up and brushed the feathers from his hair and front. Mixer stood in the doorway of the chicken coop looking at him, an eggshell stuck to his chin.

"That's it," Hook said. "I'm putting you in the next cattle car to the soap factory."

By the time Hook cleaned up and got back to the caboose, the yard had settled in for the night. He poured himself a Beam and water and sat on the edge of his bunk. Maybe Scrap wouldn't miss the eggs. What Mixer had failed to eat, he'd managed to break, making any estimate of loss impossible. Mixer, aware of the precariousness of his existence, watched on from under the table.

Hook picked up a book and started to read, but weariness soon overtook him. Boxcars bumped in the distance as a switch engine made up the smelter run.

Hook yawned and blew out the lamp. Tomorrow he'd borrow Scrap's old truck and make a trip into town. There were loose ends that needed to be tied up, but for now sleep beckoned. He pulled up the covers and soon drifted off.

THE JOLT NEARLY knocked him out of his bunk. He sat up and struggled to remember where he was. Mixer yelped from under the table and leapt into the bed next to him.

"What the hell," Hook said, shaking the fog from his head. The second jolt sent all of his books sliding across the floor and his coffeepot crashing onto the table. Hook searched for his prosthesis and put it on. Stepping into one leg of his pants, he hopped across the floor to the window. Boxcars slid by. He rubbed his face and looked again, realizing that it wasn't the boxcars that were moving but the caboose.

"Oh, for Christ's sake," he said.

Mixer tipped his head and thumped his tail, uncertain as to what kind of trouble had now befallen him.

Hook opened the door to see Scrap West's crane moving away into the distance. He stepped out onto the platform just as the engine bore down, and the caboose gathered up speed.

"Holy hell," he said. "We're coupled into the smelter run."

He went back in, grabbed the lantern, and searched his pocket for a match. In his rush, he broke the match in half and had to find another. The lantern flickered to life, and Hook ran back out onto the platform. Leaning over the railing, he swung a stop signal.

Finally, the engineer hit his whistle and brought her down.

Steam shot into the night and drifted up into the yard lights. Hook slipped on his shoes and worked his way to the front.

The engineer leaned out of the cab. "Who the hell are you?" he asked. "Don't you know it's against the law to stop a train?"

"I'm the railroad bull," Hook said.

"You don't look like no bull," he said.

"I live in that caboose you're hauling off."

"What kind of idiot lives in a caboose?"

"Climb down, and I'll show you," Hook said. "I never knew a big E what didn't need an ass kicking anyhow."

"All right, all right, take it easy. We was just clearing the siding."

"Well, take it back where you found it, and easy does it. Next time get clearance before you go messing with someone's caboose."

Once back, Hook spent an hour cleaning up the mess. He blew out the lamp and collapsed in the bunk. He listened to the smelter run pulling out onto the main line. Tunnel accidents and copper thieves be damned, one way or the other, he was going to find a way out of this madhouse.

THE NEXT MORNING, he found Scrap working on the crane. He had her shut down and the dipstick pulled.

"I need some transportation this morning, Scrap," he said. "How about a loner?"

Scrap wiped the dipstick on his glove.

"That's what a popcar's for, Hook, so you can run up and down the track. That way you don't have to worry about catching copper thieves."

"I need to check on some things in town," he said. "Maybe I could borrow your truck?"

Scrap slid the dipstick back in and turned to Hook. "Oh, sure, sure," he said. "You can have just anything you want. Maybe you'd like to have my sister, too, or the shirt off my back."

"Just your truck," Hook said.

Scrap took his pipe from his pocket and blew on the stem. "Well, I need my truck, but there's that old army jeep I guess you could borrow, seeing as how the railroad can't afford a vehicle of its own."

"I thought you sold the transmission out of it."

"Well, I put one back in. I ain't entirely helpless, you know."

"The jeep will do," Hook said.

"And you can just fill it with gas while you're at it, and you might check the goddang oil once in a while. And just 'cause I loaned her out, doesn't mean you can go tearing all over the country. I ain't the U.S. government, you know.

"Say," he said, "did you hear anything last night?"

"I haven't been able to hear anything but this crane since I came."

"A ruckus down by the back fence," he said.

"Didn't hear a thing," Hook said.

"So it must be my imagination, I suppose," Scrap said, handing him the keys. "And what's in town that's so all-fired important, anyway?"

Hook dropped them into his pocket. "You ever known men not to talk about women, Scrap?"

"They'd be more likely not to eat," he said.

"Yeah," Hook said. "That's what I figure, too."

SEVEN

BACK AT THE caboose, Hook located a can of pork and beans in the cardboard box he kept under his bunk.

Having spent his funds on books, he'd come up a little short on chow money. But payday wasn't that far away, and he'd gotten by on less in his time.

Mixer returned from somewhere with egg yolk on his mouth. "I'm not asking," Hook said, letting him in. "But if Scrap catches you down there, things could get out of hand."

Mixer, not being overly sensitive, begged for the last of the beans. Hook scraped them into his dish.

Afterward, they walked down to the shop where Scrap kept the jeep. The top of the jeep, if it ever had one, had long since been lost or sold by Scrap.

The jeep fired off and sent a cloud of blue smoke lifting over the yard. Hook slipped the gearshift into reverse and eased out the clutch. The jeep didn't move.

Scrap came around the corner with Pepe, his top hand in the yard.

Hook worked the shift and goosed the engine again. "Damn it, Scrap," he said.

"What's the matter?" Scrap asked. "Don't yard dogs know how to drive either?"

"It won't back up," Hook said.

"'Course it won't," Scrap said.

Hook drooped his arm over the steering wheel. "Why won't it?"

"It don't have a reverse," he said.

"What?"

"Jesus, Hook, a reverse. It don't have one."

"Why the hell not?"

"This is a salvage yard, not a dealership. Sometimes salvage parts don't work a hundred percent, you know."

Hook shook his head and looked over at Mixer, who was engaged in washing his privates.

"You expect me to drive this thing without a reverse?" Hook asked.

Scrap retrieved his pipe and knocked it against the heel of his shoe.

"My expectations are not so high when it comes to yard dogs," he said. "But even a yard dog might figure out that going forward is the only option when there ain't no reverse."

"My life isn't always forward, Scrap. In fact, it's mostly backward since I came to this place."

"Well now, sometimes a man has to make do with what he's got," Scrap said. "And getting huffy don't help."

Hook took a deep breath. "Do you and your employee there think you could push this pile of junk back so I can get on with my business?"

Scrap fired up his pipe and looked at Hook.

"I suppose it don't make Pepe here much difference, seeing as how he works by the hour. So he probably don't care if he's pushing yard dogs or greasing up my crane like he's supposed to be doing. On the other hand, me being the boss and being it's my time…"

"Scrap, do you know how long it takes a broken head to heal?"

"Come on, Pepe," Scrap said. "Let's push this son of a bitch onto the tracks and hope a switch engine's coming down line. Some folks don't know a favor when it's given 'em."

ONCE ON THE ROAD, Hook lit a cigarette and let the wind blow through his hair. He'd been trying to remember the name on that letter ever since he'd left the guardhouse. It was Linda Sue or Linda Lou or something like that. Maybe it was Rhonda Faye. He just couldn't remember.

Maybe his brain had turned to mush from store-bought whiskey, all that artificial coloring and perfume shrinking it away. It was probably no bigger than a key lime by now. He should have stuck with Runt Wallace's moonshine, which, like the fountain of youth, invigorated a man's mind and deepened his thought.

In Ash Fork, he pulled into the post office and admonished Mixer not to get out of the seat while he was gone.

An old man sat outside the door of the post office. His legs were crossed, and his white socks drooped about his ankles. After slicing off a plug of tobacco, he tucked it into his cheek and then nodded at Hook, who nodded back.

Inside, Hook waited for the postal clerk to finish with a customer.

"Yes?" she said, lining up her official stamps.

Her skin was as brown as a roasted Christmas turkey, and purple ink stained the tips of her fingers.

"I thought you might be able to help me," he said.

"You'll have to tell me what it is you want first," she said.

"I'm looking for a girl," he said. "Her name is Linda, I think."

"Sir, this is a post office. We don't look for girls here."

"No, you don't understand," he said.

"I think I do," she said. "Now, if you have something to mail, need postage?"

"No," he said. "I'm trying to find this Linda something or other."

"We don't give out anyone's address here," she said. "This is a federal institution, and we have rules against such things.

"Next," she said.

The woman standing behind Hook elbowed past. "Really," she said, shaking her head.

Outside, Hook looked up and down the street and then lit a cigarette.

"That dog's been sucking eggs," the old man on the bench said.

Hook looked over at Mixer, who was watching them from the backseat of the jeep. The egg yolk had dried on his whiskers, and he looked like a yellow daisy.

"He only did it once," Hook said.

"You'll have to shoot him," the old man said. "Once an egg sucker, always an egg sucker."

Hook got in, slipped the jeep into reverse, and turned to back out. The motor roared. "Damn," he said, climbing out.

Mixer jumped from the backseat and came around to the front of the jeep.

"Wouldn't shoot him here if I was you," the old man said. "There's a landfill outside of town."

"I'm not going to shoot him," Hook said. "Least not today. This jeep won't back up. Maybe you could help push it into the street?"

The old man squared his hat and came over. Together they rolled the jeep out of the parking space.

"Thanks," Hook said, helping Mixer into the backseat and then climbing in himself.

The old man wiped his chin with his sleeve and studied Hook.

"It don't have a reverse," he said.

"I know," Hook said.

"Means you can only go forward."

"Yeah, I know."

"You can't park like you just done, or you'll have to push it out. I might not be around to help next time."

"Thanks," Hook said.

"Had a Buick once that would only go backward," he said. "Plowed my garden with it. Put a hell of a kink in my neck, though."

Hook paused and looked at the old man. "You haven't seen Linda Sue, have you?"

The old man spit between his legs. "Sure."

"You have? Where?"

"At breakfast over to Blue's Café, just like always."

"Blue's?"

"Down about a block. Wouldn't pull in, though."

"Why's that?"

"No reverse," he said.

LINDA SUE COULDN'T have been over five feet two and had a waist that would fit in a man's hands. She chewed gum, and a pencil stub had been slid behind her ear. She moved from window to table with the grace of a ballerina. The men laughed and joked and looked at each other knowingly.

Hook took a booth near the back and studied the menu. Remembering that he was broke, he dropped it back into its holder.

When Linda Sue spotted him, she whisked the coffeepot from the warmer and hooked her pinky through the handle of a cup. Without asking, she poured him a cup of coffee.

"What will you have?" she asked, taking her pencil from behind her ear.

"Coffee's fine," he said.

"Meatloaf's great," she said.

"Thanks, just coffee."

She cocked her hand on her waist. "What happened to your arm?"

Hook held up his prosthesis. "Alligator," he said.

Linda Sue stared at him for a moment. "Oh, you," she said. "Really?"

"Woman driver," he said. "Then she broke my heart."

Linda Sue snapped her gum. "You probably deserved it," she said. "The broken heart, I mean."

"Look," he said, dropping his spoon into his cup. "I'm actually here to see you."

"Me? You don't even know me."

"Linda Sue, isn't it?" he said.

"How you know that?"

"Everyone in town knows Linda Sue. You're kind of a legend." She flashed a smile and looked over the room to see if anyone was waiting for service.

"Who are you, anyway?" she asked.

"Hook Runyon. I'm a railroad bull."

"A what?"

"It's like a cop, except honest," he said. "I've been working West's Salvage for a few weeks."

"Scrap? I know him. He steals the sugar when he comes in."

"That would be Scrap," he said.

She pulled a half pack of Camels out of her pocket and checked the contents.

"What do you want with me?" she asked.

"I'm needing information on one Corporal Thibodeaux. I thought maybe you could help me out."

"William? I know William. Hey, you trying to pick me up?"

"Would you like to see my badge?"

"Not here," she said. "Blue watches everything from the kitchen."

"Who?"

"The boss. That's what they call him. Look, I get off in an hour. Meet me outside but no funny stuff."

"No funny stuff," he said. "I'll be in my jeep."

WHEN LINDA SUE slid in, she smelled of bacon and bubble gum. She lit a cigarette and turned to look at Mixer.

"What's that on his face?"

"Egg."

She blew smoke out the corner of her mouth and pushed her hair back with her fingers.

"You shouldn't feed him eggs," she said. "You'll make an egg sucker out of him."

"Can I give you a ride home?"

"I usually walk, but I guess it would be okay. I walk

lots every day at Blue's. I could probably outwalk anyone in town."

"Where do you live?" he asked, starting up the jeep.

"Turn up there. I've got five acres and a trailer just off the highway. It's nearly paid off. Someday I'm going to build."

When they got to the trailer, Hook circled around. "You can park in front," she said.

"Can't turn and I have no reverse," he said.

Linda Sue hooked her elbow on the back of the seat.

"Nothing against you, but I'll see that badge now. A girl has to be careful."

Hook showed her the badge. "Just a couple of questions," he said.

"Well, come on in. I've got to get these shoes off. My feet are killing me."

The trailer had a living area, which included a tiny kitchen and a built-in table. A beaded curtain separated the bedroom from the living area. She directed Hook to the couch while she lit a scented candle and put on a record.

"It's the first thing I always do," she said. "It relaxes me."

"Real nice," he said.

"Now, what is it you wanted to know?"

"You are acquainted with Corporal Thibodeaux, right?" he asked.

Linda Sue sat down, slipped her shoes off, and leaned forward on her elbows. She wore small gold earrings, and her eyes were round and soft. She dropped a hand on her throat and looked up at him. He could see why the corporal might be taken with her.

"For about a year or so, I guess," she said.

"And do you know what he does for a living?"

"Sure. He guards the tunnel. Everyone in Ash Fork knows that. They think it's nuts. Why would anyone guard that silly tunnel out there in the middle of nowhere?"

"How would you describe your relationship with the corporal?"

"That's kind of personal, ain't it?"

"Just for the record," he said. "Are you engaged, anything like that?"

"We have a good time, dancing, going out, stuff like that, but we're not getting married or anything. He mentioned it a time or two. I've been married before, though. I don't need another boss. One boss in my life is enough."

"Do you know Sergeant Joseph Erikson?"

Linda Sue's face darkened, and she searched out a cigarette.

"I heard he killed himself in an accident," she said. "I heard they were shipping his body back to his home."

"Did you know him personally?"

"No," she said, shrugging. "William's mentioned him a time or two, I guess."

"Did William like him?"

"Once, he said that he'd been passed up for promotion because of a bad write-up Erikson gave him, but he never said more after that. I guess they worked it out."

"Do you know if Sergeant Erikson had a girlfriend?"

Linda Sue sat up and wove her fingers together in her lap. "No. I mean, I don't know. None that I ever heard about."

"Do you know if he was depressed about anything or in trouble, maybe?"

"Look, I'm real sorry about the sergeant, but it was an accident, wasn't it? I mean, it's not like he died in the war or anything."

Hook looked out the window to check on Mixer. "Thanks," he said. "You've been helpful. I better be on my way."

"Sure," she said. "Maybe you can come back sometime when you're not on business. They have a dance out at the armory every Saturday night."

"Thanks," he said, "but I'm not much of a dancer."

"It don't bother me, you know," she said.

"What doesn't?" Hook said.

"The arm," she said. "It don't bother me a bit."

BACK AT THE salvage yard, Hook parked the jeep and sent Mixer on his way. The crane clanked and growled in the distance, and the pushers idled on the siding.

He found Scrap's office empty. Taking the card from his pocket, he dialed Lieutenant Capron's number. A man answered but declined to give Hook any information. Hook explained who he was. The man paused and then gave him a different number to call.

She answered the phone herself. "Lieutenant Capron."

"Hook Runyon, here," he said. "You still want to talk to that engineer?"

"I can't file my report until I do," she said.

"Come to my caboose at West's Salvage Yard in the morning if you can. He's coming in on the eight o'clock."

"All right," she said. "I'm still in town, but it's pretty clear what happened out there."

"Not to everyone," he said.

"What do you mean?"

"I'm just a yard dog," he said. "But I've been around enough to know that when two men are involved with the same woman, trouble isn't far behind."

EIGHT

HOOK WATCHED THE engineer walk down the tracks.
He carried a lunchbox and had his hat cocked. Mixer
growled, and Hook sent him to the corner.

The engineer propped his foot up on the caboose step
and pushed his hat onto the back of his head.

"You Runyon?" he asked.

"That's right."

Over the top of the engineer's head, Hook could see
an army staff car pulling into the yard.

"I'm Ted Benson," the engineer said. "I understand
you need to talk to me."

Hook buttoned his shirt and stood to the side. "Come
on in, Ted. I see Lieutenant Capron just pulling in. The
army's involved with this as well."

The lieutenant, in full-dress uniform, stopped at the
bottom of the steps. Her hair sprang in curls from underneath her hat, and her shoes, shined to a high polish,
glistened in the morning sun. She looked up at Hook.

"A caboose?" she said.

"It's where I live," Hook said.

"Really?"

"The engineer just got here. If you have a problem
with the caboose, we could meet in Scrap's office."

Mixer stuck his head between Hook's legs and
looked her over.

"Does he bite?" she asked.

"Not often."

"Very well. I've wondered what these things looked like inside. I had no idea they were inhabitable."

"That's still up for debate," he said. "Go lay down, Mixer." Hook started to take her by the hand to help her up the steps, but she took hold of the grab iron and pulled herself up. "Lieutenant, this is Ted Benson, the engineer involved in the incident at Johnson Canyon Tunnel."

"Hello," she said, stepping in. "Oh, my, there isn't much room, is there?"

"Sleeping and eating," Hook said. "For the most part. But then that's what living's all about. Anyway, where I go, she goes. Sometimes where she goes, I follow."

"I beg your pardon?"

"Talking to myself," he said. "Comes from living alone."

The engineer had taken his seat next to the window. Sweat glistened on his upper lip. Mixer rose to check out the lunchbox that the engineer had left on the floor next to his feet. Hook pointed for Mixer to go away, which he did with some reluctance.

Hook moved some books off the bench and motioned for her to sit down.

"You've quite a collection there," she said.

"It's an addiction that keeps me on the brink of bankruptcy," he said.

She dropped one leg over the other and opened her purse. Her nails were manicured. He couldn't help but wonder how a woman like her wound up in army transportation. She looked out of place, like a crystal vase in a junkyard.

"Okay," she said, taking out a notepad. "I'm ready."

"Would you care to start, Lieutenant?" Hook asked.

"It's your railroad, Mr. Runyon."

"Ted," Hook said. "An investigation is conducted by the railroad on all deaths that take place on company property. It doesn't necessarily mean you've done anything wrong. Do you understand?"

"Yeah," he said, glancing over at the lieutenant. "They told me everyone has to do the report. This is a first for me."

"A first?" the lieutenant asked.

"Most engineers go through this sooner or later," he said. "I've been lucky up until now."

"You mean where a person has been killed?" she asked. "It happens often?"

"Most engineers experience it sooner or later," Hook said. "But it's not in the job description."

"I've hit plenty of critters," the engineer said. "It happens all the time, dogs, cattle. I ran over a pinto horse outside Amarillo, but I've never hit a man before."

"Did you see anyone else around that night?" she asked.

"No, but then you don't see much out there at night, especially coming down that grade."

Hook picked up his book and fanned the pages. Some bastard had dog-eared a page.

"At what point did you know that you couldn't avoid the impact?" he asked.

The engineer dabbed at his mouth with his sleeve. "The minute my glimmer lit him up. In that instant, I knew I was about to kill a man, and there wasn't a goddamn thing I could do about it."

"Didn't you apply the brakes?" the lieutenant asked.

"We were coming down the steepest grade on the

continent, ma'am, and with forty loaded cars at our back. No brakes or God's own hand could have slowed that train down one iota. Most folks don't have the least idea how long it takes to stop a train."

"Where exactly was the sergeant when it happened?" Hook asked.

"Standing midtrack just east of the curve. Why the hell they put a curve in a tunnel, I'll never know. The wheel carriages sounded like they were going to tear right out from under the engine."

"You didn't see anyone else in the tunnel?" the lieutenant asked.

"There's no room for a crowd in that tunnel," he said.

"Was he tied up or anything like that?" Hook asked. "Anyone forcing him to be there?"

"He was just standing there, right out of the darkness, just like that, and us barreling into that mountain. He stood with legs apart, facing the engine. There was no turning back for either one of us."

The engineer turned to Lieutenant Capron. "I wanted to be an engineer my whole life. As a kid I used to stand at the crossing and watch the trains coming and going. I dreamed about being up there in that cab ever since I can remember.

"And being an engineer turned out to be everything I thought it might be, the engine, the power, folks watching along the way. But I never thought to kill a man. I never thought that."

"What happened afterward?" Hook asked.

"I locked her down. When I got her stopped, I left the switchman with the engine and ran back."

"Through the tunnel?" the lieutenant asked.

"There's no other way to get to the guardhouse, 'less you want to climb a mountain."

"What did you see at that point?" Hook asked.

The engineer searched for a smoke and lit it up. "I saw what a train can do to the human body, and I'll never forget it."

"Did you see evidence of anyone else having been in there?" Hook asked.

"Dark, you know, and quiet, quiet as death."

"You called from the guardhouse?" Hook asked.

"That's right. Division said to finish the run. Come back in for this interview."

"And Corporal Thibodeaux answered the door that night?" Hook asked.

"That's right."

"Was he wearing his uniform?"

"To tell the truth, I don't remember. He could have been stark naked."

"Anything else you'd like to ask, Lieutenant?" Hook said. "Do you have any knowledge of why Sergeant Erikson might have stayed in that tunnel so long?" she asked.

He rubbed at his face with both hands before looking up at her.

"No," he said. "We were on schedule. You'd think a man who walked that tunnel every day would have known better than to cut it close. There are lots of reasons why a run can be late, early, too, for that matter, but we were right on the button that night.

"It was a bad mistake, and it's sad for the sergeant's people. But he's not the only one who has to pay, you know. I got to live with this the rest of my life. It's the last thing I think about at night and the first thing in the morning. No, sir, that sergeant ain't the only one who lost out on that run."

Hook turned. "If there's nothing you'd like to add, that should wrap it up. If we need you again, we'll contact Division." The engineer checked his pocket watch and walked to the door. He paused.

"There is just one thing," he said. "It keeps going through my mind."

"What's that?" Hook asked.

"That sergeant held up his hand right at the last second as if he had it in his power somehow to stop that train. I'll never forget that look on his face."

AFTER THE ENGINEER had left, Hook turned to the lieutenant. "Well?" he asked.

"I think the engineer had it right. Maybe the sergeant had gotten too comfortable. Maybe he just got careless, cut things too close in the end."

"It's possible," he said.

"But you don't think so?"

Hook opened the door to let Mixer out. "And don't run off," he said.

She picked up her purse. "The engineer believes that to be the case. I don't see any reason to think otherwise. As far as I'm concerned, this investigation is complete."

"The engineer's account didn't provide much more than what we already knew," he said.

The lieutenant rolled her eyes. "And your answer?"

Hook picked up his book and worked the dog-ear out with his thumb.

"I haven't found a good answer yet," he said. "That's my problem."

"Mr. Runyon," she said. "I admit that my experience may not be as extensive as yours, but I can't help but wonder if you don't have a vested interest in keeping this case open."

"Oh? And why would that be?"

"Perhaps a man who's guarding salvage cars prefers instead to be investigating a murder case."

"I'm just interested in the truth, no matter where it leads or who is implicated, Lieutenant."

"Really?" she said. "You were quick enough to delegate the personal details of this case as I recall."

"It may be the army is more concerned about following the rules than finding the truth," he said. "I'm not cut that way."

"Are you insinuating that we're ignoring evidence?"

"Sometimes it's necessary to look beyond the evidence, Lieutenant."

"I see. And what is it that you think I've overlooked?"

"For one thing, I'd bet my next paycheck those two guards were sleeping with the same woman. Men have been known to kill each other over that sort of thing."

A blush crawled up the lieutenant's throat. "Even if this was true," she said, "it only proves that men are capable of deception, which comes as no surprise to anyone. But it doesn't necessarily equate to homicide."

"No, but it does require consideration."

She walked to the door of the caboose. "So, what are you suggesting?"

"I want to go back and question that guard again," he said. Lieutenant Capron stepped out onto the platform of the caboose.

"Really, Mr. Runyon, is that necessary?"

"Yes," he said.

"I'll have to be there, and there are a good many other things I need to be doing."

"It's necessary."

The lieutenant sighed. "When?"

"Right now. We can take the popcar out if you want. It's a straight run from here."

"The popcar?"

"The motorcar," he said. "The railroad provides me one on occasion."

"Doesn't that violate some sort of railroad rule?"

"Not so long as I'm enforcing them," he said, picking up his coat. "Did you bring a wrap?"

"No."

He reached for an old work coat from behind the door.

"Take this one," he said. "Like me, it's a little worn around the edges, but it still does the job."

NINE

LIEUTENANT CAPRON CLIMBED aboard the popcar as if it might shoot out from under her. Mixer begged to go along, but Hook sent him back.

"Oh, my," she said, holding on to her hat as they gathered up speed. Her eyes glistened against the wind. She sat at the end of the seat, as if to distance herself from any sort of communion. She threw up walls, this one, and he couldn't help but wonder why.

He bent below the windshield and lit a cigarette. He leaned back.

The lieutenant took off her hat and stuffed it into her purse. Her hair whipped about her face as they moved into the countryside. She pulled a strand from her eye and grew quiet.

Hook said, "Riding the rails is like book collecting. Once it gets into your blood, there's no turning back."

But the lieutenant didn't answer, turning instead to study the passing landscape.

Ahead, survey flags dotted the right-of-way. The crew paused to get a good look at the lieutenant as the popcar came by. Hook understood why. Though charm had long since given way to army procedure, one couldn't deny her beauty.

"What are they doing?" she asked.

"Upgrade," he said, pointing to the flags. "Looks

like they're going to reinforce the roadbed, but then it's been a while since I've been invited to a board meeting."

The lieutenant only nodded. As they topped the run and plunged toward the canyon, she blanched and gripped the seat.

"Don't worry," he said. "This is what every engineer sees just before hitting the tunnel. It's like jumping off a cliff blindfolded. Makes me nervous to this day."

As Hook brought it into the siding, the lieutenant took a deep breath and combed her hair back with her fingers. She put on her hat and squared it onto her head. Climbing off the popcar, she placed her foot on the step to dust off her shoes. Hook searched for his cigarettes.

CORPORAL THIBODEAUX CAME out of the tunnel with his rifle propped across his arm.

"Oh, Lieutenant," he said. "I thought I heard a train coming. Near scared the life out of me."

"Corporal," she said. "Something has come up, and Mr. Runyon would like to ask you a few more questions."

The corporal glanced over at Hook. "But I've told you everything I know."

"You've been helpful, Corporal. But we need some clarification," she said.

He shrugged. "What is it you want to know?"

"Are you acquainted with a young lady in Ash Fork by the name of Linda Sue?" Hook asked.

"Yes," he said. "There ain't nothing wrong with that, is there?"

"How long have you known her?"

"About a year, I guess. We met at Blue's."

"How would you describe your relationship?" Hook asked.

"What does that have to do with anything?"

"Please answer the question."

He leaned his rifle against the popcar. "I guess you could say we were close."

"Lovers?" Hook said.

The corporal's face flushed. "Now look, that's none of your business."

Hook walked around the popcar. "Corporal, no one is interested in your love life except as it might relate to the sergeant's death. Now, please answer the question."

"Yes," he said. "Lovers."

"Were you having trouble recently?" Hook asked. "Were you fighting about anything?"

"No more than usual, I guess," he said. "Spats, you know. Linda Sue has a way."

"What kind of way?" he asked.

"Of flirting with everybody, like a puppy wagging its tail. It doesn't make a difference to Linda Sue, you know, young or old, men or women. She flirts with everybody."

"But sometimes people take it the wrong way?" Hook said.

"Yeah, sometimes," he said.

"Doesn't that make you jealous?"

"Sure. I been mad but then you got to know Linda Sue."

"What about Sergeant Erikson?"

"What do you mean?"

"Did Linda Sue flirt with him as well?"

"Sometimes. The sergeant didn't always know where his rank ended," he said.

"And where would that be?" Hook asked.

"Look, I did my job out here, everything he told me to do. But he had no say about Linda Sue and me."

"Is that what you told him?" he asked.

"Damn right," he said.

"But he kept going over to Linda Sue's while you were on duty, didn't he?"

Corporal Thibodeaux's eyes hardened. He turned away and then turned back.

"So I told him, see. I told him, 'Take off them god-damn stripes, and we'll see who's boss.'"

"And did he?" Hook said.

"He knew it to be a big mistake, I guess."

"But that didn't end it, did it?" he asked.

"Sergeant Erikson wrote up a bad evaluation on me. It cost my promotion."

Hook lit a cigarette and offered one to the corporal. He shook his head no.

"So you figured out a way to get him in the tunnel and to let the hotshot do the getting even for you," Hook said.

The corporal clenched his jaw. "I know how it looks, and I can't say I'm all that sorry about the sergeant. But I didn't kill him. He managed that his own damn self."

Lieutenant Capron looked at Hook and then back at Thibodeaux.

"I'm going to have to report this, Corporal. It could change things."

"I'm under arrest?" he asked.

"No," she said. "There are no grounds for that yet. You'll have to do the best you can out here until I can arrange for someone to come."

"Yes, ma'am."

"And you best start telling the truth, Corporal," she said. "Guarding this tunnel is paradise compared to a military prison."

"I ain't lying, ma'am. That's for damn sure," he said. "We had words now and then, but that's as far as it went."

They watched Corporal Thibodeaux work his way to the guardhouse. At the top of the steps, he looked back for a moment before going inside.

"Well," she said, adjusting her hat. "I can see that the corporal might have a motive here, though there doesn't seem to be any hard evidence."

Hook walked to the trestle and looked down into the canyon.

"Linda Sue worked both sides of the shift," he said. "Such a situation seldom ends peacefully. Add on a poor evaluation, and a man could get mad enough to kill."

"Erikson signed out on patrol before Thibodeaux even got to the guardhouse," she said. "And he checked the board like always. Suicide is unlikely. Homicide is a possibility, I suppose. Perhaps I should send out the military police. The security of this tunnel is an imperative."

"An arrest could jeopardize the investigation," he said. "In my opinion, we'll learn more without that just yet."

"I thought that's what you wanted?"

"I said it was worth considering, and that's what I'm doing. I'm just a yard dog and a little slow on the uptake, but I prefer to sleep on things before charging someone with murder."

"Well," she said. "You sleep on it. In the meantime,

I'll have to report this to Command and make arrangements for replacements."

"It's a little late for worrying about that tunnel and the war, isn't it, Lieutenant? You've heard about the atomic bomb?"

"Army orders stand until they're rescinded."

"Even if they don't make sense?"

"Even so," she said.

Hook picked up a rock and threw it into the canyon. "I'd like to take a look down there before we go, if you don't mind."

"And what do you expect to find down there?"

"Just a look," he said.

She checked her watch. "I guess the army isn't the only one who does things for no apparent reason."

"It won't take long," he said.

"Then I'll go with you."

"It's a pretty steep climb, Lieutenant."

"Mr. Runyon, I've been through army training and was the top in my squadron. I'm not afraid of a climb."

"Okay," he said. "We best get started then."

THE PATH TWISTED through the basalt rock like a corkscrew. The air cooled as they descended into the canyon. At times the trail dropped away, the rock loose and precarious beneath them. The lieutenant, not dressed for such an excursion, struggled to maintain her balance in the rocks.

Soon the trestle rose above them, its beams frail against the blue sky.

The path narrowed, and rocks jutted up from the ground like the bows of sinking ships. Animal tracks and scat were everywhere along the trail, the canyon serving as both shelter from the heat and cover from predators.

As they neared the bottom, Hook waited for the lieutenant to pick her way through the jumble of rocks. When she reached him, she dabbed the perspiration from her forehead with her sleeve. A rip in her nylon ran the length of her shin.

"Are you okay?" he asked.

"I'm fine," she said.

At the bottom of the trail, cigarette butts were scattered about, and the vegetation had been worn away.

"Looks like a resting spot for the patrol," he said. "I'm going to work my way over to the trestle."

"I'm coming, too," she said.

"With those shoes?"

"The shoes are just fine," she said.

Hook shrugged. "Have it your way, Lieutenant."

The descent steepened, and brush grew thick from out of the rocks. At one point, a dry-gulch nearly four feet across cut between them and the trestle. Hook jumped over.

"I'll be back," he said.

"Wait," she said.

Slipping off her shoes, she threw them across and then jumped over herself. He caught her under the arm and pulled her in. He could feel the heat from her body and the tremble in her arm.

Once they got to the trestle, they came to a deep ravine that cut directly beneath it. Hook knelt down and looked over the edge. Pieces of boxcars and wheel carriages were scattered about at the bottom.

"Looks like she's claimed her share of equipment over the years," he said.

"It wouldn't take much to bring the whole thing crashing down," she said. "Rail transportation would be disrupted for a good long while. That's precisely why the military is involved out here."

"Yeah," he said. "I suppose they're right about that. Blow the bracings and she'd collapse like a row of dominoes."

"Well, then," she said. "Have you seen enough, Mr. Runyon? I need to get back."

Just as Hook got up, a ray of sunshine broke over the rim of the canyon and into the rocks below.

"Wait," he said. "I saw something."

"Really, Mr. Runyon," she said. "Is this necessary?"

"We've come this far," he said. "Just as well take a look." Lowering himself over the edge of the ravine, he worked his toes into the cracks and eased his way to the bottom. "Found it," he called up.

The lieutenant leaned over the side. "What is it?"

Hook didn't answer but climbed his way back up. "Flashlight," he said, handing it to her.

She turned it over, studying it. "It's army issue," she said.

Hook nodded. "Whoever dropped it had to be on the trestle at the time."

The lieutenant looked up at the trestle and then back at Hook. "I didn't see Sergeant Erikson's flashlight, did you?"

"No," he said. "Not until now."

TEN

THEY'D GONE ONLY a few miles on the popcar when Lieutenant Capron slipped on Hook's old jacket. Her hands disappeared into the sleeves, and the collar came up to her ears.

"It's freezing on this thing," she said, shivering.

"I knew a rail inspector froze up on a popcar coming out of Chicago. When they found him, he was stiff as an icicle."

"That so?" she said.

"The popcar ran out of fuel in Kansas City, or I guess he would have just kept on going. They had to chisel him loose with a railroad pick."

"Thanks for the coat," she said.

The air smelled of the desert as they clattered along the tracks.

She pulled a crumpled pack of his cigarettes out of his coat pocket and then put them back in.

"How long have you been a railroad detective?" she asked.

"Well now," he said, scratching his head. "Some would say I've never been a real one. Most of what I know I learned riding the rails. Eddie Preston says an agent who isn't a Baldwin Felts graduate might just as well be picking cotton."

She turned and looked at him. "You were a hobo?"

"Of the highest order," he said.

"But why? How?"

"I hit the skids when I lost my arm. I been about everywhere a train can go and a few places it can't."

"How is it you became a railroad detective?" she asked.

"Time heals, they say. Fact is, it doesn't heal so much as it deadens, but the result is the same. Takes a lot of energy to keep a hatred going full tilt.

"In the end, I pulled it together long enough to land this job. It's as close to being a hobo as a man can get and still earn a paycheck. Turned out to be the right choice for me, but there was a time it could have gone either way."

"And the caboose?"

"Men were hard to come by because of the war. The railroad agreed to the caboose, figuring I would give it up soon enough. Guess they were wrong about that one."

"And the books? Isn't that a little peculiar for a hobo?"

"Or for a yard dog or for anybody in his right mind. Yeah, it's a lot peculiar, but it's not illegal. So there you have it."

The moon popped onto the horizon and lifted into the black sky. The lights of Ash Fork shimmered in the distance, and the rails shined like ivory ahead of them.

"Is your name really Hook?" she asked.

"I sign my checks Walter," he said. "And is your name really Lieutenant?"

She turned and adjusted her collar against the breeze. "Allison," she said.

"Were you born a lieutenant?"

"Army brat," she said. "My father was a first sergeant for over twenty years. I've lived all over the world."

"And here you are an officer."

"My father taught me to never be ashamed of the fact that he was enlisted. Any officer worth his salt knows that a good sergeant will save his hide a hundred times over."

"And so you decided to join the army like him?"

"Had I been a man, I would have been on the front lines. It's hard being left behind because of what you are."

"I can't disagree with that," he said.

"I joined in forty-three as a WAC. This country finally decided that we, women that is, could do something in addition to nursing. I've been with the Department of Transportation at Los Alamos since then."

"Home of the bomb," he said.

"I'm in Support. It's a base with all the needs of any base. Transportation is a part of that. Keeping the tunnel staffed and safe is just one of my responsibilities, one that hasn't turned out so well, as you know."

"Can't see that it's your fault," he said.

"I try to do my job, though it can be rather pedestrian, I suppose."

"All work counts in a war," he said. "And is worthy of praise, so long as it's for our side."

"How much farther?" she asked.

"We're about there, which is a good thing because there's an eastbound due in about an hour."

Ahead, a small light bobbed off into the darkness and then disappeared. Hook idled back, coasting to a stop.

"What's wrong?" she asked.

"I saw a light."

"A light?"

"We've been plagued with copper thieves," he said. "Can't seem to catch up to them. They're moving big quantities somehow."

He shut the engine off and listened. "You hear that?" he asked.

"It sounds like a motor," she said.

"I've been trying to nab these boys for a good long while. You wait here. I'm going to see what's going on. Scrap's getting damn hard to live with, and Eddie's sworn to keep me in the junk business until I catch them."

"I'll come with you."

"Thanks the same, but this is railroad business."

"Take this flashlight," she said. "You might need it."

"They'd spot me sure. The moon's high, and I can follow the tracks."

"I don't know how to drive this thing."

"Don't worry," he said. "I'll be back."

Working his way down line, he crouched now and again to listen. When he heard voices and smelled tobacco smoke, he knew they couldn't be far away. Soon he spotted moonlight glinting from a windshield in the right-of-way. He'd found his boys at last.

Hunkering down in the shadows, he pulled his sidearm. He could make out two distinct voices, maybe three, too damn many to cover all at once. He'd have to separate them out, take them one at a time. But he couldn't be certain how well-armed they might be.

Either way, cornered men could be dangerous and unpredictable. Given a choice, he'd not attempt it alone, but he'd been after these bastards for a long time.

Letting them get away now meant more time in Scrap's junkyard. He'd had all that he wanted.

One of the men climbed up the embankment. Hook lay low between the tracks. The man stopped, his head just visible in the moonlight, and lit a cigarette. Unzipping, he stood with his back turned from the men below.

Hook crawled down the center of the tracks, the cinders scrubbing his knees raw. He peeked over the rail. The man drew on his cigarette, a red button in the darkness, and started to work his way back down.

Hook moved in from behind and clipped him with the butt of his P.38. His legs wilted under him, and his cigarette dropped into the dirt. Hook caught him and lowered him into the weeds.

He slipped forward to where he could see. A truck had been backed into the culvert that ran under the tracks. One man worked in the back of the truck, while two others carried goods from out of the culvert. There were too many for rushing, but at some point they would miss their buddy sleeping in the weeds.

If he could slip in from the other end of the culvert, maybe he could even up the odds. If not, then someone else could worry about salvage cars.

He double-checked his man in the weeds, who still slumbered, and then he made his way down the back side. From there he could see into the culvert.

The men were loading what appeared to be copper radiator cores into the truck. They must have taken them off a sided car and stored them in the culvert for picking up when the way was clear.

One wore a ball cap and gloves. He huffed as he heaved a core onto the back of the truck.

He bent forward, his hands on his knees. "Where the hell is Leon?"

The guy in the truck bed paused. "Taking a leak, the lazy son of a bitch."

Hook moved into the shadows and waited. The man with the cap came back for another core. When he stooped to gather it up, Hook stepped in and caught him under the chin with the toe of his boot. He snorted once and spilled forward. Hook grabbed him under the arms and dragged him out of the culvert.

Donning the ball cap, Hook picked up the core and carried it to the truck. With his head down, he hoisted it into the back. When the stacker stooped to get it, Hook snagged him by the collar with his prosthesis and yanked him out the back of the truck and onto his head.

Hook rolled him onto his back. His nose, having taken the brunt of the fall, bent to the side, and dirt plugged his nostrils. A front tooth dangled from a string.

"Watch your step," Hook said.

Hook started to stand but stopped when the cold muzzle of a gun shoved into his cheek. He knew instantly that he'd failed to count the driver, the one guy with a weapon.

"Don't even breathe," the driver said.

He smelled of whiskey and tobacco, and a copper arthritic bracelet hung from his wrist.

"I quit breathing about a minute ago," Hook said.

"Who are you?" the driver asked.

"Railroad security," Hook said.

"A one-armed yard dog?"

"I came cheap," Hook said.

"Won't be much of a loss, then," he said. "You showed up at the wrong party this time, mister."

Over the years Hook had been threatened before, and they came in different degrees of sincerity. This one ranked ten on a ten-point scale. Sooner or later, he figured it would come to something like this, though dying in a culvert over a radiator core had never occurred to him.

The hammer clicked back, a sound as hard and cold as the knot in his belly, and Hook closed his eyes.

ELEVEN

THE DRIVER'S GUN spun across the culvert when the lieutenant hit him on the head with the flashlight.

His eyes closed, and his weapon fell between his feet. He pitched forward onto Hook's chest, his arms dangling over his shoulders.

Hook lowered him to the ground. "Good Lord," he said, looking up at the lieutenant. "Are you nuts? You could have been killed."

"Am *I* nuts?" she said. "You were the one with a gun in your face."

"I hadn't figured on so many of them," he said, rubbing the back of his neck. "I thought I told you to stay put."

"Does ingratitude come with the job, or is it just a natural part of your personality?" she asked.

Hook searched the man's pockets and then popped the clip out of his sidearm.

"I admit to not being thrilled about dying over a load of scrap copper," he said.

"How many of them are there?" she asked.

Hook lit a cigarette. "Three here. One up there in the weeds."

"What do we do now?"

"Turn them over to the local boys for prosecution."

"Shouldn't we get some help?" she asked.

Hook looked around. "We could load them in the truck," he said. "Can you drive one?"

The lieutenant shrugged. "Never have," she said. "Why don't we just take the popcar for help?"

Hook shook his head. "Because you can't be driving the popcar. It's against regulations, for one thing, and I can't leave you here alone with copper thieves.

"Maybe we can tie these boys up, put 'em in the back, and you can guard while I drive the truck."

"Okay," she said.

"Thing is, I need a little help. It's a chore tying up crooks with one hand while pointing a gun with a prosthesis at the same time."

The lieutenant cocked her arm on her waist. "That's an odd way of asking," she said. "Anyway, it seems railroad business to me."

"Goddang it, Lieutenant," he said. "Are you going to help or not?"

"I'll help," she said. "But your attitude could use a little improvement."

"All right," he said. "Goddang it, will you please give me a hand?"

"That's better," she said.

"First, how about checking the truck for pliers?"

When she returned with the pliers, she said, "Found them on the floorboard. How did you know they'd be there?"

"Where would scrap thieves be without pliers? Wire's in the back of the truck. Cut a length of it and bring it here. We'll bind them and toss them in."

While she retrieved the wire, Hook dragged the men together side by side. He watched on with his P.38 as the lieutenant secured their hands. The moon cast highlights in the red of her hair as she worked, and when she'd finished, she stood.

"Good job," he said. "Look like a string of fish, don't they?"

"Now what?" she asked.

"There's one more up by the tracks. We better get him wired up before he comes around."

Just as they started to climb the embankment, a sound came from far away. Hook stopped and lowered his head. The lieutenant's breath came in short strokes behind him, and the old truck creaked as it cooled down in the night.

"What's the matter?" she asked.

"Did you hear something?"

Lieutenant Capron turned her ear into the wind. "No," she said. But then it came again, a wail rising and falling somewhere off in the distance.

Hook turned and looked at her. "Oh, Christ," he said.

"What? What is it?"

"It's the eastbound," he said.

"The eastbound?"

He looked up the embankment and then back at the lieutenant.

"The popcar's sitting on the tracks," he said. "And the eastbound's coming in."

"You must be mistaken," she said.

Hook grabbed her by the hand. "Come on," he said, pulling her up behind him. "Maybe we can get it to the siding."

"A train?" she said, as she struggled to keep up. "For God's sake, a *train's* coming?"

Hook ran as best he could, though the ties kept throwing off his stride. They'd gone but a short way when the whistle wailed again, louder this time. Hook's heart beat in his ears.

"Come on," he yelled over his shoulder. "We can make it."

"We've got to get off these tracks. I'm not getting killed by a train for some stupid popcar."

"This is my job we're talking about," he said. "Come on. Run." The lieutenant struggled to keep up. Hook reached back and took her arm.

"Faster, faster," he shouted.

The whistle lifted into the night, piercing and shrill, and the thud of the driver wheels rode in on the rails.

No sooner had they reached the popcar when the train's glimmer bobbed onto the horizon, lighting up the tracks.

Hook put his shoulder against the popcar. "Push!" he yelled. The lieutenant fell in beside him, and together they heaved against the dead weight of the car. The popcar edged back.

The light shot into their eyes, and the earth rumbled under their feet as the engine charged toward them.

"Push!" Hook yelled again.

She dropped her head between her arms and bore down, and the car picked up speed.

Once there, Hook threw the switch, and they pushed her onto the siding.

No sooner had he thrown the switch back when the train roared past, her whistle screaming. Dirt spun into their eyes, and the speeding cars sucked away their breaths.

The lieutenant collapsed into the seat of the popcar as the train sped on down the tracks.

Hook searched for his cigarettes. "Damn," he said. "Those boys were in a toot, weren't they?"

Lieutenant Capron, her hands clamped in her lap, stared down the tracks.

Hook lit up. "Why so quiet?" he asked.

The lieutenant turned to him, her eyes narrowed. "I'm deciding whether or not to kill you," she said.

"Well," he said. "It's a plan, I suppose, but you better wait until we get back. We've got copper thieves to round up."

As they walked back down the tracks to the culvert, they could hear the eastbound's whistle in the distance as she made the Ash Fork crossing.

Hook searched the weeds with his light but found the man gone. He climbed down to the culvert to discover that not only had the others been cut free, but the truck and the copper were missing as well.

The lieutenant, who was waiting for him up top, called down. "Is everything all right?"

Hook climbed up the embankment. "They're gone," he said.

"What's gone?"

"Everything."

"The truck, too?"

"Everything is everything," he said.

"All of this was for nothing?" she asked.

Hook shrugged. "Come on," he said. "Let's go back for the popcar. We'll be home in no time."

The lieutenant climbed in and waited for Hook to crank the engine. It fired off, coughed a couple of times, and died. He tried again, but this time it failed even to fire.

"Now what?" she asked.

He cranked again. "She was running fine earlier."

"Well, something's wrong," she said.

"It's the equipment," Hook said. "Maintenance is not what it should be, what with the war."

"You have fuel, don't you?" she asked.

"'Course," he said.

"Are you sure?"

"I'm pretty sure," he said.

She looked at him, and he could see the fire in her eyes even in the darkness.

"I don't remember you checking the fuel before we left," she said.

"I'll check it now, if that will make you happy," he said.

He unscrewed the gas tank lid and shined the flashlight into it. "I'll be," he said. "It's that Scrap West siphoning gas again."

"You mean we are stuck out here?" she said. "You can't expect me to walk all the way to town."

Hook screwed the lid back on. "It's a nice night," he said. "And not such a bad walk."

THEY WALKED BACK to West's Salvage Yard in silence. When they reached the staff car, the lieutenant took off his jacket and dusted off her uniform, which now looked a good deal like Scrap's overalls.

"Your coat," she said, holding it out.

"Why don't you wear it home," he said. "It's pretty chilly."

"No thank you," she said. "I intend to erase this entire day from memory."

Hook started to respond but decided against it. Instead, he lit a cigarette and watched as she drove off. When her lights had disappeared, he walked to Scrap's office.

Scrap had both feet up on his desk and was working the slug out of his pipe with a screwdriver. When he saw Hook, he pushed his hat onto the back of his head.

"You get in another fight down at the pool hall, Hook? I ain't doing no fines."

Hook pulled up a chair. Brushing off his knees, he sat down.

"Maybe I have and maybe I haven't, if it's all the same to you."

Scrap fired up his pipe. "If you'd spend your time hunting them copper thieves instead of brawling, life might be more rewarding, and maybe I could turn a profit around here."

"Now there you go jumping to conclusions," Hook said. "What you think I've been doing?"

Scrap dropped his feet and studied Hook over the desk. "You caught 'em?" he asked.

Hook worked at a burr buried in his sock. "Four of them," he said. "Under the culvert just beyond the siding. They probably throw the copper off as the cars are made up for a run, stash it in the culvert, and truck it out at their pleasure."

"I'll be damned," he said. "I take everything back what I said about you, Hook, and most of what I thought."

"Thing is, they overpowered me and got away."

"They got away?"

"For the time being."

Scrap lit a match and sucked his pipe back to life. "But you saved the copper?"

"Not exactly."

"The thieves got away and with my copper to boot?"

"They weren't anxious to stick around for another go after I worked them over," Hook said. "No need for thanks."

Scrap laid his pipe in the Chevy hubcap that doubled as a paperweight for his car titles. He scratched his head.

"You're telling me you caught 'em, but they got away?"

"Yes, sir, that's more or less how it happened."

"And you saved my copper, but now it's gone?"

"That's the short of it."

Scrap shoved his hands into his pockets and started for the door. About halfway there, he turned.

"Just what am I supposed to do now?"

Hook stood and squashed out his cigarette.

"Scrap," he said. "That's the one question you might not want to ask."

TWELVE

THE NEXT DAY Hook waited until he heard the crane start up before he went to the office to call Eddie Preston.

"Security," Eddie said.

"Eddie, this is Hook Runyon."

"Runyon, what the hell is going on out there?"

"Chasing thieves, Eddie. I hear that's what security is supposed to do."

"I get a call from the engineer on the eastbound hotshot. He says he dang near hit a popcar that had been left on the tracks outside Ash Fork. He says he damn near ran over some fool pushing it down track. So I says, 'Don't worry about it. We got all kinds of dead people up and down the track out there. What's another one more or less?'"

"That's a real cynical point of view, Eddie."

"So, I'm thinking to myself, what kind of a dumb ass would leave a popcar on the tracks with a hotshot coming in, and guess who came to mind?"

Scrap opened the door and commenced searching for his pipe tobacco.

"Hello, hello," Eddie said. "Damn it, Runyon. Don't hang up on me."

"Copper thieves, Eddie," Hook said. "First thing I know the eastbound's coming in. I almost managed to nab those copper thieves, but the bastards outnumbered me."

"Count on an investigation," Eddie said. "The railroad frowns on leaving popcars on the main line. And then there's that other thing, too."

"What other thing?"

"That orphanage formed a committee. They're unhappy about the government using tax money to buy rubbers for soldiers."

"They use tax money to buy bombs," Hook said. "Anyone worried about that?"

"They ain't happy about them rubbers."

"Can't they just destroy them?"

"They're government property. It's against the law."

"Well, give the rubbers back to the railroad."

"The railroad don't want them, Runyon. Nobody would have known anything about this if you hadn't set that car loose."

"Next time I'll just let them shut the main line down," Hook said.

"And what about that Johnson Canyon Tunnel deal?" Eddie asked.

"What about it?"

"You wrapped it up?"

Hook lit a cigarette and looked over at Scrap, who was taking a nap under his hat.

"I don't think it was an accident," he said.

"Well, it damn sure wasn't natural causes, unless you count being run over by a train natural."

"There was a love triangle, Eddie."

"A what?"

"Those two guards were sleeping with the same woman."

"I don't care if it was a circle jerk, Runyon. The railroad's getting ready to pour a lot of money into that line, and I don't want delays."

"I found that guard's flashlight at the bottom of the trestle. Why would he go into the tunnel without his light?"

"Maybe he didn't want to see the train that was going to run over him."

"And maybe he dropped the flashlight during a struggle on the trestle," Hook said.

"If you think there was a love circle, turn it over to the military, Runyon."

"Triangle," Hook said.

"What?"

"A love triangle, Eddie. Jesus, you need to get out of the office once in a while."

"Whatever," he said. "In the meantime, see if you can't stop those copper thieves before they shut down the whole system. That's why you're out there, you know."

"Little static on the line, Eddie. I'm having trouble hearing. Are you still there? Hello. I'll check back later, Eddie."

Hook hung up the phone and searched out a cigarette. Scrap scratched his chin and tossed his hat onto the toe of his boot.

"What's this about rubbers?" he asked.

"Don't start, Scrap."

"You got rubbers, Hook, I got a right to know."

"There were army condoms on a railcar that turned over, that's all. The damn things wound up in the wrong hands."

Scrap blew on his pipe and reached for his tobacco. "The army's got rubbers?"

"Where you been all your life, hanging out with Eddie?"

"What do they do with them?"

"Jesus, Scrap, what do you think?"

After filling his pipe, Scrap hung it in the corner of his mouth. He studied Hook.

"What color are they?"

"What color are what?"

"Try to concentrate, Hook. We're talking rubbers here."

"Army green. Hell, I don't know. What difference does it make?"

"All those rubbers will be coming back as surplus," he said. "I figure a man could pick 'em up cheap."

"And what would you do with army surplus rubbers?" Hook asked, shaking his head.

"Sell them. What do you think? Just 'cause the war's over don't mean people are going to stop making unwanted babies."

"Just forget it, Scrap. You can't sell green army rubbers out of a salvage yard."

Scrap lit his pipe and hooked his thumbs under his overalls' straps.

"I don't know why not. I sold two hundred boxes of sanitary napkins one time. Bought from a trucker what tipped over his eighteen wheeler. I knew the time of month of every woman between here and Flagstaff."

Scrap sucked at his pipe and looked at Hook. "Did you know them things come in different sizes? Now that's something to ponder, ain't it?"

"No, it isn't," Hook said. "How about loaning me the jeep for a few hours?"

"Oh, sure. Why not?"

"You haven't taken the motor out of it yet, have you?"

"Something's been sucking eggs down at my chicken coop," he said, ignoring Hook. "Eggshells everywhere. Looks like it snowed, and all the chickens are walking around in a daze."

"Are you going to loan me the jeep, Scrap?"

"All right, take it," he said, handing him the keys.

"There's a place in heaven set aside just for you," Hook said.

"Well, that's good 'cause I sure wouldn't have to worry about yard dogs no more," he said.

Hook found Sheriff Roscoe Mueller in city hall, sitting at his desk. His blue uniform, leftover fat clothes by the looks of them, hung on his frame like a sack. The collar of his T-shirt had been frizzed by an overabundant beard, and hair sprang from his nostrils, the tops of his ears, and fingers. In a different setting, he might be mistaken for a gorilla or orangutan. His badge, big as a jar lid, looked like something from a kid's cowboy outfit.

The nightstick lying on top of his desk had been the same one he'd offered to break Hook's head with at the pool hall skirmish. The sheriff had backed off upon realizing that Hook was a railroad dick. Hook had learned over the years that some of the most dangerous cops could be found in the backwash towns of America. A good many were less than concerned about lawful procedures.

Sheriff Mueller looked up from his paper. "Well," he said, "if it ain't the yard dog. How's the junk business these days?"

"Never any shortage of junk," Hook said.

"Heard someone left the popcar on the main line,

Hook. Trains run on those main lines, in case you didn't know."

"Yeah," Hook said. "The divisional supervisor filled me in on that.

"Look, Sheriff, I got boys stealing Scrap's copper right off the cars. Where do you figure they are selling it?"

"Any salvage yard in the country," he said. "Say, I hear tell that sergeant at the tunnel tried to stop a hotshot with his hand, and it didn't work out so well?"

"It's not altogether clear," Hook said.

The sheriff rolled up his paper and tossed it in the trash basket. "I figured to help sweep up out there, but that lieutenant said the army would be taking care of things.

"The digger said they shipped the body back. Why is this *your* problem, Hook? Don't you have enough to worry about?"

"You know how the railroad is," Hook said.

"I sure don't remember lieutenants looking like that when I was in the army," the sheriff said.

Hook pulled up a chair and fished out a cigarette. "The world's changing, Roscoe. Going to leave you behind."

"That's for sure," he said, hiking his boot up on the desk.

"You managing to keep the peace around here?" Hook asked.

"Now that you ain't busting up the pool hall, things been pretty quiet."

"Sorry about that little bang-up," Hook said. "Appreciate the professional courtesy, though."

"Well, Ben Hoffer's been asking for an ass kicking

most of his life," he said. "Guess he was waiting for you to come along to do it."

"I try not to break the law most of the time," Hook said. "Sometimes it just can't be helped."

The sheriff reached for a pencil and dug a wad of gum loose from under the heel of his boot.

"I figure Ben started things, or I'd have run you in, Hook. That's the way it is. You might want to keep your eyes open. Ben Hoffer ain't one to take a beating and forget it."

"Thanks. I'll do that, Sheriff."

"I figure you ain't here to ask forgiveness, Hook, or to check on how my day's going."

"Been wondering if you know anything about Corporal Thibodeaux?" he said. "He's one of the guards out at the tunnel."

"Thibodeaux? Yeah, I know him. He's living here in Ash Fork. Been staying at Linda Sue's, the waitress over at Blue's Café."

"You got anything on him?"

"Hot checks," he said. "Thibodeaux's got a problem getting from one payday to the next on his own funds. Never nothing big, just piddling shit. But I'm getting damn tired of chasing him down. I told him next hot one and he gets sack time in my hotel. He don't show for duty and the army eats his ass. He knows how it goes."

"What about Linda Sue?" Hook asked.

"Been waitressing most her life. No one works harder than Linda Sue, but she ain't got a notion when it comes to men. She can spot a goddang bum a hundred miles away, and there ain't nothing she likes better. Her and Corporal Thibodeaux were born for each other."

"And what do you know about Sergeant Erikson?" Hook asked.

"I spotted him coming out of Linda Sue's a time or two. I figure those boys were sharing more than a guardhouse. Linda Sue ain't nothing if not generous."

"No trouble from Sergeant Erikson?"

"Quiet and kind of spooky. Always on the outside looking in. You know the type."

Hook squashed his cigarette out in the ashtray. "Thanks, Sheriff. I'll let you know if anything comes up."

WHEN HOOK GOT back to the jeep, someone had pulled in front of him.

"Damn it," he said.

He tried to push the jeep back with his one hand, but the wheels rode up against the curb.

Just then the old man from the post office came around the corner. Hook leaned against the hood to catch his breath.

The old man sank his hands into his overalls' pockets. "Where's the dog?" he asked.

"He isn't here," Hook said.

"Shoot him?"

"Not exactly," Hook said, turning around and leaning into the jeep.

"Shoot him behind the ear," he said. "He'll never know what hit him."

"You think you could help me push this jeep back?" Hook asked.

"Got to have a reverse to back up," he said. "No reverse, you got to park with no one in front of you."

"Someone pulled in," Hook said. "Maybe you could give me a hand. I'll steer if you'll push."

The old man turned his back to the jeep, putting both hands under the bumper. He rocked her a couple of times, and the jeep rolled back into the street.

"Thanks," Hook said, getting in.

"No reverse, you got to plan ahead," he said. "Sometimes I had to park my Buick on the edge of town. Going backward everywhere ain't easy, you know. Sometimes a man gets confused about which is the right side of the road."

"I'll be more careful in the future," Hook said.

"People get tired of pushing after a while," he said. "People will get where they won't push no more."

"Thanks again," Hook said, pulling off.

He drove by Blue's Café to talk to Linda Sue, but Blue said that Linda Sue didn't show up for her shift. So on his way back to the salvage yard, Hook swung by her house and knocked on the door. No one answered.

The sun had set by the time he pulled into the salvage yard.

When Mixer heard him, he came out from under the caboose steps wagging his tail and stretching.

Once inside, Hook slipped off his prosthesis and fixed himself a whiskey and springwater. Both the pushers were gone from the siding, but he found the quiet more unsettling than comforting. He thumbed through a few of his latest acquisitions and then tossed them aside.

The more he tried to gather up the loose ends of the sergeant's death, the more they unraveled. He figured a man careful enough to check the board and sign the log had a fair notion of the schedule going in. For Erikson to get caught short in the tunnel just didn't fit. And he'd been on the right side of the curve for spotting the glimmer when she broke over the canyon. And then there was Linda Sue, the love nest, and the flashlight under the trestle.

He pulled the covers over him as the night deepened. Maybe the army would come up with some answers. The lieutenant had promised to keep him informed, but it struck him that she didn't push like she ought, leaving the hard questions for him. Maybe this sort of investigation was out of her league. With her being in Transportation and all, maybe she didn't deal with love triangles and dead bodies in tunnels every day.

Even though he preferred working his cases alone, at this point he'd take all the help he could get. And the possibility of seeing the lieutenant again didn't bother him much at all.

THIRTEEN

A STEAMER WITH a line of salvage cars in tow rattled the window as it blew past the caboose. Hook rolled over and groaned. Living in a caboose was like living inside a concrete mixer.

He found the coffee grounds swelled to twice their size in the coffeepot, and the ashes hadn't been cleaned out of the coal stove in days. After shaking them down, he dumped the ashpan outside. He put in enough fresh coal for breakfast coffee, and soon the aroma filled the caboose.

In the summertime, it took the coal stove about five seconds to turn the caboose into an oven and three hours for it to cool down to a tolerable temperature. Eddie had promised to update the old caboose with electricity, but somehow he had never gotten around to it.

Hook sat on the edge of his bunk and rubbed at the stubble on his chin. He needed a shave, which meant more hot water, which meant more misery as the sun bored through the cupola.

When the coffee had finished, he poured himself a cup at the table. From there he could see Scrap's office and the crane rising into the morning sun. He lit a cigarette and watched Scrap working his way toward him through the yard.

The military had yet to file charges or close the tunnel investigation, so in the meantime he figured to see if

he could find where the thieves fenced the copper. He'd
follow Sheriff Mueller's advice and check out the other
salvage yards in the area. Nothing stopped a thief faster
than drying up the money source. Once those copper
thieves were rounded up, he'd petition Eddie to move
him back to civilization.

Scrap knocked on the door before sticking his head
in. "You up, Runyon?" he asked.

"Why don't you run some electricity out here, Scrap?
I'm going blind with that kerosene lantern."

"So's you can read half the night, I suppose. Did you
bring my jeep back?"

"It's back," Hook said. "Half of Ash Fork's popula-
tion has taken a turn pushing it down the road."

"You got to park it where you don't have to back it
up."

"I hadn't figured that out," Hook said.

Scrap shrugged. "I've got a transmission just come
in. If you'd park it long enough, I could drop her in."

"I've been thinking I might check around, see if I
could find where those boys are fencing that copper,"
Hook said.

"Just 'cause I'm losing half my profit don't mean you
have to do nothing rash, Hook."

Hook took out his pocketknife and worked at a burr
that had been gouged into his prosthesis.

"Scrap," he said, "if a man brought a load of copper in here to sell, how would you know if it was stolen or not?"

"Junk's junk, and there ain't no telling where it's
been or where it's going."

"So, you figure you might have bought some stolen
copper yourself one time or another?"

He fished out his pipe. "Never bought stolen copper in my life," he said.

"How do you know?"

"Because I'm a law-abiding citizen."

"Except it *might* have been stolen?"

"If it was, I wouldn't buy it."

"Jesus," Hook said.

Scrap lit his pipe and thought it over. "I got rules about buying stolen salvage, Hook. If it's stolen, I don't buy it. That's about as plain as I can make it."

Hook slipped on his shoes and looked over at Scrap. "Sometimes it's like talking to a goddang echo," he said.

"And where's that dog?" Scrap said. "My chickens been roosting in the rafters like turkey buzzards."

"Now don't go picking on Mixer. He's got a sensitive nature."

"He pinned a dog three times his size in the yard last week," Scrap said. "He lay on his back for an hour in fear that killer might show up again."

"How about borrowing the jeep for a few hours today, Scrap?" Scrap went to the door.

"I wonder how the goddang railroad operated before they found me," he said.

THE OWNER OF the Flagstaff Salvage Yard pushed his goggles onto his forehead and snapped off his acetylene torch. White circles punctuated the black soot that had gathered on his face.

"You buy copper?" Hook asked.

The owner laid down his torch and lit a cigarette. "Copper, brass, and iron. No farm machinery and no appliances."

"I got a load of copper to bring in," Hook said.

He took out an oil rag and wiped his hands. "What you got?"

"Radiator cores."

"They bring top market price," he said. "Easy to handle and high quality."

"Great," Hook said. "You need records or anything?"

"They'll be on their way to the smelter before you get home," he said. "Who has time for records?"

"Thanks," Hook said. "Might be a few days."

The owner picked up his torch, fired his flint, and snapped the torch to life. He brought the yellow flame to blue with practiced turns of the knobs.

"I pay cash," he said, dropping the goggles over his eyes.

As Hook drove back to Ash Fork, the sun drifted low in the sky. There were other salvage yards he could check, he supposed. But it was pretty clear that copper thieves could sell their wares on the open market and with no questions asked. Cutting off the money source wasn't going to work.

Circling through the yard, he parked the jeep where he could pull out. Scrap's office light was on, and he could see Scrap bent over his desk. When Hook opened the door, Scrap pushed back his chair.

Scrap fished out his pipe and loaded it. "I've been thinking," he said.

"Oh, hell," Hook said. "Batten the hatches and hide your daughters."

"I been thinking they'll be bringing all them tanks home after the war. A man could buy some up, convert them to dozer tractors, and sell them back to the government. You know, turn swords into plowshares. Not only would it be the patriotic thing to do, but a man just might make a keen profit in the process."

"It takes about five hundred gallons of fuel just to start one of those bastards up," Hook said. "I don't think it would work out so well."

Scrap fired up his pipe. "Some folks just live to rain on a man's parade."

"Well, don't worry about it, Scrap. You always got army-green rubbers you could sell."

"That lieutenant called and wanted you to call her back. She left a number."

"Oh? Mind if I use your phone?"

"Shut off the lights when you're done," he said, putting on his hat.

Hook dialed the phone and waited through four rings. He was about to hang up, when the lieutenant came on line.

"Hook, here," he said. "Scrap said you called."

"Thanks for calling back," she said. "Something's come up. I don't have a guard at the tunnel. I hate to ask this, but I need someone out there."

"What's going on?" he asked.

"I'll be over first thing," she said. "But I can't leave that tunnel unguarded. I know this is short notice."

Hook paused. "All right," he said. "I'll take the jeep out."

FOURTEEN

UNCERTAIN THERE'D BE anything to eat at the guardhouse, Hook finished up the last can of beans and washed it down with tepid water. He stopped in at the office and made a call to the operator in Ash Fork. The line was clear.

Scrap rarely locked his office since he lived in quarters at the back of the yard. The little house had been abandoned, and Scrap had procured it from the city for the price of a move.

Hook took the jeep, leaving the lights off so as not to disturb Scrap's rest, and headed for the Johnson Canyon Tunnel. Pulling duty for the army hadn't been something he'd planned on this evening. Why the fuss over that damn tunnel escaped him, but if that's what the lieutenant wanted, a night away from the salvage yard might be a relief. In the past, the army had been less than anxious to have a one-armed man in its ranks. But then he could hear the concern in the lieutenant's voice, and he figured he owed her one.

The road to the canyon turned and twisted in the darkness, forcing him to take his time. He could easily get stuck, and without a reverse, it would be impossible to get out.

As he approached Johnson Canyon, the moon broke, setting the canyon walls aglow in its light. The trestle stood like a giant skeleton over the canyon, and the tracks struck off into the black hole in the mountain.

Hook shut the jeep off, and the silence of the canyon washed over him. Maybe he should have brought Mixer along for company, but then he'd be chasing him down half the night. He checked his sidearm and fished the flashlight out from between the seats.

He didn't know what had set the lieutenant off, and she hadn't been as forthcoming as he'd like. But checking out the tunnel and the trestle might be a good place to start. If nothing else, he'd sleep better knowing that no one had been about.

Moon shadows slid out from the rock peaks, and the smell of creosote rose up from the track bed as he worked his way down. Clicking on his light, he entered the darkness of the tunnel.

The silence loomed in the absence of Scrap's crane and the rumble of idling pushers. His light beam drew to a point in the blackness ahead, and the weight of the mountain pressed in about him. The air felt still and damp, and the smells of life dropped away. Each step resounded in the confinement of the rock.

When he came to the curve, his stomach tightened. A train could be charging in at this very moment. A violent death could be headed his way. Only a split second would pass between the time a train entered the tunnel and the end of his life. To stand at this point in the tunnel, to wait for the trembling of the earth and the certainty of an oncoming locomotive, would be a terrifying experience.

As Hook moved in, he found where the bridge and building gang had been removing the support beams.

In their place, they had lined the interior of the tunnel with boilerplate.

A few yards more and he turned back until he could see the moonlight at the end of the tunnel. This is where Sergeant Erikson met his fate. Hook smelled earth and felt the warmth from the outside world. From there, a train's headlamp could be seen coming down the grade. From there, the possibility of escape would still exist. Why would a man who had checked the board and signed out as usual stand midtrack and watch the train rushing toward him? How could he not make a run for a last chance at life?

Once outside, Hook clicked off his flashlight. He paused at the trestle to listen. He'd learned as both a hobo and a yard dog that sounds and smells could save a man's life. He'd learned, as well, that both patience and attention were essential to the process.

Stars rode overhead, and the moon hung like a lantern above the canyon. He moved onto the trestle, his steps deliberate. Every few seconds, he paused to re-establish his equilibrium. When in the middle of the trestle, he stopped. The moonlight cast into the canyon, but the bottom lay in darkness.

For a moment, he thought he saw a flicker of light in the distance, but on a night such as this, the moonlight could reflect off a shard of broken glass, a beer bottle, a piece of tin. He knelt and waited, and when satisfied that all was clear, he made his way back to the guardhouse.

Finding the door unlocked, he panned the room with his light before entering. Corporal Thibodeaux's things were strewn about, and his bedding lay in disarray. The ashtray contained cigar butts, and an empty cola bottle lay on its side next to his bed.

Hook walked to the window and looked down at the tunnel. The moonlight reflected from the trestle rails. This would have been lonely duty for anyone but especially tough for young men in the prime of their lives.

He pulled the bedding off the corporal's bunk and covered the mattress with an army blanket he found folded in the closet. Lying down, he listened to the sounds of the night. He wondered why the lieutenant had called on such short notice. It would take a while for her to come all the way from Los Alamos. Perhaps Corporal Thibodeaux had been relieved of duty, or perhaps they had been alerted to something.

Weariness swept over him, and he slept a disturbed sleep. Sometime during the night, the moonlight cast through the window had awakened him. He turned on his side and watched the beam of light edge beneath Sergeant Erikson's bunk. Hook lifted onto an elbow. He could see a backpack that had been pushed far beneath the bunk. It must have been overlooked when the sergeant's things were packed.

He got up, found a broom, and dragged the backpack out. Dumping the contents onto the mattress, he sifted through the things: a pair of hiking boots, civilian jeans and shirt, a jacket, and a pair of leather gloves. Tucked into an envelope were ten one-hundred-dollar bills.

He lit a cigarette and sat on the edge of the bunk. Why would Sergeant Erikson have a backpack readied and cash money stowed away? Perhaps he'd had all the Johnson Canyon Tunnel he could take and had planned to go AWOL. But with the war nearly at an end? A few more months, and he would have mustered out anyway.

Unable to go back to sleep, Hook sat at the table and waited for the dawn.

THE NEXT MORNING he brewed a pot of coffee and ate from a box of crackers he found in the pantry. After that, he made another run through the tunnel and then worked his way down to the base of the trestle.

By the time he got back, the bridge and building crew had arrived and were busy attaching boilerplate onto the tunnel wall. Since foremen frowned on chitchat during working hours, Hook went on down the track where he came upon a survey crew hard at work.

He lit a cigarette and watched as the men set their flags. When someone tapped him on the shoulder, Hook's hand moved to his sidearm. He turned to see a man standing behind him with his hands on his waist. A shock of red hair sprang from beneath his hat, and his hands were the size of hams. Freckles covered his face and his arms and the tops of his hands. His belly rose up under his shirt, and he peered at Hook through thick glasses.

"Who are you?" he asked.

Hook moved his hand off his sidearm. "Hook Runyon, the railroad bull, and who are you?"

The man lifted his chin and studied Hook. "Rudy Edgeworth," he said. "Value Survey Inc."

"What's going on with the line?" Hook asked.

"Upgrade," he said.

"Upgrade for what?"

"You'd need to check with the big boys for that."

"The railroad's contracting the surveying, right?" Hook asked.

Edgeworth reached into his hip pocket and retrieved a package of chewing tobacco. With three fingers, he loaded his jaw. "That's right," he said.

"What they doing to the tunnel?" Hook asked.

"Taking out the timbers," he said. "They catch fire from the smokestacks now and again. No one thought about that when they built her, I guess."

"I guess not," Hook said. "Your crew going to be working out here long?"

"All the way to Kingman," he said.

"You boys didn't happen to see anything the day that guard died?"

Edgeworth pushed his glasses back up on his nose. "I've seen the hotshot that killed him," he said. "He's a highballer and doesn't like stopping for no army grunts."

Hook turned to leave and then paused. "Where's your home base?" he asked.

"Kansas City," he said.

"You mind if I talk to your boys?"

"My crew answers to me, not the railroad."

"You might be right about that, long as you aren't on railroad property. At the moment that isn't the case."

Edgeworth spit between his legs. "They were with me the whole time. They didn't see nothing."

"Thanks," Hook said. "You be careful in these rocks. There's rattlesnakes the size of anacondas out here."

Hook sat smoking on the porch of the guardhouse when a military staff car and jeep pulled in. Lieutenant Capron got out of the staff car and waited as two soldiers unloaded duffels from the backseat of the jeep. Hook watched them climb the steps.

The lieutenant leaned against the porch railing to catch her breath.

"This is Sergeant Folsom and Lance Corporal

Severe," she said. "They'll be taking over the guard duty here at the tunnel."

Hook dipped his head. "Hope you boys brought plenty of reading material," he said. "It's a tad quiet out here."

"I thought you might show them the patrol area," the lieutenant said. "They've been briefed on procedure."

"I don't see why not," he said.

"If you have time, I'd like to visit with you before you leave," she said.

"All right," Hook said. "Come on, boys, I'll give you the tour."

The lieutenant sat on the steps and waved them over upon their return.

"You men go on up to the guardhouse and get settled," she said. "I'll be up shortly."

After they'd gone, Hook said, "What's going on, Lieutenant?"

"I wanted to thank you for helping me out."

"You're welcome," he said.

Her eyes lit green in the sunlight. He'd underestimated her beauty. With looks like that, life couldn't be easy in the army.

"I take it Corporal Thibodeaux is gone?" he said.

"After I got back to the base, I called the guardhouse. I had this feeling. No answer, and I haven't been able to locate him anywhere. The tunnel couldn't be left unguarded, so I called you. I couldn't think of any other way."

"Well, there's not much to worry about out here," he said.

She leaned back against the step and locked her eyes on his. "I wouldn't have bothered you about this, but the army has a thing about showing up for duty, even if it's standing guard over a water fountain. I'm afraid Corporal Thibodeaux is in serious trouble. I would have been, too, if I'd left this place unguarded."

"By the way," he said. "I think you should know that I found a backpack under Sergeant Erikson's bunk. It had a change of clothes and a thousand in cash in it. I left them on the table."

"A thousand in cash? Is that so? I must have overlooked it."

"Do you know of any reason why he'd have that much cash hidden away under his bunk?"

The lieutenant shrugged. "I don't know, emergencies maybe. I'll see that it's sent to his people."

"It seems a large sum for an enlisted man."

"Frugality is not unheard of in the army," she said.

"No, I suppose not. So, I'll be on my way," he said.

She slipped her purse off of her shoulder. "Have you talked to that girl yet?"

"Thibodeaux's girl? Not yet," he said. "I've been guarding a tunnel."

"I'd like to go along when you do."

"I'd figured to check her out in the morning"

"Yes," she said. "Tomorrow would be fine. I'll pick you up."

Hook walked to the jeep and paused. "Did you have the prints checked on that flashlight?"

"Yes," she said.

"Did you find any?"

"Yes," she said. "Mine."

Hook got into the jeep, and, just as he started up, Sheriff Mueller pulled in behind him. Hook shut off the engine and waited for him to come over.

"Hook," he said.

"Sheriff. What's going on?"

"I can't talk long. Got a call on the way out. Some idiot turned a truckload of sheep over on the highway. You folks ain't seen that Corporal Thibodeaux, have you?"

"He's missing," the lieutenant said. "We've been unable to locate him anywhere."

"I figured as much. The banker in Ash Fork says a soldier showed up at the bank to cash a paycheck."

"Lots of folks cash checks at banks, don't they, Sheriff?" Hook said.

"That they do," he said, "but generally not the paycheck of a feller just run over by a train."

FIFTEEN

THE LIEUTENANT PICKED Hook up at the salvage-yard gate. He moved her briefcase and leather gloves over and slid in.

She leveled her gaze on him. "Where to?"

"Blue's Café," he said. "It's on Main."

She backed up and turned toward Ash Fork. "Nice to have a reverse," he said.

"Excuse me?"

"Nice car," he said. "I've been driving Scrap's jeep."

THE LIEUTENANT TURNED into the parking space in front of Blue's and shut off the engine.

"Why here?" she asked.

"This is where Thibodeaux's girlfriend works. I'm hoping Blue will have some information."

"Blue?"

"Her boss and owner of the café. I'll be right back," he said.

"I'm going with you," she said, opening the door.

Blue looked out of the service window. A grease-spattered apron hung about his neck. His eyes were black as night and closely set. He had a weak mustache that sprang out from under his nose.

"Linda Sue don't work here no more," he said, pushing out a plate of ham and eggs.

"Do you know where she is?" Hook asked.

"I don't know," he said.

Hitting the bell, he peeked out at the dining room. "She came in here with that army boy and told me she quit. Not so much as an hour's notice. These kids nowadays. And then I came up fifty dollars short in the till."

"She had Corporal Thibodeaux with her?" Allison asked.

"Looked like he'd had a few, if you know what I mean. Why am I the only one left in the world who has to work for a living?"

"Did he say anything?" Hook asked.

"He just kept standing between the service window and the cash register so I couldn't see. Being a nice guy gets you nowhere, I can tell you."

"You didn't report this to Sheriff Mueller?" Hook asked.

He scoffed. "I didn't want to get Linda Sue in trouble, you know. She's just a dumb kid. Anyway, I couldn't prove nothing. They stole cash, didn't they?"

"Thanks," Hook said. "If we recover your money, we'll let you know."

"Shoot that corporal, and the money is yours," he said.

Once outside, Hook lit a cigarette and looked down the street.

"Now where?" the lieutenant asked.

"Linda Sue lives on five acres outside of town. Maybe they're there."

The lieutenant pulled behind the shrubbery in the driveway and shut off the ignition. Several minutes passed. Finally, she said, "Well?"

"No signs of life," he said. "They're either gone or in there hiding."

"So what do we do?"

Opening the car door, he said, "We go find out."

Hook circled around the house with Lieutenant Capron at his heels. At the back door, he stopped and listened.

"This is crazy," she whispered. "There's no one home. Can we go now?"

"We can't be sure without looking," he said.

"You can't go in there. It's against the law."

He reached for his sidearm and clicked off the safety.

"I'm not one to break the law," he said, turning the doorknob. She rolled her eyes and followed him into the house. The air smelled stale, and the sink overflowed with dirty dishes. Hook checked each room before holstering his sidearm. "Maybe they'll be back," he said.

The lieutenant pursed her lips. "A waitress doesn't leave dirty dishes to come back to, and I can't find her makeup. I think they're on the run."

"Yeah," he said. "You might be right."

"Could we get out of here now before we both wind up in jail?"

"Right," he said. Back at the car, Hook rolled down the window and lit a cigarette. "Blue thought the corporal may have had a buzz going. Let's check out the pool hall. Maybe someone there knows something."

She looked over at him. "I haven't done much hanging out in pool halls."

Hook said, "And you call yourself cultured?"

The pool hall smelled of tobacco and urine, and the sunlight, filtered through window grime, failed to penetrate the gloom. Cue sticks and racks lined the walls, and a jukebox sat silent in the corner. In the back, a man worked at the bar with a rag. Balls clacked from the back of the room, and men cursed.

"I don't think this was such a good idea," the lieutenant said, stepping in close to Hook.

"Won't take long," he said. "You wait here, and I'll check with Harry, the manager."

"I'm going with you," she said.

Hook lit a cigarette. "All right. Have it your way."

Harry took a final swipe at the bar before looking up. "Hook," he said, "I don't want no trouble."

"I wasn't the one looking for trouble that night, Harry. You know that."

"Maybe so, but that's Ben Hoffer back there now. His nose don't look so good, and he ain't happy about it."

"You haven't seen Corporal Thibodeaux, have you, Harry?"

Harry looked over at the lieutenant. "Last time I saw him he had a snoot full."

"You don't know where we could find him, do you?" she asked. "He's left his post. He's AWOL."

"No, but then I see enough of these boys without following them home, if you know what I mean."

"He have his girl with him?" Hook asked.

"She picked him up out front. Most women don't care much for coming into a pool hall, no offense, ma'am.

"Say, I heard that sergeant got himself killed in the tunnel," he said.

"Human flesh and trains don't mix," Hook said.

"Jesus," he said. "Too bad."

"Thanks, Harry. Sorry about the scuffle."

When Hook looked up, Harry's face had blanched. The lieutenant said, "Those men…"

Hook turned to see Ben Hoffer and two of his

friends, each with a cue stick, standing between them and the door.

"Harry, take the lieutenant out the back way," Hook said.

"No," she said. "I'm staying."

Hook looked at her. "I'll step in front. When I do, reach under my jacket and take my sidearm. Don't use it unless you have to."

After she had lifted his gun, Hook walked over to the men. Ben Hoffer stood in the center. His left nostril, red and swollen, sported a half-inch gash where Hook had snared him with his prosthesis. The other two men stepped out to form a semicircle. "Ben," Hook said. "Sorry about the misunderstanding the other night."

Ben's lip curled, and he touched his nose. "I'll bet you are. If you weren't carrying, I'd settle up."

Hook glanced back to see that the lieutenant had moved to the end of the bar.

He pulled his jacket back. "No weapon, Ben, but why don't we call it even."

"We'll be even when I tear off your other arm," he said.

On signal, Ben's running mates lifted their cue sticks and stepped forward.

"I wouldn't do that, boys," the lieutenant said from behind Hook. "This is a sharpshooter medal you see on this uniform. Now, drop those cue sticks."

The men looked at each other and then at the lieutenant and then at the barrel of the P.38 she had pointed at them. Their sticks clattered onto the floor.

Ben started to move, but Hook snared his ear and yanked him forward. Ben squealed and danced on his toes. Hook let him loose before clipping him hard across the skull with his prosthesis. Ben dropped to the floor as if shot.

Hook turned to the other men. "Ben can't play no more today, boys."

HOOK AND THE lieutenant sat in the staff car outside the pool hall. She handed him back his sidearm. Hook lit a cigarette and looked down the street.

"Sorry about the trouble," he said.

"I can't talk right at the moment," she said. "Because I can't breathe."

"The problem is that we don't know any more than when we started," he said. "I guess it's too late to do more today. Where will you be staying?"

The lieutenant took a handkerchief out of her purse and dabbed at her mouth.

"Motel," she said. "Out on the highway."

"How about a nightcap?" he said. "We'll talk this out."

"A nightcap? Where?"

"My caboose."

She rocked the steering wheel and looked over at him. "I've had enough trouble for one day," she said.

"Just so you know, I don't cross lines without an invitation."

"I've heard *that* before," she said.

"No more than a drink."

She looked over at him. "All right," she said. "But understand there's nothing personal in this."

"Understood," he said. "By the way, is that really a sharpshooter medal?"

She lifted her lapel and looked at it. "Good conduct," she said. "It took three cycles before I finally qualified on the rifle range."

SIXTEEN

MIXER GREETED THEM at the steps of the caboose, and the lieutenant stooped to pat his head.

"What's that smell?" she asked.

"Mixer favors skunk. One time he worked six hours digging one from under a stack of ties. He came home with his eyes watering and his nose running, but I never saw a happier dog."

"There's no accounting for taste," she said.

Hook lit the lantern and pointed her to a seat. "That's a fact," he said. "I've known a few folks who couldn't tell from a skunk either."

The lieutenant went through the stack of books that were piled on the table.

"Speaking of odd behavior," she said. "What about these?"

Hook took glasses from the cabinet. Poured her a Beam and water and handed it to her. "No ice," he said. "Sorry."

"It's fine," she said.

"Not everything a man does has to make sense, you know. I knew a fellow once who collected rail spikes."

"How did this all start?"

"I worked as a hobo before I took this job," he said. "The pay wasn't that good, so going out to restaurants and movies and taking overnight trips on my yacht didn't work out so well. I spent a lot of time in local libraries. They're warm, you know, and free. No one there to bother you. I did a lot of reading, and I could always catch a snooze in the Daughters of the American Revolution section. They usually provide an easy chair, and the references are rarely used."

"So one thing led to another?" she said.

"In a thrift, I could get a sack of books for a dime. I branched out best I could, but collecting is a rich man's game. Still, rare books can crop up about anywhere, so even a bo gets lucky once in a while."

"You don't strike me as the studious type," she said.

"You could ask any of my old teachers about that, I guess, but I've always been curious. Maybe that's why I like being a yard dog."

"So what kinds of books do you read?"

"Big ones," he said.

She picked one of the books up and studied it. "Are these of value?"

"I suppose a man could sell them, but no real collector is willing to part with his books unless he's trading up. I've never been tempted to sell, but I *have* been tempted to steal."

She took a sip of her drink. "Good," she said, running her finger around the rim of the glass. "Has anyone ever told you that you're a little eccentric?"

"One time a bo in El Paso said I had book madness. He was right about that, I guess. But then he made the mistake of trying to start a fire with one of my books."

He looked up at her. "Now, I have a question for you, Lieutenant."

"Go ahead."

"You're with the army's Department of Transportation?"

"That's right."

"And those guards at the tunnel are, too?"

"Yes."

"Why isn't the military police in charge of security out there?"

The lieutenant pushed her drink to the side. Her hands were small and free of the abuse manual labor can inflict.

"My commander says that if he's the one responsible for transportation, which he is, then he has to be the one who controls its security."

She took another sip of her drink. "But aren't you really asking why they would send a woman instead of a man?"

Hook reached for a cigarette. "Hadn't crossed my mind," he said.

Just then a knock came at the door, and Mixer's hackles rose. "Who is it?" Hook asked.

"Eisenhower," Scrap said. "Who do you think?"

Hook got up and opened the door. "What is it you want?"

Scrap took a moment to check out the lieutenant. "Beg your pardon. I didn't know Hook had company."

"This is Lieutenant Capron," Hook said. "She's handling the tunnel security."

"Hello, Ike," she said.

Scrap pushed his hat back, revealing a line of smoke and grime across his forehead.

"Name's Scrap West, Lieutenant. I don't mean to frighten you, ma'am," he said. "But some folks might think this is just a caboose and safe enough for having a drink and such. But they'd be mistaken."

"Oh?" she said. "What do you mean?"

"This here is a spider's web."

"A spider's web?" she said.

"Occupied by a one-armed spider."

"Scrap," Hook said. "Are you here to scare away my company?"

Scrap took out his pipe and knocked it against the palm of his hand. His nails were black from the day's work.

"Doing my civil duty's all," he said, grinning. "Anyway, that division supervisor called on my phone again. He wants to talk to you. I says to him, 'Hell, I'd be glad to go get him. Why would I mind setting aside my work and walking up to Hook Runyon's spiderweb, given all the copper thieves he's caught for me?'"

"Thanks, Scrap."

Scrap turned. "Now, Lieutenant, I'd hit the road and not look back if I were you."

The lieutenant smiled. "Thanks for the warning, Scrap. I'll stay on my guard."

"Well," he said. "I've done my duty."

"Sorry, Lieutenant," Hook said. "I'll be back in a minute."

AT THE OFFICE, Hook dialed Division and lit up a cigarette. "Security," Eddie said.

"Eddie, Hook Runyon."

"Runyon, I got a problem."

"Eat more fruit, Eddie."

"Maybe you can get a job as a comedian, Runyon, because your current employment is hanging in the balance."

"I forget about your keen sense of humor, Eddie. What's going on?"

"Someone waylaid an engineer on that siding just

west of Williams. They lifted his wallet, and he's in the hospital with a headache."

"Do they know who did it?"

"That's what yard dogs are for, Runyon, to find out who did it. You think I called to make nice?"

"That hadn't occurred to me, Eddie."

"Get over to that hospital and see if you can come up with anything."

"Engineers don't have much to say even without a headache, Eddie."

"Just stick to the facts for once, Runyon."

"What about that other thing?" Hook asked.

"The orphanage?"

"Yeah, that."

"It's off. I guess they figured every rubber in use could mean one less atheist in the world."

"That's real sensitive, Eddie."

"But that popcar is a different situation. Leaving one on the main line is a serious infringement of the rules."

"I was rounding up copper thieves at the time, Eddie."

"They said you signed out for the popcar, that it had been abandoned on the main line and could have resulted in a derailment, which in turn would have cost the company a lot of money."

"What did you tell them?"

"That it wasn't the first time."

"Thanks for the support, Eddie."

"You know how I feel about you, Runyon."

"Yeah, I feel the same way about you."

After he'd hung up, Hook lit another cigarette and sat in the darkness. He laid his cigarette in the hubcap and called the operator in Ash Fork.

"Hook Runyon here. Did those guards out at the Johnson Canyon Tunnel check the board tonight?"

"Two calls came in," the operator said.

"Two?" Hook said.

"Yeah," he said. "Guess they are a little worked up about that sergeant's death out there."

THE LIEUTENANT SAT with her chin in her hand as Hook told her what Eddie had said about the engineer getting robbed.

"I think someone other than the new guards at the tunnel has been checking the train schedule," Hook said.

"Who?"

"Could be Corporal Thibodeaux."

"Thibodeaux? Why do you say that?"

"That's a remote siding out there at Williams. Whoever robbed that engineer must have had some idea that he would be there."

"By calling in?"

"Exactly. Thibodeaux knows the system," he said. "One call and he's got all the information he needs to be waiting at the right siding at the right time."

The lieutenant walked to the door. "Seems like a lot of trouble just to lift a wallet."

"Not much chance of anyone catching them that far out in the country."

"What are you going to do?" she asked.

"Division wants the engineer questioned. I'll wait until morning to go over. Right now he's nursing a pretty big headache."

"Look," she said, "I'll be going back to the base

tomorrow. Why don't you ride over with me? I want to be in on the questioning."

"Well," he said. "I don't know. It's really a railroad matter, given it took place on railroad property."

"If the corporal's involved, I need to be there."

"I guess I could catch a train back."

"Good. I'll see you in the morning then."

"Another drink?" he asked.

She picked up her purse and opened the door. "Said the spider to the fly."

SEVENTEEN

Lieutenant Capron, wearing her uniform, picked him up just as the morning sun lit the sky.

"Morning," she said. "Did you sleep well?"

"Spiders have to stay alert," he said.

She reached for a thermos. "I stopped at Blue's and picked up coffee."

"Thanks," he said. "How's Blue doing today?"

"He said that Linda Sue had been one of his best workers, except she had a taste for the wild side and that it usually came in the form of a knucklehead."

"No shortage of those," Hook said.

As they drove into the countryside, he cracked his window. The morning smelled clean and new.

"You have kin, Lieutenant?" he asked. "Brothers? Sisters?"

She shook her head. "Only child."

"Spoiled?"

"I received lots of attention, if that's what you mean. Contrary to what most people believe, being an only child is not always so easy. You grow up with only adults around, and you're expected to be an adult yourself. My father, being military, believed in discipline, you see, and excuses were not well received."

"Hard duty, I guess. For a kid, I mean," he said.

"At times, but it's served me well."

"I grew up in a large family," he said. "Not much

attention to go around. They just threw me into the pen with the others."

"Oh, really, that's not true."

"Like you, it has served me well."

"We all have to adjust to our situations," she said. "It's a matter of backbone, isn't it?"

Her hair turned out in perfect curls, and her eyes snapped with spunk. But there was something about her, as if she had her arm stuck out in front of her to keep everyone at bay.

"You're a pretty smart lady," he said. "Once you get your shooting skills polished up, you'll be about perfect, I guess."

"I doubt that you think anyone perfect."

Hook lit a cigarette and hung his elbow out the window.

"My experience is that intelligence is where you find it, and I've found it in some mighty unexpected places."

"But intelligence has to be applied, doesn't it, or it's of little value to anyone?"

"Some folks don't even know they have it," he said. "I once saw a bo memorize the numbers of every boxcar in a forty-car freighter as it passed over the crossing at twenty miles an hour. He could repeat the numbers forwards and backwards."

"Oh, really."

"Not only that but he could tell you which cars were sealed and which were open. He thought everyone could do it."

The lieutenant lifted her brows. "I never know when you're telling the truth and when you are lying."

"About fifty-fifty," he said. "So, what happens to Lieutenant Capron when this war's wrapped up?"

She moved the mirror before answering. "I've yet to figure that out," she said.

"That bomb's likely to change the world," he said. "It's like holding a lit stick of dynamite in a gunpowder factory. You don't know whether to keep it or throw it."

"Things could go either way now, good or bad," she said. "The world is scrambling for position. The next few years could be dangerous for us all."

"An old steamer is enough power for any man," he said. "But then no one has ever asked me how I want the world to go."

THE MINUTE THEY walked into the hospital room, Hook recognized the engineer as his old pal. Frenchy sat on the side of the bed in his hospital gown. If ever a man looked out of place in a hospital gown, it had to be Frenchy.

"Frenchy," Hook said. "What the hell happened?"

Frenchy reached back and clamped his gown together. "Hook? I'll be damned. What you doing here?"

"This is Lieutenant Allison Capron. She's with the army's Department of Transportation," Hook said. "One of those guards at the tunnel has gone AWOL."

"Lieutenant," Frenchy said. "I'd stand, but this here dress ain't been sewn together."

"Nice to meet you," she said. "I gather you two know each other?"

"Oh, hell, yes," Frenchy said. "I knew Hook when he was a bo. He used to hitch my train."

"Never did," Hook said. "A man could starve to death riding one of your crawlers."

"Hook here has a nose for trouble and a way of taking care of it when it comes," he said. "Wouldn't want him to know it, though. Give him a compliment, and he'll follow you around like that dog of his."

Hook took a look at the lump on Frenchy's head. "You got a skull thick as boilerplate," he said.

"They're letting me out of this place anytime now. It's a good job, too, 'cause I don't have my cigars. A man without his cigars might do just about anything. I knew a feller once killed his whole family with a railroad pick when they hid his cigars from him."

"How did you manage to get robbed, Frenchy?" Hook asked.

"We were laying by for a hotshot. You know that siding west of town?"

"Someone haul you out of the cab?"

"Nobody gets in my cab without my say-so. You know that, Hook."

"Did you get a look at who did it?" the lieutenant asked.

"Not exactly. The end man came up to tell me he'd spotted a hotbox not far up from the bouncer and that I should go take a look. He stayed with the fireman while I worked my way back. Firemen have to be watched nearly every second, you know.

"So I head back, though it's against my better judgment. Walking track in the dark can end up any number of ways, most of them not good. Hell, there's rattlesnakes out there been known to drag men off into the desert."

The lieutenant asked, "So, what happened?"

"About halfway back, somebody steps up behind me, sticks a gun in my back, and says, 'Give me your money, or I'll be blowing your head off.'"

"Did you?" she asked.

"Damn right," he said. "It ain't much of a head, but then it's the only one I got."

"But you didn't see him?" Hook asked.

"About that time the hotshot comes charging full bore down line. She's got her glimmer on bright as morning, and she's blowing steam. This bastard lowers his gun for a second. I turn, see, and get a look at him."

"Did you know him?" the lieutenant asked.

"Not as I recall, but he wasn't alone. This girl stood off behind. 'Turn around, you son of a bitch,' he says. When I do, he hits me with the butt of his rifle."

"Are you certain it was a rifle?" she asked.

Frenchy rubbed his head. "Could have been the world's biggest pistol, I suppose."

"Did you know the girl?"

"I've never seen her before. Next thing I know, I'm in this dress talking to a goddang yard dog and a female lieutenant."

"Thanks, Frenchy," Hook said. "We have a pretty good idea that the man is Corporal Thibodeaux, one of the guards out at Johnson Canyon Tunnel, and the girl is a waitress he took up with. They're on the lam and probably picking up cash where they can get it."

"I heard about that sergeant out there," he said. "Too bad, for him and the engineer what killed him. That tunnel has taken its share of lives over the years."

"Did they call in an engineer to finish your run?" Hook asked.

"Naw," he said. "I'm deadheading empty cars to West's Salvage over at Ash Fork. Picking up a load there and taking it to Williams Salvage. Soon as they've got a full train made up, I'll be making a run to the smelter.

The railroad ain't in no hurry long as I get there this year or next."

"That's where I'm working," Hook said. "Eddie's got me chasing copper thieves."

"You still living in that old louse box?"

"Still home," he said. "How about a lift back to the salvage yard, Frenchy?"

"Well, long as I don't have to listen about them books," he said. "I've already called in for clearance. The crew's out there now bringing up a head on that ole calliope. Soon as I shed this dress, we can go, providing you got a car."

AFTER FRENCHY HAD climbed into the cab of the steamer, Hook got out of the staff car and went around to the lieutenant's window.

The lieutenant looked up at him. "What about the corporal and his girlfriend?" she asked.

"We can't be sure which direction they're headed," he said. "But I figure we'll be hearing from them soon enough."

"You'll let me know if anything comes up?"

"They'll be needing cash," he said.

"I'll be in touch, then," she said.

Steam shot from the engine and floated up into the blue as Frenchy brought her up.

"Right," Hook said, turning to leave. "And…"

"Yeah?" he said.

"Cast that web of yours far. It's important to the army that Corporal Thibodeaux be apprehended."

EIGHTEEN

HOOK CLIMBED INTO the cab and stowed away behind Frenchy's seat. The old steamer hissed and moaned, and steam shot from her belly. The fireman looked into the firebox before settling back.

Frenchy took off his hat, tapped a gauge with his pliers, and checked for the brakeman's signal. Hook could see where a spot of blood had soaked through the bandage on his head. Frenchy took his pocket watch out of his overalls, looked at it, and then slipped it back in.

"You ready, yard dog?" he asked.

"I've been ready for twenty minutes," Hook said, winking at the fireman.

Frenchy eased the throttle forward. The engine reached down and bumped out the slack, sending a ripple the length of the train.

"Want me to get out and push?" Hook asked.

"Just sit there and play with your gun," Frenchy said. "This here's a working man's job."

With each stroke, the old girl gained momentum. She soon settled in at a steady clip. Hook loved the throb of the engine, the way it pooled deep within him. Rendered by fire and water, she came as close to being alive as ever a machine could. Her strokes hauled left and right and left again, her great hulk swaying down line like a giant horse.

Hook lit a cigarette and leaned over on an elbow. "I thought you were going to retire, Frenchy?"

Frenchy put his hat back on and checked a gauge. "Someone has to haul yard dogs up and down line, don't they?"

"Ain't it grand he doesn't have to be a genius to do it," Hook said. "Given a train runs forward and backward on a rail. Even an engineer should get it mastered somewhere between hiring and retiring."

"Well, it ain't the smartest man what points it out this far from the next stop," Frenchy said.

"You figure I could catch a ride back out to the tunnel when you leave Ash Fork, Frenchy? I need to do some checking on things. I'll hitch the pusher coming back to town."

"Oh, sure," Frenchy said. "Maybe you could help me out on going forwards and backwards while we are at it."

"Thing is, I thought I might check on my dog while you're switching out in Ash Fork."

"Maybe you'd like to do your laundry while we're there, too. We'd be glad to hold up the line. Just because the security of the country depends on keeping this corridor open don't mean we shouldn't wait while you feed that goddang dog.

"Why don't you use your popcar, Hook, given you cinder dicks got more perks than a union boss?"

"Some idiot left it on the track, and a hotshot damn near gave it a lift into town. Eddie's not happy."

"Did the idiot have one arm?" Frenchy asked, grinning.

"Copper thieves, I figure," Hook said. "Can't turn your back for a minute."

As they came down the final leg to the tunnel, Frenchy got a slow signal. Construction crews and dirt-moving equipment lined the tracks. The section gang had heavy rail strung down the right-of-way, and a pile driver had been sided for trestle work. "What the hell's going on?" Frenchy asked. "They got the whole countryside tore up."

"Upgrade, I guess," Hook said. "It don't make sense to me. Looks like they're going to underpin the trestle, and they're lining the tunnel with boilerplate."

As they rolled into the tunnel, the roar of the engine magnified, and the smell of steam and smoke filled the cab.

Frenchy shook his head and shouted above the din. "That's the railroad for you, ain't it. Build too much too late at too big a price. I guess no one's told the railroad the war is all but over."

WHEN THEY CAME upon the wigwag crossing outside Ash Fork, Frenchy lay in on the whistle and shifted his cigar to the other side of his mouth. Within moments West's Salvage Yard came into view. Mountains of scrap metal rose into the sky. There were piles of washing machines, refrigerators, and crushed cars rising up like volcanoes.

One stack contained hubcaps, another hot water heaters, and yet another nothing but horse-drawn farm machinery. Scrap, convinced at one time that the horse was on its way back, had bought up every bit of machinery within a hundred-mile radius of Ash Fork.

When Frenchy slowed, Hook swung down off the engine and made his way to the caboose, where he found Mixer sleeping in the shade. When Mixer spotted him, he lifted his head and thumped his tail. Bits of shell clung to his whiskers, and his belly rose up like a balloon.

"It looks like you been eating well enough without me," Hook said.

He headed across the yard to catch up with Frenchy, who waited for the pusher to bump a line of empties off the siding.

Scrap spotted Hook from the crane and waved him over. Hook waited while he climbed down.

"I don't have all day to chat, Scrap. I'm headed back out to the tunnel with Frenchy."

Scrap fished out his pipe and pushed his hat back. Dirt had gathered in the creases of his face, and his glasses were fogged with dust.

"That dog's been sucking my eggs, Hook."

"Coons," Hook said. "Once they get started, you can't get them shut down."

"I know dog tracks when I see them."

"I'll have a talk with him," Hook said.

"And another thing, I had a load of copper weigh in light again. Those bastards know I got copper going out before I do."

Hook reached for a cigarette. "You hired any new people lately, Scrap?"

Scrap loaded his pipe with tobacco. "Same crew I've had all along. Once they work for Scrap West, they're spoiled for any other job."

"You trust those boys, do you?"

"I watch them every goddang minute."

Hook lit his cigarette and studied the line of cars. "You got any copper going out today?"

Scrap fired up his pipe, and a cloud of smoke drifted off. "They're tearing down an old power plant over to

Kingman, and a scrounger's trucking in the copper pipe. It's high quality and a good profit in it, if I could ever get it to the smelter."

"Give me a little time on it, Scrap. I'm getting closer."

"Well, now, if you got a plan, Hook, I'd sure like to hear it."

"These things can't be rushed, Scrap. They require thought. Patience is required when it comes to solving crime."

"Thing is," Scrap said, "I'm near bankrupt from copper thieves, and I find myself rubbing up against old age to boot."

"You wouldn't have a grease pencil, would you?"

Scrap dug his pencil from his pocket and blew away the lint. "Every good junkman carries a grease pencil," he said. "I expect you'll be giving it back?"

"I'll see you later, Scrap. Frenchy's about got the train made up."

Hook walked the line looking for Scrap's copper car, finding it at the end. He swung up on the ladder, threw back some of the pipe, and swiped a few with Scrap's grease pencil.

Dropping down from the ladder, he made his way to the front. Just as he climbed up on Frenchy's engine, the pusher coupled in at the tail.

Frenchy looked over his shoulder at Hook and then blew his whistle.

"Another second and you'd been left at the gate," he said.

"Might want to be more respectful of the law," Hook said. "Seeing as how I'm the only thing between you and trouble."

"Trouble's my best friend," Frenchy said.

"You stop this teapot anywhere else before you get to the smelter, Frenchy?"

"Sure. Make up the rest of the train at Williams," he said. Frenchy eased the throttle forward, and with the pusher at their backs, they were soon up to speed. The sun lowered in the west, and the smells of the country rode in through the window.

As they made a bend, Frenchy leaned out and checked the line for blazers, bad wheel bushings that could turn white-hot and set half the countryside afire. Frenchy cultivated his reputation as the most cantankerous engineer on the corridor, but no man knew better how to tease out the best in an old steamer.

When they hit the grade, the engine bore down. She rumbled and thundered and blew steam out her stack as they crawled up the ascent. Black smoke from the pusher boiled skyward as she hauled in behind. Even so, by the time they'd exited the tunnel once again, they'd slowed to walking speed. Hook spotted one of the guards climbing up the trestle path.

"I'm bailing here," he said, swinging out on the ladder. "When you coming back through, Frenchy?"

"Few days probably," he said. "Don't you want me to stop, Hook? Ain't no wonder you got more Brownies than the Girl Scouts."

"I've jumped off more of these teakettles than you've seen in a lifetime, Frenchy. Thanks for the lift. I'll buy you a whiskey and branch water when you come through."

LANCE CORPORAL SEVERE climbed the last few steps up the trestle path. He looked up to see Hook sitting on a bracing having a cigarette.

"Quite a climb, isn't it?" Hook said.

Corporal Severe nodded. "Sure is," he said. "What you doing out here?"

"Just checking to see if you boys need anything."

The corporal leaned his rifle on a rock. Lines pulled at the corners of his eyes, lines that can come from too much experience at too young an age.

"We're a little short of girls and hooch," he said.

"Yeah," Hook said. "It can get dry out here. You living in the guardhouse, are you?"

"Just duty hours," he said. "Found a place in town. It isn't much, but it beats staying in this canyon twenty-four hours a day."

"Guess there haven't been any German invasions?" Hook said, smiling.

"Yesterday I thought I spotted a patrol coming up the canyon. Turned out to be a herd of range cows."

"Cigarette?" Hook asked.

"Thanks," he said, slipping one out of the pack.

"I hear you boys been careful about checking the board before going in."

Corporal Severe lit his cigarette. "After what happened to Sergeant Erikson? You bet your ass."

"The operator said he got two calls on the same run. Can't say I blame you, though."

The corporal sat down on the rock and pulled his knee into his arms. "Wasn't us," he said. "Though I can't say I haven't wanted to call more than once just to make certain. The operator could make a mistake, you know, wrong time, wrong day, wrong train. Hell, could be anything, couldn't it? Walking that tunnel can make a man jittery."

"You wouldn't be headed for town soon, would you?" Hook asked.

"I'm off duty now. You want a lift?"

"I'd appreciate that," Hook said. "I won't have to wait on that pusher to get back. Anyway, I've had about all the engineers I can take for one day."

HOOK WAITED IN the jeep for Corporal Severe to get his things out of the guardhouse, and as they drove off a cloud of dust boiled up behind them. The road had taken a beating from the increased construction traffic. When it leveled out, the corporal settled back against his seat.

"Where you from, Corporal?" Hook asked.

The corporal shifted gears and eased the jeep over a dry wash.

"About everywhere, I guess," he said. "My old man didn't like to stay in one spot very long."

"You been stationed at Los Alamos for quite a while?"

"About a year. Before that I saw a little action. Picked up shrapnel in my back, and they sent me stateside. They said if it moves, I could wind up in a wheelchair."

"What do you do at Los Alamos?" he asked.

"Civil Engineers. You know, fixin' shit, for the officers' wives mostly."

"You and Sergeant Folsom both are assigned to Civil Engineers?"

"Yeah, that's right," he said, pulling out onto the highway. "Where to?"

"West's Salvage Yard," Hook said.

By the time Corporal Severe pulled up at the gate, darkness had set in. Scrap's floodlights lit up the yard.

"You live here?" the corporal asked.

"That's right," Hook said. "In a caboose."

The corporal looked at the mountains of salvage and then over at Hook.

"I'd about as soon live out at the canyon," he said.

"Yeah, me too," Hook said. "But then I'd miss all of Scrap West's brilliant conversation. Thanks for the lift, Corporal."

HOOK COULD SEE the office light still on, and despite his better judgment, he stopped. Scrap, engaged in doing something at his desk, didn't look up for several moments.

"I'll be a son of a bitch," he said, dropping his pencil.

"What now?" Hook said.

"I've got three hundred and twenty-eight car generators in this yard."

Hook sat down and rubbed at his shoulder. Sometimes his prosthesis hung as heavy as a side of beef.

"That's great," Hook said. "If you've got a call for car generators."

"If a man put all those generators to spinning, he could sell electricity. I figure there's a fortune just waiting to be made."

Hook dropped his forehead into his hand. "And how you going to spin three hundred and twenty-eight car generators?"

"Well, I hadn't thought that out just yet," he said.

Hook stood. "I'm going to bed, Scrap. Between you and Frenchy, my head feels like it's going to fall off."

"By the way," Scrap said. "That Eddie Preston called again."

"Yeah? What did he want?"

"He wants you to call."

"What for?"

"Someone held up the Albuquerque operator or something."

"Jesus," Hook said, looking at his watch. "Eddie hates to be called at home. I'll do it first thing in the morning."

NINETEEN

HOOK WOKE UP to the thump of the pusher engine as she came up to steam outside his caboose. Climbing out of bed, he peeked out the window. In the distance, the whistle of a freighter sounded, her voice soft and throaty in the morning.

The pusher engineer leaned out of the cab, his arm big as a tree stump, and checked on the train coming down line. The caboose trembled beneath Hook's feet as the freighter rolled in.

He made coffee, poured himself a cup, and checked his watch. Eddie should be at work by now. Eddie raised hell when Hook called him at home. In fact, Eddie didn't like to be called anywhere by anyone for any reason. How someone so averse to being disturbed wound up as head of security was one of life's mysteries. But then if the world made sense, he would have been Walter Runyon, bookstore owner or professor of literature, instead of Hook Runyon, yard dog.

On his way to the office, he met Pepe, who had just clocked in for the day.

"You seen Scrap?" Hook asked.

"He's greasing the crane."

"Thought that was your job, Pepe."

Pepe rolled his eyes. "I'm taking out generators."

"You don't mean Scrap's serious about that hare-brain scheme?"

Pepe nodded. "I made two hundred flower planters out of old tires one time. He didn't sell a one."

"What did he do with them?"

"Burned them for heat in the woodstove down at the shop. By the end of the winter, my hat stank so bad I had to throw it away."

"Keep smiling, Pepe."

He shrugged. "I get paid by the hour."

HOOK PUT HIS feet up on Scrap's desk and called Eddie. "Security," Eddie said.

"This is Hook, Eddie."

"Why didn't you call last night, Runyon?"

"It was after working hours."

"Security is a twenty-four-hour-a-day commitment, Runyon. Some of us take our work seriously."

Hook rubbed at the pain that drilled into his forehead. "You're an inspiration, Eddie. What's going on?"

"Someone robbed the Albuquerque operator on second shift last night."

"Who?"

"You think he checked in with me first?"

"Was anyone hurt?"

"The operator's got a fat lip, and his wallet's missing. It could have been a hell of a lot worse if he'd missed a call and sent a couple of trains together. How would you explain that one, Runyon?"

"I don't have to, Eddie. I didn't rob him."

"It's high time Bonnie and Clyde were shut down before they destroy the entire line."

"Got it, Eddie," he said, lighting a cigarette.

"Get over to Albuquerque and see what you can come up with."

"There's a highwheeler coming through about ten. I'll catch it over."

"You got those copper thieves yet?"

"Closing in, Eddie. I'll check that Albuquerque thing and get back to you," he said, hanging up.

AT TEN, HOOK waited on the platform as the highwheeler came to a stop. He showed his pass to the conductor and worked his way to the back of the car. The train wasn't the *Super Chief,* the most glorious ride on the line, but it was good enough to get him there and provide him a nap along the way.

He'd called the lieutenant's number and left a message about the robbery. Whether she'd come or not he didn't know. He had mixed emotions about it anyway. Working a case with someone else cramped his style. And he couldn't shake the feeling that she knew more than she was sharing.

Just then the kid across the aisle spotted Hook's prosthesis. He stuck his finger into his nose and whispered something to his mother.

"Hush," she said, squaring him back into his seat.

Hook rolled up his jacket and lay his head on it. The clack of the wheels soon lulled him to sleep. When he awakened, the woman and the little boy were gone. In their place an old man snored beneath his paper.

When the train slowed for Albuquerque, Hook checked his watch. The second trick would be on now. With luck, the same operator would be working the shift.

When he stepped off the train, the lieutenant waved at him from across the platform.

"Well," she said, moving up beside him. "We meet again."

He took her by the arm and guided her through the crowd. She smelled of soap, and her heels clicked on the brick platform. They moved behind the baggage cart and out of the way of the crowd.

"You think it's them?" she asked.

"Can't be certain, but it sounded like it might be our corporal and his girlfriend."

"My commander's anxious to get this guy rounded up," she said. "The army isn't happy about one of its soldiers looting his way across country."

"The operator will be busy until the train departs. Let's grab a cup of coffee."

"All right," she said.

They found a booth near the back of the café. The lieutenant ordered an RC Cola and settled her purse in next to her. Through the window, they could see the passengers boarding the highwheeler. The service crew milled around the engine with their oilcans. One of the crew set a blue flag and then crawled beneath the engine.

"What's the flag?" she asked.

"The engine can't budge as long as that flag is there, and no one is permitted to move it except the guy under the engine. Even at that, crawling under a live locomotive isn't the most comfortable thing in the world."

"What's he doing under there?" she asked.

"Checking bushings for the most part," he said. "These old steamers require a good deal of attention."

She folded a napkin and set her drink on it. "So how's Mixer?"

"Scrap says he's sucking eggs," he said.

"Is he?"

"The evidence is circumstantial, though Scrap makes little distinction between that and hard facts."

"And what do you think?"

"Well, it's true Mixer's weight gain is unexplained. But I prefer to give him the benefit of the doubt until proven otherwise."

"He's earned your loyalty?" she said.

"Mixer? He's earned nothing but my suspicion."

The man crawled from beneath the engine and removed the flag. By the time the highwheeler released her brakes, the platform had emptied of passengers. The conductor signaled a go, and air shot from the brakes. The engine chugged out of the station.

"Well," he said. "You ready?"

She finished her drink and pushed it aside. "Let's go."

THE OPERATOR TOUCHED his fat lip and rolled his chair back. He crossed his legs and bobbed his foot.

"Yeah, I'm the guy," he said with a lisp. "A man and a woman showed up here late in the night. The man had a rifle big as a cannon, and the woman kept blowing these boobles."

"Boobles?" the lieutenant asked.

"You know, gum," he said. "I hate that."

"Oh, bubbles," she said.

"Did anyone else see these two?" Hook asked.

"They waited until the depot emptied," he said. "I think they hid in the bathroom or something. First thing

I know this bastard has a rifle pointed in my face. 'Give me your cash,' he says, 'or I'll blow your eyebrows off.'"

"And you gave it to him?" she said. "Because they are the only eyebrows you have."

"No, I've another pair in my locker," he said. "So, I gave him what cash I had in the box. But then he says, 'Now your wallet.' And I says, 'That's my paycheck you're taking, mister.' And he says, 'You been sitting on your ass while the rest of us been fighting Germans, so divvy up.' And the girl laughs, see, and blows a booble big as her goddang head.

"So I says, 'Hadn't been for me, you'd been walking to the war,' and that's when he smacked me."

"Did they have a car?" the lieutenant asked.

"He told me to keep my head down for five minutes, or he'd come back. I didn't see nothing."

"You've reported this to the local police?" Hook asked.

"They came by and took a statement, but they're too busy giving out traffic tickets to worry about robberies on railroad property."

"Anything else you'd like to add?" Hook asked.

The operator touched his lip. "Not in front of the lady."

"Thanks," Hook said. "We'll be in touch."

"Wait for me in the car," she said, as they started to leave. "I'll only be a second."

HOOK SAT IN the staff car waiting for her to come from the depot. June bugs circled the streetlight, and the day's heat slipped away in the desert evening.

He moved the lieutenant's briefcase to the side and lit a cigarette. The case, made of heavy cowhide, had been riveted at the seams, and the handle reinforced with extra layers of leather.

After checking the door of the depot again, he opened the briefcase and retrieved a file folder. In it he found a single sheet of paper with a notation that read, "Deliver J.B. as scheduled on the 7th. Departure, 0100 hours. Secure all points."

"What do you think?" the lieutenant asked, sliding in.

"That's our couple, all right," he said.

"And we haven't heard the last of them, have we?" she said.

"They're gutsy but green," Hook said. "It's a combination prime for mistakes. In the meantime, we can only hope no one gets hurt.

"Are you going back tonight?" he asked.

"In the morning," she said.

"I'm staying in the sleeping rooms. Thought I might do a little book scouting tomorrow. On the way over, I spotted an estate sale in the paper. It's the early bibliophile who gets the book. You wouldn't care to come along, would you?"

"I think not," she said. "I've some things that need attention."

"There's this Mexican restaurant," he said. "I try never to miss it. Would you like to eat?"

"Thanks, anyway, but I'd be glad to drop you off."

"Okay," he said. "I'd appreciate it."

Hook gave directions and watched the sun lower on the horizon.

"By the way," he said. "I hitched a ride into town with one of the new guards at the tunnel, Severe I think was his name. Nice kid but inexperienced. You did say both guards worked in the motor pool?"

She turned into the parking lot and pulled up. "That's right. They had men to spare, I guess."

Hook got out and leaned back in the window. "Thanks, Lieutenant."

"You will contact me if something comes up in the meantime?"

"If I hear anything," he said, "I'll let you know."

The adobe walls of the café extended into a courtyard at the rear. The waitress led him to a table shaded by an arbor. Sunlight darted through the vines and played on the table. The aromas from the kitchen wafted in on the breeze.

He would have preferred to not eat alone, but he never missed a chance for a good meal if he could help it. Living in a caboose and eating out of cans made one appreciate fine food. This restaurant provided exactly what he had in mind.

He ordered Mexican beer, which arrived in a frozen mug rimmed with margarita salt and a slice of lime.

When the food came, he sat back and took it in. There were beef enchiladas swimming in melted cheddar, refried beans and rice, all topped off with a nest of shredded lettuce and tomato. On the side were sliced jalapeño peppers, salsa, *queso blanco*, a basket of chips, and a warmer stacked full of corn tortillas. When finished, he topped the whole thing off with sopapillas and honey.

Outside the restaurant, he lit a cigarette and watched the moon slide over the city, a perfect evening for a short walk back to the sleeping rooms. Tomorrow, he would get in a little book scouting. A railroad bull had few vacations, and detective work never ended at quitting time. He'd learned long ago that he had to take his enjoyment where and when he could, and the only thing he liked better than a great meal was a great book find.

THE NEXT MORNING, Hook dug the city map from his back pocket and checked the address. The house, a frame bungalow, sat in the middle of a modest neighborhood. A single outbuilding leaned to the left, and the yard had degraded into its natural state. Cars lined both sides of the street, and pickers made their way across the yard.

Some of his best finds came from the most unlikely places. He figured this to be the home of a widow. She probably lived here alone for twenty years after her husband died and took the opportunity to do exactly what she'd always wanted to do. In that little house was everything she had owned, but also, more importantly, those things she'd always dreamed of having. Married people sometimes made sacrifices for each other, putting their own wants and needs last.

He preferred estate sales to auctions, everything set out and priced by someone who most often didn't have a clue about value. By the end of the day, there would be nothing left but the ironing board.

The tiny house churned with people digging through the hundreds of boxes that were stacked about on tables. The prices had been marked in red crayon, and a lady in rimless glasses took money near the door.

Hook worked his way through the crowd. Now and then he stopped and examined the contents of a box. The house smelled of burnt toast and old clothes, and the windows were gray with dust and grime. A few pictures were leaned against the wall, including one of

Jesus ascending into heaven, another of the Last Supper, and yet another of Jesus breaking loaves.

It was not until he climbed the narrow stairs to the bedroom that he found the boxes of books. The owner's reading practice had been insatiable and eclectic. There were novels, religious books, travel books, and three boxes of biographies. One box contained Bertrand Russell's *Religion and Science,* another Faulkner's *The Unvanquished* and Hemingway's *For Whom the Bell Tolls.*

He'd found that people's reading lives could be as unpredictable as their sex lives. You just never could know what went on behind closed doors.

Hook made his selections and paid the bill on the way out. Now, he'd have to tote the books all the way back, but he didn't care. They were great copies. Had he the money and the time, he would spend his days doing nothing else. There would be no rare books left in the world that he didn't own. But he knew, even as he hoisted the box, that there would never be enough. He would always want more.

THAT EVENING HOOK checked the board and found a short haul heading for Kingman. The engineer agreed to give him a slow at West's Salvage, so Hook rode in the caboose, which turned out to have a broken window. He plugged it with a grease rag to stop the cold draft and then he stretched out on the bench. The train clacked along as steady as a heartbeat.

After going through his finds one last time, he lit a cigarette and thought about the last few days. There were more questions now than when he began. Why hadn't the army placed military police at the tunnel from the beginning? It only made sense to use trained personnel. What could that note have meant in the lieutenant's briefcase: secure all points. And what was Sergeant Erikson doing with all that cash stashed under his bunk? And what about the flashlight? And, the most puzzling of all, why did the lieutenant tell him the guards were from the motor pool when Severe claimed they were from Civil Engineers?

He rolled over and closed his eyes. He liked the lieutenant, liked her a lot, but he'd learned long ago that when things didn't add up, there was either an error in process or in the facts. Maybe it was time he double-checked the facts.

TWENTY

THE ENGINEER BLEW a slow for West's Salvage Yard, and Hook took measure of the speed before swinging down off the grab iron. Reaching up, he snatched his box off the bottom step and gave a wave to the engineer, who responded with a short blast of his whistle.

Hook lit a cigarette and struck out across the yard. Scrap stepped out of the office and motioned him over. One of his overalls' straps had twisted over his shoulder, and he had a cup of coffee in his hand.

Scrap tossed out his coffee dregs. He opened his tobacco pouch and smelled it.

"About that dog," he said.

"You accusing my dog again, Scrap?"

"That chicken coop looks like someone had a pillow fight in it, Hook."

"Could be a raccoon. Could be a bo. Could be mass suicide for all I know."

Scrap lit his pipe, and a cloud of smoke drifted off. "Could be that dog, too," he said.

"I'll let that go, Scrap, seeing as how you're uncommonly attached to those chickens, and it's probably affecting your reasoning."

Hook could see Mixer coming across the yard, his belly swinging to and fro like a hammock.

"And another thing," Hook said. "Pepe says he's been pulling generators. Now, I'm not one to criticize entrepreneurship, but even you ought see the lack of promise in such an enterprise as making electricity with car generators."

Scrap relit his pipe again and pushed his hat back. "I'm not one to rush to judgment on such matters, particularly where there's a great deal of money hanging in the balance.

"So, I've set up a small-scale experiment. If that works, I'll move on to a full-blown operation. I intend to be in on the ground floor. 'Course, being the man I am, I'll not be saying I told you so when the money starts rolling in."

Hook rubbed at the base of his neck.

"Well, before you start up your power plant, you suppose you could give me a little information?"

"That depends," Scrap said.

"On what?"

"On whether you're wanting my generator plans or not."

"Well, I'm not."

"Then what kind of information do you want?"

"Does your copper car carry a number?"

"Yes, it does."

"Do you think you could give it to me?"

"Depends."

"On what?"

"On what you're going to do with it?"

"I'm going to try to find your copper thieves, Scrap. You got a problem with that?"

"Hardly none at all," he said.

"Well?" Hook said.

"The number is SF-48032. I've had that same copper car three years now. West's Salvage cars are towed to

Williams. When there's enough for making up a train, they haul them on over to the smelter and deadhead the empties back."

Mixer waddled up and flopped down on Hook's feet. "I got one other request, Scrap."

"This is the only clean shirt I got, Hook."

"I need to borrow the jeep. You put in a new transmission yet?"

"Yes, I did."

Hook took out his handkerchief and dabbed at his face. The sun beat down hot as an engine boiler, and it wasn't ten o'clock yet.

"It has a reverse, doesn't it?"

"Why do you think I changed it out?"

"So it's in working order?"

"'Course it is, so long as you don't need high gear."

Hook looked at him. "It doesn't have a high gear? Jesus, Scrap, why would you do that?"

"'Cause I was sick and tired of listening to you complain about no reverse. This ain't no Cadillac dealership, as you well know."

"Jesus, Scrap, now I know why those chickens committed suicide."

"I'd like to stick around and listen to you complain some more, Hook, but I got work to do. Providing transportation for the railroad don't come cheap. Someone has to put in a day's work around here. You might consider putting in a little gas while you're gallivanting around the country."

At twenty miles an hour, the motor roared like a buzz saw, and a dust cloud drifted up from the wheels and settled onto the dash. Hook cut down Main and headed for Sheriff Mueller's office. When the old man sitting in front of the post office saw Hook coming, he leaned over onto his knees and pulled his hat down.

Sheriff Mueller looked up from his desk when Hook walked in.

"I was just getting ready to call Washington," he said. "I thought the Japanese were attacking."

Hook pulled up a chair and lit a cigarette. "It's Scrap's old jeep," he said. "It doesn't have a high gear."

"You can't drive without high gear," the sheriff said.

"Listen, I'm doing a little background work on that Sergeant Erikson who was killed out at the tunnel."

Mueller scratched at his beard. "Don't know a whole hell of a lot," he said. "As you know, the army took care of most of that."

"You don't have his home address, do you?"

"That lieutenant didn't give out much information. Not that I cared one way or the other. Cleaning up runned-over corpses ain't my all-time favorite thing.

"Say, rumor is you had another upset with Ben Hoffer over at the pool hall."

"Ben heats up pretty fast, as you know, Sheriff, but I talked him down."

"Sorry I can't be of help with the sergeant thing, Hook. But I figure when a military man gets killed on railroad property, the law ain't much in it one way or the other."

Hook stood. "I better be on my way, Sheriff. Twenty's top speed on that pile of junk out there, and I want to get back to the salvage yard before dark."

Sheriff Mueller turned in his chair. "You might check with Fred Colson, the mortician. He picked up the body as I recall. His place is a couple doors north of the pool hall."

HOOK FINALLY LOCATED Fred Colson eating pie at Blue's Café.

"Yeah, I'm Fred," he said, loading his fork. "You got a call for me?"

"No call," Hook said. "I'm the railroad detective staying out at the salvage yard. Sheriff Mueller thought you might be able to provide me a little information."

"Sit down," he said, pointing his fork at the seat. "Pie?"

"Thanks, no."

"Not that I'm wishing anyone harm," he said, "but I sure could use a call. I got a payment coming up on that new hearse."

"Things are a little slow?" Hook asked.

"In a town like this, folks die faster than they're born. You might think that's good for business, but it ain't. Without replacements, sooner or later no one's left, and business dries up. 'Course, there's the occasional accident and such, but they don't come along often enough to keep a man going."

"Well, maybe things will pick up."

Fred scraped the last of the pie from his plate and shoved it aside.

"Now, what kind of information you looking for?"

"I understand you were the one who made the run on Sergeant Erikson out at the tunnel."

"That's right," he said, sipping his coffee. "What was left of him."

"I'm gathering up background on the sergeant and thought maybe you could help me out."

"I could give you a description," he said, "but you might lose your dinner."

"Were you the one who shipped the body?"

"There's regulations about that sort of thing, you know. Not just anyone can do it. There's embalming and having the right shipping container. There can't be no leaks. The health department hates a leak."

"Sounds complicated."

"Folks got no idea how tricky shipping a cadaver can be. 'Course, I'll be dead myself by the time the army reimburses me."

"You don't happen to remember where the body was shipped?"

"Kansas City, as I recall. I got the records over to the shop."

THE TRANSMISSION WENT out halfway back, and Hook had to walk into the yard. He found Scrap in the office working at his desk.

"You can't be hot-rodding my equipment and expect it to hold up, Hook."

"I was going fifteen miles an hour, Scrap. That's not exactly speeding."

"Did you try reverse?"

Hook lit a cigarette and rubbed the back of his neck. "What good would that have done?"

"It could have saved me a trip for one thing."

"I can't be backing all the way from Ash Fork."

"Ain't no wonder you can't hold down a real job," he said.

"I'll just let that pass, Scrap, seeing as how I carry a weapon, and my temper can get out of hand."

"I'll have to go get it my own damn self," Scrap said.

"You want me to go with you?"

"Thanks just the same. I'll take Pepe. He's less particular about going backwards, and he don't carry a gun."

DARKNESS HAD FALLEN by the time Hook pulled up on the grab iron of the caboose. A strange whishing noise emanated from somewhere, and a light flashed briefly through the caboose window.

Hook slid back into the shadows and pulled his weapon. Someone must have broken in. There was no shortage of bums passing through, and they would steal anything not tied down. The light came again and then faded.

Hook tried the handle and eased the door open. He paused to listen. Bums rarely carried weapons, but they were not shy about using anything at hand to crack a man's head. The light glimmered again, and he cocked his pistol. Swinging open the door, he leveled it into the darkness.

Just then an electric light bulb began to glow over the kitchen table. It brightened and then faded to an eerie orange.

Hook retrieved his flashlight from the cabinet just as the bulb went out once again. He panned his light under the table and then under the bunk but found no one. After that, he went outside and checked under the caboose. When the whishing noise rose up once again, he whirled about, bringing his sidearm to bear. Only then did he see the windmill blade atop the caboose. A fan belt ran from the blade to a gear that turned a car generator that had been bolted to the frame.

"Scrap," he said, lowering his weapon.

HOOK WAITED IN the office as Pepe backed the jeep in. Pepe walked off without a word, rubbing his shoulder the whole time. Scrap opened the office door and rolled his eyes when he saw Hook sitting at his desk.

"That dang Pepe can't drive backward worth a damn," he said. "Three times we went in the bar ditch.

"What the hell you want now, Hook? You can't be borrowing my jeep again, that's for sure."

"I'm not here to borrow that broken-down jeep," Hook said.

Scrap fished out his pipe and looked inside the bowl.

"When a yard dog shows up, it ain't no social call, that much I can tell you."

"I want to know who put that contraption on my caboose?"

"That's the first generator model of the Headlight Electric Company. Seeing as how you've been asking for electricity and seeing as how we're friends, I thought to permit you the privilege. In addition, I won't be charging for the electricity, not right away at least."

"The damn thing goes on and off like a crossing signal, Scrap. A man could go into convulsions."

"You'd think a feller would be more appreciative of having his electricity provided for free."

Hook rubbed at the first signs of a headache that had sprung up between his brows.

"I need to use your phone, Scrap."

Scrap buried his hands in his pockets and rocked back on his heels.

"Criticize a man's electric company and then ask to use his phone. There just ain't no explaining some people."

When Scrap had gone, Hook called Division. "Eddie, this is Hook."

"You know what time it is, Runyon?"

"Security is a twenty-four-hour commitment, Eddie."

"You figure out some way to derail the *Chief*?"

"I'm making a run to Williams tomorrow, Eddie. Something's come up on this copper deal."

"You called me for that?"

"I'm going on over to Kansas City from there."

"What the hell is in Kansas City?"

"Look, Eddie, I'm on Scrap's phone, and he's raising hell. I'll call you later."

Back at the caboose, Hook unscrewed the light bulb from over the table. Across the way, the pusher engine rumbled and sighed on the siding. He took off his prosthesis and lay down in his bunk. Everyone else had accepted Sergeant Erikson's death as an accident. Why couldn't he? Life would be a hell of a lot easier for him if he could.

The wind swept in, and the windmill blade squeaked and squawked atop the caboose.

Perhaps if he could find Sergeant Erikson's people, get an understanding of what kind of a man he was. Perhaps then he could let it go.

TWENTY-ONE

THAT AFTERNOON HOOK waited on the depot platform for the eastbound short haul to come in. He recognized Frenchy's whistle pattern from as far away as the wig-wag crossing.

Frenchy brought the old steamer into the platform and leaned out the cab window.

"Don't you yard dogs have anything to do but beg free rides all day?" he asked.

"Catching one of your trains is like drinking bad hooch, Frenchy. It isn't good, but it beats sobriety."

Frenchy pushed back his hat. "Well, I suppose I could use someone to talk to. This bakehead ain't said a word since Needles. I think he might be dead."

The bakehead lifted his brows. "I wish I was," he said.

"Where you headed, Frenchy?" Hook asked.

Frenchy flipped his cigar butt out the window. "I'm deadheading hoppers to Flagstaff. You ever catch that son of a bitch what stole my wallet?"

"Solving crimes is a complicated and slow business, Frenchy."

"Well, it's for damn sure slow," he said.

"You going to give me a lift, Frenchy, or just complain all day?"

"I guess you can hitch to Williams long as I don't

have to listen about no book writers," he said. "Last time I thought my head was going to crack open."

Hook settled in at the back and waited for the bakehead to bring up steam. The old teakettle hunkered down as she bumped out the slack, and they were soon clipping across the countryside.

Frenchy unwrapped a new cigar and wet her down.

"What you doing in Williams, Hook, looking for a place to lay down and read?"

"Tracking copper thieves," he said. "I'm sick of listening to Scrap West bitch."

"Bitching is like breathing to Scrap, 'cept more so. I figure he's going to make a fortune, what with the war over."

"Scrap West with more money? That's a scary notion," Hook said.

Frenchy lit his cigar and pinched off his match. "I figure the world has changed forever and not for the better. What with this atomic bomb, there ain't no one in the world safe no more. They say a peanut-size piece of that uranium could blow up Africa and Australia, with enough left over for a wiener roast."

"I'm not so sure about the wiener roast," Hook said. "But before it's done, Scrap West will have figured out a way to make money from it."

Frenchy checked the end of his cigar and then puffed it into a cloud.

"They say the whole world's scrambling for the bomb now, that there's Russians and Germans and Japanese behind every rock. Some say they're out to steal our bomb, and they figure to send her right up our pants."

"You got to lay off that Mexican beer, Frenchy."

Frenchy pushed his hat back. "Me, I like my world

simple. I like knowing how much steam's in the boiler before she hits the grade."

"Yeah," Hook said. "And how do you do that?"

"The more sweat on the fireman's head, the more steam I got. It's a surefire method."

The bakehead took out his bandanna and dabbed at his face. "Frenchy's happy so long as he's not doing the sweating."

"Learned that from watching yard dogs," Frenchy said. "A man ponders his navel long enough and someone else will wind up doing the sweating for him. Ain't that right, Hook?"

"All I want is to get to Williams without a nervous breakdown," Hook said.

HOOK DROPPED DOWN from the ladder at the Williams Salvage spur and gave Frenchy a wave-off. The piles of junk glimmered in the twilight, and the smell of rust and iron filled the air. Hook lit a cigarette and waited for the evening to darken. He would be on private land and just as soon not have to explain his presence.

When darkness fell, the yard lights blinked on in the distance. Hook worked his way down the track, pausing from time to time to listen. A switch engine rumbled off as she shuffled salvage cars through the yard.

Keeping low, Hook made his way along the fence until he came upon a low spot. Stooping under the fence, he crept along to the line of cars on the siding spur. Voices drifted from across the yard, and the chug of the switch engine thudded under his feet.

After a search, he spotted SF-48032 sitting under one of the yard lights. He double-checked to make certain he was alone before climbing the ladder to look in. By his estimation, the load had been lightened by at least a third.

He circled the perimeter of the yard, coming in close to where he could see the switch engine and a truck that had been parked alongside the tracks. In the distance, men cursed and then laughed.

Hook slipped through the shadows and pulled himself up for a peek in the truck. It brimmed with copper pipe. Just then the switch engine blew her whistle and bumped the line of cars forward. Hook dropped off the truck and moved into the darkness.

When the steamer pulled under the lights, Hook recognized it as one of the pushers from out of Ash Fork. And the copper arthritic bracelet dangling from the engineer's wrist looked exactly like the one he'd seen that night at the culvert.

"I'll be damned," he said to himself. "So that's how they're doing it."

Hook waited until the switch engine had cleared the spur before checking his watch. The copper thieves would just have to wait until another time. He had less than an hour to catch the *Super Chief* to KC, and she was seldom late.

THE *SUPER CHIEF,* purring like a giant cat, slid into the Williams depot. Hook flashed his badge to the conductor and stepped into the air-conditioned car. The train was no longer called the *Chief,* but the *Super Chief,* and for damn good reason. Luxurious as a fine hotel, she raced across country at unheard-of speeds. Forty hours from Chicago to San Francisco, sometimes less, and with a guest list to rival the Ritz.

Decked with teak and ebony, she gleamed like a fine

hotel lobby. She smelled of leather and linen and sported original art.

Hook loved to ride the *Super,* not so much for the speed as for a moment's escape from the rudeness of the world. Here in this train, and at the speed of lightning, the world came as close to perfect as it ever could. For a few brief hours, he drank the best booze, ate the best food, and received service normally reserved for kings.

As they raced into the desert, he napped, and when he awoke, he went to the lounge car and ordered a scotch on ice. He sat in a chair big enough for two that had been adorned with a colorful Navajo motif. He watched the scenery race past the picture window as he smoked a cigarette.

After that he went to the diner, with its vaulted ceiling and linen napkins. He ordered cold salad with blue cheese and croutons, leek soup, and baked bass. Everything arrived on Mimbreño turtle china and was served with the most exacting care. For dessert he had layer cake and topped the whole thing off with black coffee.

Unwilling to spend his entire ride sleeping, he sat in the passenger car and listened to the clack of the wheels as the *Super Chief* charged through the American heartland.

ONCE OUT OF the Kansas City depot, Hook checked the address and hailed a cab. He rolled down his window as they edged through the traffic. The smells and noise of the city assaulted him from every direction. He watched the people at the stop signs, the way they turned inward as if surrounded by mirrors.

The cab traveled for miles until they were on the outskirts of the city. When at last they pulled up, Hook stuck his head out the window to see where the cabby was pointing.

"That trailer up there," he said. "You want me to wait?"

"I won't be long," Hook said, climbing out.

The land had developed around a body of water that now struggled under the onslaught of people. The lots were littered with trailer houses, old cars, and livestock, including a half dozen goats that languished in the shade of an abandoned dump truck.

Hook knocked, and a dog barked from somewhere inside. The man who opened the door wore shorts, sandals, and a T-shirt with a frayed neck. Blue veins knotted up his legs.

"Mr. Erikson?" Hook said, showing him his badge.

"Yeah," he said.

"I'm with railroad security. Could I ask you a few questions?"

The dog came to the door and growled. Erikson kicked at it. "What about?"

"Your son's death."

"They said the army would take care of the burying expenses."

"Just some things I need to clear up."

He paused. "Well, the place is a mess, but come on in."

Hook pushed aside the stack of newspapers and sat down on the couch.

The old man dropped into the easy chair across from him, took out his cigarette papers, wet the corner of his finger, and peeled one off.

"What is it exactly you wanted cleared up?" he asked.

"As you know, your son's death has been deemed an accident. And as you probably know, a thousand dollars was found under his bunk. Given his pay scale, it's a rather large sum of money. Would you have any idea why he would have it?"

The old man folded the cigarette paper around his finger. Taking a can of Velvet from the coffee table, he tapped a row of tobacco along the length of the paper.

"About a thousand reasons is all," he said, sealing his cigarette with his tongue.

"Like what, Mr. Erikson?"

"Take a look around," he said.

Hook scanned the room, the dishes in the sink, the pile of dirty clothes in the hallway, the window screen that bulged out in the middle.

The old man lit his cigarette and squinted his eye against the smoke.

"I guess you'd have to put me high on the list of reasons. Joseph and me didn't always see eye to eye, if you know what I mean. I came up hard, see. My schooling was hit-and-miss, mostly miss. A man without an education can't provide for his family like he ought. It's back-work mostly, and back-work don't count for much. We got by, but that's about all."

"Joseph wanted more?" Hook asked.

"Shamed, wasn't he?" he said. "So, he joined the army the minute he could. Money meant more to him than anything, even his own folks. When he came home on leave, he didn't stick around much, always had some place to go, something else to do."

"What about his mother?"

"Died in childbirth. Joseph came into the world to be laid in the arms of his dead mother. I remember it like yesterday. You could hear that boy mewling halfway across Kansas. I think he always blamed himself for her death." He paused, drawing on his cigarette until the end drooped in a red point. "I think maybe I blamed him, too.

"Want to hear something funny?" he said. "That train run over Joseph on his birthday. Ain't that the funniest goddamn thing? Joseph had too much want in him for his own good. A boy that hungry can never be happy until he has it all. He can never get enough, you see."

Hook got up. "Did he have girlfriend trouble, anything like that?"

The old man flipped the ash off his cigarette onto the floor.

"Joseph didn't fret much about women, not that he was funny or anything like that, but he could take them or leave them. I never knew a woman *I* didn't want. Guess being randy don't run in the blood."

Hook walked to the door. The cabby stood behind the cab taking a leak.

"There is one thing," the old man said. "Last time Joseph came home on leave, a feller showed up one day and asked to talk to him."

Hook turned. "What about?"

"He didn't say."

"Did you know him?"

"Never saw him before," he said, "but Joseph left with him. He came back and laid up back there in the bed for a couple of hours. When he came out, he said he had to leave. I never saw him alive again."

"Do you remember what the man looked like?"

He shrugged. "Big hands, like goddamn journal jacks. Glasses, I think. Men all look the same, don't they."

BACK AT THE depot, Hook checked in with the operator.

"Mind if I use your phone? I need to make a call to Division," he said.

The operator pointed out a side office. Hook closed the door, lit a cigarette, and dialed Division.

"Security," Eddie said.

"Eddie, Runyon here. I'm in KC. I'll be heading back to Ash Fork soon."

"Runyon, this ain't your personal railroad, you know."

"It's a long, hard trip all the way up here, Eddie, but I figured I owed it to the company."

"Don't blow smoke up my skirt, Runyon. What do you want?"

"I got a hot lead on those copper thieves."

"I need you in Wichita," Eddie said.

"Wichita?"

"That's right, Wichita. It's in Kansas."

"I know where Wichita is. What's going on?"

"The cops picked her up."

"Her who, Eddie?"

"The one who robbed half the depots in your territory."

"I'll catch the *Super* back in the morning."

"Catch something sooner, Runyon. This can't wait."

TWENTY-TWO

HOOK HUNG UP the phone and waited for the heat in his ears to subside. He'd as soon be punched in the belly as talk to Eddie.

The operator leaned back in his chair and looked at Hook. "What happened to the arm?" he asked.

Hook held his prosthesis up. "My old man yanked it off when I was a kid."

The operator rolled his eyes. "I never did know a yard dog could tell the truth," he said.

"Listen," Hook said. "I need to get to Wichita. Anything headed that way?"

"Why don't you wait and catch the *Super*? She's coming in later."

Hook shook his head. "You'd have to ask Division about that." The operator checked the board. "There's an old battleship deadheading stock cars back to Dodge City tonight. She's in the yards getting a drink. I'd as soon ride a razorback hog myself."

"I've ridden worse in my day," Hook said. "Least I'll be on the inside."

"I'll let the engineer know," the operator said. "But you better get on out there."

"Thanks for the phone," Hook said.

"By the way," the operator said. "What did he do with it?"

"Do with what?"

"The arm."

"We didn't buy groceries for damn near a week," Hook said.

"Jesus, I should ask," he said, turning back to his desk.

As Hook left the depot, he noticed a man leaning against the building. Hook turned his back and lit a cigarette. Through the reflection in the window, he could see the man pull his hat down before moving off into the shadows.

THE ENGINEER STOPPED halfway up the engine ladder and looked down at Hook over his shoulder.

"Yeah," he said. "We're pulling out shortly."

"Where you want me?" Hook asked.

"There's an old drover's caboose on the tail, but it don't smell so good back there. Those stock cars ain't been cleaned in a hundred years."

"I'll be clearing in Wichita," Hook said. "No need to stop. Just give me a slow, will you?"

"All right," he said, climbing into the cab. He stuck his head out the window. "This old rattler don't move so fast, though. You might be dust by the time we get there."

Hook worked his way down line. The stink of cow manure and rotting carcasses permeated the night. Moving live cattle on stock cars came with a price. Cows got down and were crushed under the weight of the others. They died of thirst and broken limbs and all manner of mishaps. Nothing in the world moved freight as well as the railroad, except when it came to live animals. Mortality rates were high and the deaths often brutal. Hook had seen all of it he cared to.

The drover's caboose, designed to overnight cattle owners, was larger by a margin than a regular caboose. It smelled of whiskey and cigarettes, and he could see the rails through a hole in the floor. Taking off his coat, he rolled it up for a pillow and lay down on the wooden bench.

A ripple worked down line, and Hook braced himself as the caboose lurched forward. The lights of Kansas City faded behind as they rumbled off into the darkness. The stink of the cattle cars rose up through the hole and settled into his clothing.

Hook watched the stars through the window as they slid through the blackness. He thought about Linda Sue. Why had she been picked up and Corporal Thibodeaux hadn't? And who was the guy lurking outside the depot?

He turned his back against the cold breeze that churned up from the floor. A drover's caboose was a far cry from the *Super Chief.* But then his life had always been a matter of extremes. Why should it be different now?

HOOK ARRIVED IN Wichita just as dawn broke. He stood at the operator's window to check for a sleeping room.

"Yeah," the operator said. "There's one on the second floor. There's a shower at the end of the hall, too. You might consider using it."

"Thanks," Hook said.

Hook showered, washed out his socks by hand, and hung them over the end of his bunk. His back ached, and his eyes burned from lack of sleep. He collapsed into bed and yawned. A few hours in the sack would be welcome relief.

He awoke at two and dressed. When he stepped outside, he lit a cigarette and scanned the area. A man reading a newspaper sat on a bench across the street, his hat slung onto the end of his shoe. The man peeked over the top of his paper at Hook before returning to his reading.

Hook hailed a cab for the police station. The desk sergeant checked Hook's credentials and called for the deputy to fetch Linda Sue to the interrogation room. While he waited, Hook browsed a *Time* article on the *Enola Gay.* He lit a cigarette, and when he looked up, Lieutenant Allison Capron stood in the doorway.

"Hello," she said, setting her purse on the seat next to him.

Hook stood. "Lieutenant, what are you doing here?"

"I thought I might sit in on the interrogation," she said.

"How did you know I was here?"

"Got a call. I was on my way to Chicago anyway. I hope you don't mind."

"They're getting Linda Sue now. Do you know what's going on?"

"No," she said. "Do you?"

"Only that she's been picked up. I guess we'll find out together."

The deputy led them into a small room with a table and chairs. It had a single small window that had been secured with bars.

"Wait here," he said.

Within moments, he returned with Linda Sue in tow. Both of her eyes were blackened, and her hair lay in strands. Hook pulled out her chair for her.

"Linda Sue," he said. "This is Lieutenant Allison Capron, U.S. Army."

Linda Sue glanced over at the lieutenant. "I never meant no harm to anyone," she said.

"Tell us what happened," Hook said.

Linda Sue shrugged. "William said he'd take me away. That we'd have a wonderful time, and I wouldn't have to work at Blue's no more."

"Corporal William Thibodeaux, right?" the lieutenant asked.

Linda Sue nodded her head. "He said that he had money and that we'd go places and do things I'd never dreamed of." She pushed her hair back. "He was right about that, I guess."

"What happened to your eyes?" the lieutenant asked.

Linda Sue glanced over at Hook. "He hit me," she said.

"But why?" the lieutenant asked.

"Sometimes William couldn't control his temper."

"He hit you before?" Hook asked. Linda Sue nodded. "Jealous?"

Linda Sue clamped her hands in her lap. "You got a cigarette?"

Hook gave her a cigarette. She leaned over for Hook to light it.

"Did he ever talk to you about his work?" the lieutenant asked.

"Just that he guarded the tunnel, that the only thing worse than guarding a tunnel in the middle of the desert would be having permanent army KP."

"And that's all?"

"William don't talk much about anything, really," she said. "After he robbed that engineer, I got to thinking that maybe I had made a big mistake. I didn't want no trouble, and I had my five acres. It's nearly paid off, you know."

"But he didn't want you to go back?" the lieutenant asked.

"He said that he knew about me and…about Sergeant Erikson."

"And what he heard was true, wasn't it?" Hook asked.

"Well, I wasn't engaged or nothing like that, and Sergeant Erikson always had plenty of money. He used to take me places, buy me things."

"And so Corporal Thibodeaux hit you?" the lieutenant asked.

"He said that I was a whore and always would be."

"Where is he now?" Hook asked.

"I don't know," she said. "I went into the bathroom to clean up and when I came out, he was gone."

"Do you have any idea which direction he might have taken?"

"He talked about home, Louisiana." She stubbed her cigarette out in the tray. "You'd have thought no other place on earth existed."

"And then you were picked up by the police?" the lieutenant asked.

"I sat there for a long time before deciding to turn myself in. I tried to talk him out of robbing those people, you know, but he said it was the only way we could get the money. He said people like us would never have nothing if we didn't take it. But I ain't no criminal. I worked all my life and never robbed no one."

Hook walked to the door and then back to the table. "Did he ever talk to you about Sergeant Erikson's death?"

"He said he was glad he was dead, that Erikson had ruined his promotion."

Hook sat back down at the table. "Do you think he killed Sergeant Erikson?"

"No," she said.

"But you said he was jealous of you and angry about the promotion, so why wouldn't he kill him?"

Linda Sue studied her hands before answering. "Because he was afraid of him."

"And were you afraid of him, too?" the lieutenant asked.

"Yes," she said.

The lieutenant glanced at Hook. "Why were you afraid of him?"

"I don't know," she said. "I just was."

Lieutenant Capron and Hook sat in the staff car. She took a mirror out of her purse and checked her makeup. She dropped a fingernail against the corner of her mouth.

"Do you think she's telling the truth?" she asked.

"Yes," Hook said.

"So," she said, clamping her purse shut. "Where have you been?"

Hook searched out his cigarettes, but he'd given the last one to Linda Sue.

"Pickpockets up north," he said. "There's no end to them."

"Do you have a theory about Thibodeaux?" she asked.

"He's developed a taste for easy money," he said. "We'll be hearing from him again, I expect."

"Are you going back to Ash Fork?" she asked.

"Tomorrow," he said. "I've a hot lead on those copper thieves. You?"

"I plan on staying at the Broadview here in Wichita tonight and then on to Chicago tomorrow. Army business."

"The Broadview? The army must not be so bad as everyone says."

"Could I drop you?" she asked.

"I'd appreciate that."

"Mind if I stop by the hotel first? I'm expecting a call."

"No problem," he said.

HOOK BOUGHT A pack of cigarettes at the bar and then waited in the lobby while she checked at the front desk.

"Would you bring up my luggage from the car?" she asked. "I'm in room 204. I've requested room service to send a bottle of Beam up. That is your preference, isn't it?"

"Sounds good to me," he said.

Hook found only a single suitcase in the car. He knocked on the door and waited.

"Come in," she said, opening the door. "I've drinks fixed."

He took a seat, and she handed him a whiskey on the rocks. "Thanks," he said.

She sat across from him and sipped at her drink. "Do you think Corporal Thibodeaux is still in the area?"

"It's possible," he said. "But I don't think so."

"Perhaps he's gone back to Louisiana like the girl said."

"Thibodeaux's smart enough to know that home is the first place the army would search for him."

"Where do you think he might be?"

"Well, that I couldn't say, but he's leaving a pretty clear trail, isn't he?"

"There must be something that can be done?"

Hook lit a cigarette. He stirred the cubes in his drink with a fingertip.

"It strikes me that the army's particularly keen to catch a soldier who's just gone AWOL," he said. "I'd think that such a thing might happen fairly often in the army, especially when a war's on. Guarding that tunnel out there in the middle of nowhere had to be pretty lonesome duty for a young fellow like him."

"You're forgetting that the corporal has managed to commit a couple of felonies along the way."

"That's a fact," he said. "And he's likely running scared. It's pretty clear he's not a master criminal. He'll be sticking his head up again soon enough."

She settled back in her chair. "Perhaps you're right. Let's change the subject."

Hook finished his drink, and she got up to fix him another. "You've never talked much about what happened to you, I mean, about the arm and all that," she said over her shoulder.

She handed him the drink. "There's not much to say," he said. "I lost it in an accident. I felt pretty sorry for myself for a while, but sooner or later you either die or get up. I wasn't ready to die, I guess."

"At first, I thought you were just arrogant," she said. "I don't think that anymore."

"You were probably right about that," he said. "A man with one arm has to believe in himself a little more than the normal. Some folks might take it as arrogance.

"I never did thank you properly for saving my life that night at the culvert," he said.

"It was nothing," she said.

The phone rang, and the lieutenant went over to the desk to answer it. She sat down and held the phone with her chin.

"All right," she said. Reaching for a pen, she jotted something down on the hotel notepad. "Right," she said, tearing off the page and slipping it under the corner of the lamp. "Yes, thanks for calling."

Hook stood. "Everything okay?" he asked.

She looked in the mirror and brushed her hair back. "Yes," she said. "Army business. Everything's fine."

"Well," he said. "Thanks for the drink. I best be going."

"I'll get my wrap and drop you," she said.

When she opened the closet door, Hook glanced at the notepad where she had written down a phone number and, in perfect hand, "Contact John Ballard, American Locomotive Company, Schenectady N.Y."

HOOK WATCHED FROM the depot window as the lieutenant pulled away. He checked his watch. He had plenty of time before his train's arrival.

The operator unlocked the office door for him.

"Phone's there," he said.

"Thanks," Hook said.

He dialed Eddie and lit a cigarette. When he crossed his legs, he noticed that he'd put his socks on wrong side out.

"Security," Eddie said.

"Eddie, this is Hook."

"Where are you now, Runyon, Bermuda?"

"I'm in Wichita, Eddie, and with cow manure in my pockets from riding on a stock train."

"You interview that girl?"

"Yeah. The bastard blacked both her eyes before he dumped her. She turned herself in."

"And where's he?"

"On the lam."

"Jesus, Runyon," he said. "Do you ever catch anyone?"

"I'm heading back to Ash Fork, Eddie. I'm closing in on those copper thieves."

"I don't want any more diner bills run up on the *Super,* Runyon. You ain't Clark Gable, you know."

"Listen, Eddie, what do you know about the American Locomotive Company out of Schenectady?"

"Just that they're the biggest supplier of steam engines in the world, Runyon. Where the hell you been?"

"One more thing, Eddie. Did you call Lieutenant Capron about Linda Sue's arrest here in Wichita?"

"You think I have time to take care of your business and army business, too?"

"Gotta go, but I always know where to come for information. You're full of it, Eddie."

TWENTY-THREE

HOOK FOUND SCRAP and Pepe atop the caboose. "What's going on?" he asked.

Pepe took out his bandanna and wiped the sweat from his eyes.

"Loco," he said.

Scrap climbed down and searched out his smoking tobacco. "A man ahead of his time has to deal with the ignorance and narrow-mindedness of others," he said.

"Mexico calls," Pepe said. "I think it's time Pepe listens."

Scrap lit his pipe and looked down his nose. "You bastards go ahead and make fun. One day you'll be begging to be a part of the Scrap West empire, but it's going to be too late, ain't it?"

Scrap pinched off his match and flipped it away. "You catch those copper thieves yet by any chance?"

Hook said, "No, I haven't, but then what can you expect from ignorance and narrow-mindedness?"

"I've got another load of them copper pipes coming in today," Scrap said. "I was hoping they might get to the smelter."

"I've been working on it," Hook said.

"It's a sorry state of affairs when a law-abiding citizen has to stand by while he's being robbed of a living."

Hook looked over at Pepe, who had taken up a seat on the caboose steps.

"Well," Hook said. "I have to have evidence before standing someone up against the wall and shooting them."

Just then Hook heard something coming from under the caboose. He whirled around.

"What the hell was that?" he said.

"Hogs," Scrap said.

"Hogs?"

"They've taken a liking to sleeping under your caboose," Pepe said.

"Top-notch rooters," Scrap said. "None better in the state." Hook looked under the steps and found a half-dozen sows stretched out in the shade. They grunted and peeked over the tracks at him.

"Hogs under my caboose?" he said again. Hook dropped his head and rubbed his face. "What the hell you doing, Scrap?"

"Them porkers didn't cost me a dime," he said. "Traded out that old station wagon for 'em. I figure they'll turn a neat profit."

"What are you doing with hogs, for Pete's sake?"

"You ain't got a lick of free enterprise in your blood, Hook. Them sows breed like rabbits. Tell him, Pepe. I'll have hogs fence to fence and three deep by summer's end."

"You have to feed hogs, Scrap, or hadn't you thought of that?"

"Hogs eat anything, even rattlers. Makes them randy. Bosely said he had a boar eat a rattler once, and it mounted three sows in a row before falling over dead."

"That's just crazy," Hook said. "My dog sleeps under there, and by the way, where *is* Mixer?"

"Gone," Scrap said.

"Gone where?"

"He just went off down the tracks with his nose stuck in the air."

"Jesus," Hook said. "Maybe I'll just move on myself where there's no hogs or lunatics to deal with."

Scrap said, "Hear that, Pepe? And what would I do with my phone and jeep? Who knows but what someone might even steal my copper."

"You just leave Pepe out of this," Hook said. "He's got enough misery.

"I got to go find Mixer now that his feelings are hurt. He could be lost, or worse."

"He'll be back when it's time to eat," Scrap said.

Hook looked down the tracks. "I need to borrow the jeep, Scrap."

Scrap knocked out his pipe and stuck it back in his pocket. "It's currently in a state of disrepair," he said.

"You sold the transmission again?"

"Back tires and for a dang good price."

"How am I to find my dog? He might be halfway to Williams by now."

"The daily operations of a salvage yard take a good bit of time and thinking, Hook, and that dog ain't high on my worry list."

"You'd think a man who owns a salvage yard could keep at least one vehicle running."

"Well, if I was you, which I ain't, thank the Almighty, I'd catch Frenchy's short haul out."

WHEN FRENCHY EASED the bullgine up to the switch point where Hook waited, he stuck his head out of the cab.

"Now what is it, Hook?" he asked.

"How about a hitch out to the tunnel, Frenchy?"

Frenchy pushed back his hat. "You got a pass?"

"I got a sidearm," Hook said.

"Climb aboard."

Hook settled in at the back of the cab and waited for Frenchy to bring her up.

The bakehead opened the firebox, the heat blasting into the cab. Frenchy leaned over and checked the color.

"Blow her out," he said. "She's choked up."

The bakehead pitched in some sand, and black smoke churned into the sky. The steamer coughed and sputtered and took a deep breath.

"Why you going to the tunnel, Hook?" Frenchy asked. "Or is it a police matter what's too important to share with the rest of us?"

"My dog ran off," he said.

"I'd count that as a blessing myself," Frenchy said.

"I admit Mixer's got a few emotional problems," Hook said. "But who hasn't?"

"Me," Frenchy said. "I keep this son of a bitch running so fast and hard that problems can't catch up." He looked over at Hook. "Most of them, anyway."

"You're running pretty fast already, aren't you? I don't want to be sweeping up locals at a crossing."

"They took all the crossings out," Frenchy said. "It's an open alley, no stops, and the tracks are spanking new. I guess they figure the *Super* wasn't going fast enough to keep the celebrities happy."

Hook watched the smoke boil by the window as they hit the grade. If Mixer stayed with the tracks, he might have wound up at the guardhouse, given that they had food, and food had always been one of his priorities.

Hook studied the back of Frenchy's neck, which looked exactly like old shoe leather. Come any kind of weather, Frenchy rode with an open window where he could stick his head out. Said a man couldn't get the most out of a machine without smelling the smoke.

"Frenchy," Hook said. "What do you know about the American Locomotive Company?"

Frenchy studied his cigar. "They make the biggest, hottest engines in the country. But a steamer's like a woman, she can get too big and too hot to handle."

"Sounds like an engineer's problem to me," Hook said.

Frenchy grinned and lit his cigar. "It's the fireman what can't keep the boiler hot," he said.

BEFORE THEY REACHED the trestle, Hook lowered himself onto the steps, the ties clicking by beneath him.

"How long before you're back?" he called up to Frenchy.

"Couple-three hours," Frenchy said, "providing I can keep the bakehead awake."

"Look for me when you come through, will you?"

"You can ride anytime you want, long as you got that sidearm," he said.

Hook dropped off in a lope and waited as the train labored off toward the tunnel. He picked his way out onto the trestle, his head whirling a little at the space that opened beneath his feet. He knelt to get his bearings and to listen. Mixer, like most animals, preferred not to walk the trestle, so he may have sidetracked into the canyon instead.

Working his way over, Hook spotted dog tracks at the other end but couldn't determine if they led in or out of the canyon. From there, he could see the military jeep parked in the shade near the guardhouse. Since food was most likely there, he decided to check it out first.

He knocked on the door of the guardhouse, but no one answered. Peeking through the window, he could see no one inside. Only then did he notice the briefcase sitting on the bunk.

He looked around before trying the knob. The door opened, and he stepped in. The guard's weapon was gone, which meant that he had probably left on patrol. An empty coffee cup sat on the table, and Hook could smell the remnants of breakfast bacon.

The briefcase was army and of high-quality leather like the lieutenant's, unusual for an enlisted man to have officer issue. Hook looked out the window once again before dumping its contents onto the bunk.

He found in it a ballpoint pen, grocery receipts, and an Arizona map that had come apart at the seams. Something shiny had caught in the bottom corner of the briefcase. While he didn't know much about the army, he did know what a captain's insignia bars looked like, and he knew that they had no business being in the possession of enlisted men.

When he looked up, he could see Corporal Severe climbing the steps. Putting everything back into the briefcase, Hook went out to the porch. As Corporal Severe climbed the last few steps, he glanced up.

"Oh," he said. "It's you."

"Couldn't raise anyone," Hook said. "Figured you were on patrol."

The corporal leaned his rifle against the railing. "That's right. Is there something I could do for you?"

"Looking for my dog," Hook said. "You haven't seen him, have you?"

Corporal Severe shaded his eyes with his hand. "No dog," he said. "I haven't seen a living soul all day."

"Well, he's not much of a dog," Hook said.

"I'll keep an eye out," the corporal said.

"Thought I'd check down below. Hope the coyotes haven't gotten to him."

"Well, good luck, then," he said.

"Is the line clear?" Hook asked. "Might take a turn through the tunnel."

"It's clear for now," he said.

"Thanks," Hook said. "You boys be careful out here."

Now CLAD IN BOILERPLATE, the tunnel magnified the sounds of Hook's footsteps. The curve had remained as before, cutting off most all light.

Without a flashlight, Hook had to feel his way along the wall. The weight of the mountain pressed in, as it always did, and the smell of dampness hung in the air. When he could see the sunlit exit in the distance, he went no farther and returned instead the way he'd come.

He looked at his watch, two hours until Frenchy was due back. That should be enough time to search out a pretty good stretch of the canyon.

THE PATH TWISTED DOWNWARD, looping in hairpin switch-backs, and the air grew still as he descended. Rails and odd bits of boxcars from past wrecks twisted out of the rocks below.

At the bottom of the trail he spotted animal tracks leading down the canyon. All manner of creatures sought the protection of the canyon, and he couldn't be certain they were Mixer's tracks. A little farther along, he saw the print of a man's boot, an old track weathered away by the winds. He smoked a cigarette and watched a buzzard circle high in the blue sky above him.

He'd gone a mile, maybe more, when the walls of the canyon rose up around him, jagged cliffs that cut away the world. High above him, the rock cut back into a natural ledge, and he decided to check it out.

He climbed by working his toes into the cracks. At times like this he most missed the leverage and efficiency of two arms. Sweat ran into his eyes, and when he stopped to wipe it away, he realized that Mixer watched him from above. Hook climbed his way to where Mixer greeted him.

"You ole thief," he said, patting him. "What are you doing up here?"

Mixer wove between Hook's legs a couple of times before bounding away. He looked back at Hook and wagged his tail.

"What is it, boy?"

Mixer circled and whined, and just as Hook started to follow, he heard the whistle of a steamer in the distance.

"Come on, boy," he said. "We better get back. If we miss Frenchy, it's a long walk home."

FRENCHY ROLLED HIS EYES but didn't say anything when Hook and the fireman lifted Mixer into the engine cab. As they eased across the trestle, Mixer climbed up on the fireman's seat and stuck his head out the window. His tongue lolled from his mouth and water dripped off its end.

Frenchy said, "If that dog weren't so smart, I'd mistake him for my fireman, sure enough."

The fireman, who'd been checking the water gauge,

shook his head. "If he was smart, he wouldn't be taking no fireman's job in the first place."

Hook's feet hurt from the climb, and he was hungry. On top of that, he was feeling even more uncertain about the case.

He lit a cigarette and leaned back against the cab.

"Frenchy," he said. "What do you figure a man would have to have to hike out of this canyon?"

Frenchy looked over his shoulder at Hook.

"Hell," he said, "I don't know, food and water, I suppose. Cigars. Some way of knowing what direction to go. Maybe a gun for shooting stray dogs or himself if worse came to worst." He eased the throttle forward. Steam and smoke boiled skyward. "Anything else you need an expert opinion on?"

Hook looked back over the darkening canyon.

"I guess the real question is, *why* would you want to hike out of here?"

Frenchy took out a fresh cigar, unwrapped it, and ran it under his nose.

"There's only one reason a man would hike out of this country afoot," he said.

"And what would that be?"

He lit his cigar and propped his elbow out the window. "If he had no other choice," he said.

TWENTY-FOUR

WHEN HOOK HEARD a commotion, he sat straight up in bed. Mixer commenced barking, his hackles raised.

Hook opened the caboose door and found Pepe chasing the last of the hogs from beneath the caboose with a stick.

"What the hell is going on?" Hook asked.

"Moving the hogs. Scrap traded some for a tractor and wants them moved today," he said.

Hook pushed his hair back from his eyes. "A tractor?"

Pepe poked a sow in the butt with a stick. She squealed in protest and trotted off behind the others.

"A garden tractor. He's going to plant tomatoes," he said.

"What does Scrap West know about gardening?"

Pepe shrugged. "About as much as he knows about hogs, I guess."

"Jesus, Pepe, can't you do something about this?"

"I work by the hour, Hook. He can knit doilies for all I care."

Hook found Scrap in the office putting a nail in the heel of his shoe.

"I see you found that dog," Scrap said.

Hook wiped out a cup. "Poor thing was hiding out in Johnson Canyon for fear of being eaten by hogs.

"Pepe says you traded for a tractor?"

"That's right," he said.

"May I ask why?"

Scrap loaded his pipe. "To feed my hogs," he said.

"You don't have any land for gardening, Scrap."

"I figure to raise tomatoes between those stacks of cars in the back. What I don't feed to the hogs, I will sell in town."

"It won't work, Scrap."

He lit his pipe and blew out the match.

"You're a dark thinker, Hook. A fellow has to be positive if he's ever going to get anywhere."

"I'm positive it won't work," Hook said.

Scrap got up and dumped sugar into his coffee.

"If my attitude was as sour as yours, I'd probably be living in a caboose and eating beans."

"Did you get the tires put back on that junk pile?"

"The tires are just fine, though a bit oversized."

AFTER SCRAP HAD gone, Hook dialed the number he'd seen on the lieutenant's note. A woman answered.

"American Locomotive Company," she said. "How may I help you?"

"John Ballard, please," he said.

"Who's calling?"

"Hook Runyon, railroad security."

The woman paused. "Just a moment."

Hook watched the dust circle in the sunlight that cast through the window.

Coming back on the line, she said, "Sir."

"Yes."

"I'm sorry. We don't have a John Ballard here."

"Are you certain?"

"Perhaps you have the wrong name or number."

"Yes," he said. "Perhaps."

THE TIRES ON the back of the jeep were nearly twice the size of the front ones, and when Hook got in, he slid forward against the steering wheel. Pushing himself back with his legs, he cranked up the jeep and pulled off down the road. He hit forty miles an hour while still in low gear. The front end of the jeep whipped from side to side, and the back tires hummed against the pavement. Debris and dirt bellowed up from the side of the road.

When he got to Blue's Café, he dusted himself off before going in. Blue stood at the sink washing dishes. He'd tied his apron on in the front but had failed to turn it back. He stopped and dried his hands on the rag that hung from his pocket.

"You get caught in a tornado?" he asked.

"It's a long story," Hook said.

"So, did you find Linda Sue?"

"They picked her up in Wichita," Hook said, leaning on the pass-through. "The corporal left her behind but not before he worked her over a little."

"You get my fifty bucks?" he asked.

"What do you think?" Hook said.

Blue hung the dishcloth over his shoulder and fished out a cigarette.

"What's going to happen to her?"

Hook rubbed at the kink that had developed in his neck from the jeep ride.

"Be my guess they'll squeeze her for information and give her some time in county."

Blue checked the grill, flipping a couple of burgers

over. "Linda Sue was a hell of a waitress," he said. "She could serve a full house, flirt with every one of the customers in the doing, and make 'em all happy. My business is off twenty percent since she left."

"Sorry to hear it," Hook said.

"On top of that, the track crews are all going elsewhere for their meals. I'll be lucky to keep this place open at this rate."

"Linda Sue got caught up in something she didn't understand," Hook said. "I'd hate to see her lose her place. She says it's nearly paid off. I've been thinking maybe someone could keep an eye on it. Make sure it wasn't broken into, that sort of thing."

Blue flattened the burgers, and smoke raced up the exhaust. "What the hell," he said. "I've made a mistake or two my own damn self. I suppose I could drive by there once in a while."

"Thanks," Hook said. "I'm sure Linda Sue will be grateful."

"What's going on out there at that tunnel, Hook? They're running equipment up and down that track twenty-four hours a day."

"Upgrade, I'm told," Hook said. "I guess passenger service is likely to be big with the war over."

"I'm just a cook," Blue said. "But why didn't they go north with a new line? They wouldn't have that grade or that tunnel either one to deal with."

"The big boys don't consult me much these days. Anyway, the railroad is kind of like me, it doesn't do anything the easy way as long as there's a hard way."

The door opened, and several customers came in.

"I better run," Hook said. "I'll check out the crews'

meal schedules for you. Most times the railroad prefers spreading their business around."

HOOK LEFT THE jeep parked in front of Blue's and walked down to Sheriff Mueller's office. Mueller had his feet up on the desk and had fallen asleep in his chair. A fly preened on the top of his ear.

"Damn, what?" he said, rubbing his face.

"I didn't mean to disturb your nap, Sheriff, but thought you'd like to know that they picked Linda Sue up in Wichita."

Sheriff Mueller pushed his hair back with his fingers. "I got a call," he said.

"Blue's going to keep an eye on her place."

Mueller dropped his feet to the floor and dug at his crotch. "They haven't caught Thibodeaux yet?"

"Not yet."

"The son of a bitch," he said. "They told me he beat her up some."

"I'll let you know if anything comes up," Hook said. "By the way, anyone been looking for me?"

"Not so's you can tell," he said, adjusting his gun belt. "Ben Hoffer's been spreading it around that he's going to even things up. But he's mostly wind."

Hook walked to the door. "You aren't having me tailed for anything, are you, Sheriff?"

Mueller set his hat and picked up his keys. "Hell, no," he said. "You know what a tail costs?"

"Yeah," Hook said. "That's what I figured."

WHEN HOOK GOT back to the jeep, the old man from the post office was standing next to it. He had his hands in his pockets, and he rocked back on his heels when he saw Hook.

"Most folks have the same," he said. "Excuse me?" Hook said.

"Tires," he said. "Most folks have the same. Those tires on the back are bigger than the tires on the front. She'll run too fast in low gear, and the front end will wobble."

"The thing is, if the big ones are on the front, you can't see the road," Hook said.

The old man walked to the door of Blue's Café before turning around.

"If they're the same on the front as they are on the back, then it don't matter," he said. "You can see the road clear as day, front or back, either one."

Hook got back to the salvage yard by late afternoon. He parked the jeep in front of the office, which he found empty. As he made his way to the caboose, a cool breeze drifted in from the countryside, and the crickets struck up their chorus for the evening.

Mixer, exhausted from his escapade into the canyon, failed to get up to greet him. Hook took off his sidearm, fixed himself a whiskey and water, and thumbed through his books.

The Erikson case had consumed him far too long, and he wished for it to end. But with each passing day, it had grown more baffling and more frustrating, and then with all the time he'd spent chasing copper thieves on top of it.

How long had it been since he'd had time to peruse his books, to read them and contemplate their histories and the lives they may have touched? Such was the fun of collecting, and he'd missed not having the time to do it right.

When an engine came down line, her drivers thumping, Hook rose and looked out his window. She coupled into an empty car before crawling back by the caboose.

Downing his drink, he slipped on his sidearm, stuck his flashlight into his rear pocket, and moved out into the stacks of junked cars. By then the engine had moved the car onto the siding down line and had coupled her onto a short haul. A truck had backed in, and men were loading copper pipe off it and into the car. Hook figured it to be the truck load that Scrap had been expecting to arrive.

He circled, coming in from the back, and he waited until the men had finished and pulled away. He swung up on the ladder of the car and paused to catch his breath. Pulling a ladder one armed was one of the hardest tasks he did. Even now, after all these years, it didn't come easy.

He climbed up and dropped down into the car and took a close look at the pipe. When he spotted the grease pencil marks he'd made earlier, he leaned back against the side of the car.

The bastards were stealing Scrap's pipe off his cars when they arrived in Williams, being careful not to take so much as to be noticed, loading it in a truck, and re-selling it back to him as a new order. They might have gotten away with it, too, if they'd been dealing with anyone but Scrap, who could estimate a load of copper within a few pounds.

A westbound freighter blew her whistle on the edge of town and within moments thundered by. When she'd passed, the switch engine brought up steam and bumped out the slack on the short haul. Hook rose to get off and then changed his mind. Maybe he'd just ride her out, be there when she arrived at her destination.

As the steamer chugged through the desert, he thought about the lieutenant. At times he felt left out of things. Her information just didn't add up to the facts he'd been given, but then his thinking hadn't been so rational either. Though he'd not admitted it, not even to himself, he'd been attracted to her, and such emotions could complicate life, particularly when it came to solving a case. He hadn't planned it that way and hadn't taken into account the distraction she had presented.

Maybe he'd missed a lot in life, come up a little short on the formalities. But he could smell a lie better than most, and he was pretty certain the lieutenant had been holding back on something. Stick to the facts, Eddie always said. Maybe for once Eddie had been right.

Night fell over him as the train made its way to Williams. When it leaned into a curve, Hook took a look over the top of the car. Black smoke from the steam engine churned upward into the moonlight. He lit a cigarette and leaned back against the copper pipe.

The steam engine blew its whistle at the Williams crossing, and Hook squashed out his cigarette. Maybe he'd just spent too long on the rails, a man corrupted and cynical from living with the underbelly of society.

He checked the clip in his P.38. The engine blew its whistle, a note trailing off into the night, and they slowed for the Williams Salvage siding. If things went as they should, they'd couple onto the Williams cars and be on their way to the smelter. If they didn't, then certain trouble awaited.

TWENTY-FIVE

WHEN THE TRAIN STOPPED, Hook dropped down from the car. The lights from Williams Salvage lit the security fence beyond the right-of-way. He turned his ear into the wind to listen. Junkyard dogs could be less than understanding when it came to intruders, but only the steamer chugged in the distance. On the siding next to him, a line of old cattle cars sat like silent dinosaurs, and the stench of manure filled the night.

Just then a signal lamp bobbed on up track. Hook slipped under the car and rolled onto his side. He could just see the lamp over the wheel carriage.

He lay back. They were probably throwing the spur switch to side off the main line. Maybe they were coupling in, making up the train to go on to the smelter with a full order. Maybe he'd been wrong about this whole thing. If so, he'd catch the next freighter back to Ash Fork and call it a miss. It wouldn't be the first time. He'd never calculated his catch rate, and he hoped no one else had either.

In any case, if a go signal came, he'd have time to escape from under the car. Still, lying under rolling stock with a live engine at tow could make a man uneasy. The human body was no match for the wheels of a loaded copper car.

Bracing himself on his elbow, he took another look.

The switchman's lamp had moved down track and was nearly upon him.

"Damn it," he said.

He drew to the center of the tracks and held his breath as the switchman approached. He could smell the kerosene fumes from his lamp and could see his feet and the pistol in his hand. Not many switchmen Hook knew carried a sidearm just to throw a switch.

When the switchman moved the lamp in a frontal circle, indicating a backup signal, Hook's pulse ticked up. If he rolled out now, he'd be discovered. If he didn't, he and roadkill would have a lot in common.

The engine blew her whistle, and a rumble traveled down line. The cars bumped and groaned as the slack fell away. Hook's mouth went dry. He'd never make it under the wheel carriage if she started to roll back. Placing his feet against the track he spun around so that his head pointed downrange. The car creaked and groaned and crawled backward.

Sweat ran into Hook's eyes, and his heart hammered in his chest. With the wheel axle now only feet away, he snared his hook on an overhead bracing. It caught, and the car dragged him along like a fish on a line. Both shoes pulled off, and his heels bumped and plowed along in the gravel.

When at last the car crept to a stop, Hook waited, his breath locked. If it started forward, he'd be headed in the wrong direction again and in deep trouble. He peered over his shoulder and could just make out the switchman moving his lamp from side to side in a full-stop signal.

He worked the hook loose from the frame and checked for his sidearm, which had somehow managed to stay holstered. Clicking off the safety, he leveled in for a clear shot, just in case.

But at that moment, lights broke in the distance, and a truck clambered down the right-of-way. It backed into the car, and two men climbed out. The driver, who wore a baseball cap, approached the switchman. His passenger walked to the back of the truck and lit a cigarette.

The driver asked, "Is that West's load?"

"Yeah," the switchman said.

"The same stuff?"

"Keep it light this time, and we'll send the rest on to the smelter."

"You afraid of Scrap West catching on?"

"I ain't worried about Scrap West," he said, "but that yard dog might be smarter than he looks."

"That one-armed bull?" the driver asked.

"Yeah, the one what put three of you in the dirt by hisself."

"I hear he was a bo and a drunk 'fore taking up with the railroad."

"Maybe so," the switchman said, "but hadn't been for that popcar on the tracks, you boys would be breaking rocks at the state prison.

"Now, let's get this done. That main line ain't clear all night, you know. Unload about a third. We'll put her in that end car until we're certain things have blown over."

"You going to help load?" the driver asked.

"Loading ain't my job," the switchman said.

"Maybe it ought be," the driver said. "Given the size of your take."

"My take ain't your concern, and you don't want

Hump coming back here from the engine. He ain't as good-natured as me."

Hook waited until the two men had commenced throwing pipe in the back of the truck before working his way out the opposite end of the railcar. The switchman, who had taken up a seat on the running board of the truck, smoked a cigarette and watched them.

Hook circled around and came in at the front of the truck. He picked up a rock and tossed it into the darkness. The switchman stood.

"Who's there?" he said.

Hook caught him with a short punch in the jugular. He hit him hard and fast and with his body weight behind it. The switchman wilted to his knees. Hook slammed in with a second punch, and the man dropped into the dirt. He'd learned long ago that having an advantage didn't mean a damn thing if he didn't use it.

He made for the car ladder. Halfway up, he hung in close to catch his breath. Near the top, he waited until the driver of the truck leaned over the edge of the car with an armload of copper. Reaching up, Hook slammed him across the ear with his prosthesis. The driver hung suspended for a moment, and then pitched over the side. Hook couldn't see where he fell or what happened when he hit, but by the sound of things, he wouldn't be getting up anytime soon.

But the driver's friend, working somewhere at the back of the car, had no doubt heard the noise as well. Hook slipped over the top of the car and into the shadows. He located a short piece of pipe and cocked it on his shoulder. He could see the man's silhouette coming forward.

"Where the hell you go?" he said. "I ain't unloading this son of a bitch by myself."

When Hook hit him, the copper pipe rang like a church bell. "I'd give you a hand," he said, "but I only got the one."

Hook dropped down from the ladder. The truck driver lay at the bottom like a piece of crumpled paper. That left the engineer, but getting up to the engine cab without being detected might get tricky.

He looked down line and into the darkness. He could smell the heat from the engine in the night air. There could be a fireman in the cab with the engineer as well, though short hauls didn't always stick to regs. What with stolen goods involved, he figured they were operating lean.

THE SIGNAL LAMP, still lit, lay next to the switchman. Hook took it and donned the switchman's hat. It smelled of Wildroot Cream Oil and sat atop his head like a bird nest.

As he walked toward the engine, he made sure the engineer could see the lamp at his side. About halfway to the engine, he paused and then ducked between the cars. He waited a few moments before stepping back out. He swung the lamp in a full-body circle to signal a separated coupling. The engineer acknowledged him with two short blasts of the whistle.

Hook swung up on the grab iron, slipped off his belt, and cinched the signal lamp to the car. He pulled his sidearm out and moved between the cars again to wait. Sooner or later that engineer would be coming to find out what the hell had happened.

He didn't have to wait long before he spotted a flashlight bobbing down track.

As the engineer approached, he said, "Goddang it, Frank, what's going on?" When no answer came, he stopped. "Frank?" he said.

Hook pulled in tight against the car. If the switchman had been armed, the engineer might be, too. The engineer panned the area with his flashlight. "Frank?" he said again, uncertainty in his voice.

When the flashlight beam settled in on the signal lamp, Hook stepped out with his pistol leveled. But the engineer had moved in next to the car.

"Security," Hook said. "Raise your…"

He never finished the sentence because an explosion in his head scrambled his words into bits of light that scattered and flashed behind his eyes.

When he opened them, he lay on the ground, and Hump stood over him. Hook's sidearm lay on the ground just out of reach. At that point Hook figured he could talk or attack. Given Hump's size and disposition, he concluded that the talking phase had pretty much ended.

Pulling his leg into his chest, Hook shoved his foot full bore into Hump's kneecap. The howl that followed could have been Hump's or it could have been his, because he'd completely forgotten about his lack of shoes. His big toe telegraphed a pain, hot as boiling grease, into his groin.

Hook located his weapon and waited for the engineer to recover.

"Get up," he said.

"I think you broke my leg, you bastard," he said.

"It's the other leg I'm going to break if you don't do as I say," he said. "Now, let's move."

"What are you going to do?"

"I'm going to round up some steers for market," he said. "And you're going to give me a hand, so to speak."

Hook watched from the truck, sidearm at the ready, as the engineer loaded the others one by one into a cattle car.

Hook picked up a piece of pipe. "Now it's your turn. Climb in." The engineer hoisted himself up into the car, and Hook slid the door shut behind him. Hump hung his hands out between the slats of the car.

"You're not going to leave us out here?" he asked.

Hook jimmied the pipe into the door's latch and bent it over. "Someone will be back to get you," he said. "Providing the slaughter run doesn't get here first."

HOOK LIT A cigarette and looked down track. The steamer, now absent its engineer, chugged away on its own, and the depot light winked in the distance. He'd have to walk, he supposed, shoes or no shoes, and get the locals out here before those boys figured a way out of that car.

As he picked his way down track, he shook his head. Why he did this job, he didn't know. Maybe it was just the big money and glamour of it all.

TWENTY-SIX

AFTER THE OPERATOR had called the sheriff, he pushed his chair back.

"Jesus, Hook," he said. "You don't have no shoes on."

Looking at his bloodied heels, Hook said, "I guess it's your attention to detail what makes you such a great operator, Bill." Bill picked up his coffee cup and looked into it before taking a sip.

"I seen cinder dicks with slick knees," he said. "And bad hair pieces. I even seen one wearing a vest and a gold watch fob, but I ain't never seen one barefooted. Must be the new fashion."

"Ever seen an operator with a broken nose?" Hook said.

"No need to get sore, Hook. I think it's right stylish. Maybe you should consider painting up your toenails."

Hook squinted his eyes. "I might consider using my sidearm on smart-ass operators," he said. "The world's got too many as it is. Now maybe you could quit grinning long enough to find me something to put on?"

"Well," the operator said. "There might be something in my locker, though I can't guarantee they will be the perfect color."

"I'll make do," Hook said.

"You watch the office, and I'll go check," he said.

"All right," Hook said.

"And don't run no trains together. Just watch."

"Goddang it, Bill."

"All right, all right," he said.

Hook sat down on the lobby bench. He lit a cigarette and examined what remained of his socks. When he looked up, a woman stood in the doorway.

"Do you know when the eastbound to Chicago comes in?" she asked.

Hook rose and checked the board. "Six," he said.

"A.m.?"

"Yes," he said.

She looked at Hook's arm and then at his bare feet. She fumbled through her purse and handed him a dollar bill.

"Remember God loves you," she said.

"THIS IS ALL I could find," Bill said, handing Hook the shoes.

"Dang it, Bill, those are galoshes."

"I didn't know barefooted yard dogs were so fussy. You want them or not?"

"I guess I have no choice," Hook said, putting them on. "And they're too damn big, aren't they?"

"Well, now," Bill said. "This may look like a department store to you. Fact is, it's a railroad depot, and I don't remember any money exchanging hands. You don't like the galoshes, just take them off."

"Oh, I intend to pay you back, don't you worry about that.

"Now, do you think I could use the company phone, or is there a charge on that as well?"

Bill grinned. "Phone's back there," he said. "No charge. Don't let it be said I ain't generous with my friends."

HOOK DIALED DIVISION and waited for the phone to ring. He could see Bill pouring something out of a flask into his coffee thermos.

"Yeah?" Eddie said.

"Eddie, this is Hook."

"You got something against calling during working hours, Runyon?"

"Couldn't wait to hear your voice, Eddie."

"This better be important."

"I rounded up those copper thieves."

"About time."

"Two of them are railway employees. One of them's an engineer, Humpback or whatever his name is. Management needs to be a little more careful about who it hires, Eddie."

"You got that right. Where are they now?"

"Turned 'em over to the locals here in Williams. That short haul's sitting on the siding at the salvage yard. You better have someone get out there."

"Yeah," he said. "I'll make a call."

Hook lit a cigarette and watched the operator pour another coffee.

"Listen, Eddie, how about a transfer out of that junkyard now? It's like sleeping in a parking lot."

"What's another parking lot more or less, Runyon?"

"Scrap West doesn't need his own private security anymore."

"Look," Eddie said. "That tunnel is important. I need someone out there to keep an eye on things."

"Hell, the war's over, hadn't you heard? They dropped a bomb, and everyone is dead."

"Yeah, I know all about it. Listen, I got a call from

a guy in Ash Fork looking for you. Said his name was Blue Boy."

"Blue Boy?" Hook said.

"That's right."

"There's a Blue's Café."

"Whatever."

"Jesus, Eddie, *Blue Boy* is a famous painting by Thomas Gainsborough."

"I know that."

"Why don't you read a book, Eddie?"

"Why don't you buy a burial plot in Ash Fork, Runyon, 'cause that's how long you're going to be there?"

"What did he want?"

"Who?"

"Blue Boy," Hook said.

"How the hell would I know?"

"Glad to know you have things under control as usual, Eddie. Gotta run."

HOOK DIALED THE operator and asked for Blue's Café in Ash Fork. A woman answered.

"Blue's Café," she said.

"Is Blue in?"

"He's in the john," she said. "Hang on."

Hook lit a cigarette and watched Bill work the board. An operator could screw things up in a big way if he didn't pay attention.

Blue came on the phone. "Hello," he said.

"This is Hook Runyon. Division said you were trying to get hold of me."

"I stopped by Linda Sue's trailer on the way home like you asked."

"And?"

"I ain't no detective, but it didn't look right to me."

"Could you be a little more specific?"

"Looked like somebody's been nosing around. There's kind of a path worn through the weeds, and the screen on the window is hanging loose."

"I'm in Williams right now, but I'll have a look when I get back."

"I could sure use Linda Sue around here. The waitress I hired spends all her time smoking.

"Listen," Blue said. "You didn't get a chance to talk to anyone, did you?"

"About what?"

"About sending those crews this way for dinner once in a while. They ain't hit my place yet."

"I intended to check on that, Blue, but things turned a little hectic. I'll see what I can do. Thanks for the call."

ON THE WAY OUT, Hook stopped at the operator's cage. "When's the next ride to Ash Fork, Bill?"

Bill checked the schedule. "There's a westbound freighter with twenty blackjacks in tow."

"How long before she arrives?"

"Forty-five minutes."

"I'm going to catch her at the crossing. Give her a slow signal for me, will you?"

"Coal cars ain't the cleanest ride in the world, Hook. Wait a few hours, and you could catch the *Super*."

"I'll hop the crummy and listen to the brakeman tell lies. Helps pass the time. Let the engineer know I'll be bailing at West's Salvage in Ash Fork, will you?"

"Okay."

Hook paused. "You're a good operator, Bill. I'd hate to see the railroad lose you."

Bill pushed his glasses up on his nose. "What does that mean, Hook?"

"Thing is, too much coffee isn't good for a man. Pretty soon he gets all jittery and can't pay attention to his job. Operators have to keep their feet under them, if you know what I mean."

Bill's face ashened, and he set his cup down. "You ain't reporting me, are you, Hook?"

"I've done my share of drinking over the years, Bill, but never on the job. It's the one thing will get a man fired around here. I'm thinking that maybe you didn't understand that when you hired out."

Bill swallowed and looked over at his thermos. "I understand it now, Hook."

"Thanks for the shoes, Bill. I'll get them back next time through."

THE TRAIN SLOWED to a crawl at West's Salvage just as the sun broke. Hook swung down and made his way to the office. Scrap sat at his desk having his morning coffee. He looked over the top of his newspaper.

"You expecting rain, Hook?"

"What do you mean?"

"Them's galoshes, if I ain't mistaken."

Hook held up his foot. "It's a complicated story."

"I'll bet. Anyway, I get this call from the smelter, see. They're wondering where my copper is. Turns out the whole dang car is missing."

Hook poured himself a cup of coffee and sat down. "That car's on a siding over to Williams. I rounded those boys up last night while you were planning out your next tax-evasion scheme."

"Well, I'll be damned," he said, laying down his paper. "Who are they?"

"Two of them are railroad employees, an engineer and a switchman. I've seen the engineer working a pusher right here off this siding. I figure the others work for Williams Salvage one way or the other."

"That son of a bitch," Scrap said.

"They've been selling the same copper to you over and over again, Scrap. Steal it one week and truck it back the next. Hard telling how many times you paid for the same pipe."

Scrap stood. "I been buying back my own copper?"

"I tell you, Scrap, I'd as soon trust a Juárez hooker as a salvage man."

Scrap looked into his open hands. "I been buying my own copper?"

"Don't take it so hard, Scrap. Everyone gets taken sooner or later."

He took off his hat and ran his hands over his bald pate.

"A good businessman don't get screwed, Hook. He's supposed to do the screwing hisself."

"Well, just cut back a little on your expenses, Scrap. It will be all right. Maybe you ought stop paying Pepe by the hour. And then you got your hogs and tomato garden to fall back on if things get tough."

"I don't have no hogs," he said. "Traded them for a truckload of empty ammo boxes."

"But I thought those hogs were going to make you rich, Scrap."

"A little problem came up," he said.

"Oh."

"Everyone knows a hog will eat anything, right?"

"They're known for having a sharp appetite," Hook said.

"A hog will eat barbed wire and the posts it's strung on, given he gets hungry enough."

"It's a possibility," Hook said.

"Did you know there's one thing in the world a hog won't eat?"

"That's a lie," Hook said.

"Tomatoes."

Hook looked through his brows. "Tomatoes?"

"Hogs hate tomatoes like preachers hate sin, and I don't have enough clear land to grow anything else. My hog days are at an end and so's my life. If I had a gun, I'd end it right here."

"I got one you could borrow," Hook said. "'Cept I might want to use it on myself before this ends."

"I'm telling you, Hook, sometimes it don't pay for a man to put his boots on in the morning." He paused. "Or his galoshes either."

"All right, Scrap. I'll try to keep it quiet so people won't think you're an idiot."

"You're a true friend, Hook."

Hook lit a cigarette and blew out the match.

"Then you wouldn't mind me borrowing the jeep tonight. I need to make a trip to town."

"What's a ruined man like me need a jeep for?" he said. "It ain't like I'll be using it for business. And don't worry about putting no gas in it 'cause I got nowhere to go."

HOOK PULLED MIXER'S ears and let him into the caboose. Mixer stretched and then crawled under the bunk for a nap. Hook searched around for something to eat. Finding nothing worth the effort, he had a whiskey instead.

After taking off his prosthesis, he put it on top of the stove.

His bunk, not having been made in a few weeks, didn't look so inviting. Too exhausted to care, he lay down and listened to the pusher chug and thump from the siding. Scrap's crane soon roared into life across the yards.

He dropped his arm over his eyes and struggled to make sense of things, to put the facts in order. What could account for a man standing in a tunnel with a train speeding down a 3 percent grade? Why did Erikson have a backpack and a fistful of money under his bed? While he couldn't be certain the flashlight was Erikson's, it was army issue and a good possibility. What was it doing outside instead of in the tunnel with Erikson? And why did the replacement guards' account of their duty assignment differ from the lieutenant's, and what were captain's bars doing in one of their briefcases, anyway? Who the hell was John Ballard and what did he have to do with the lieutenant?

He turned over, and fatigue washed through him. Maybe when he awoke, things would clear up. For now, he would sleep. Come dark, he planned to be at Linda Sue's place just in case a visitor came calling again.

TWENTY-SEVEN

THE JEEP SAT in front of Scrap's office, and the keys had been tossed onto the floorboard. Hook double-checked the tires and tried out the reverse before pulling out.

As he drove away, he looked back at West's Salvage Yard. Piles of trash loomed against the setting sun, and deep in their innards, fires smoldered. Scrap's fires were perpetual, like eternal flames marking the graves of the dead.

What Scrap couldn't sell, he burned. What he couldn't burn found its way into a natural gorge that cut through the back of the yards. Someday archaeologists would puzzle over the strange society that must have existed there.

The evening breeze had cooled with dusk and blew Hook's hair across his eyes. He lit a cigarette as he turned onto the highway to Ash Fork. The old jeep hummed down the road as smooth as a showroom Cadillac. Hook figured that Scrap's propensity for robbing Peter to pay Paul must be on the decline. But then Scrap's week had been tough, first the hog debacle and then the disgrace of being duped into buying back his own copper. For a man known as a skilled haggler, it had all, no doubt, been humbling.

As the sky darkened, Hook clicked on the headlights, but nothing happened. He pulled over and worked the switch. No lights. He got out, walked to the front of the jeep, and discovered both headlamps missing from their sockets.

He kicked the bumper, and his sore toe fired off a bolt of lightning.

"Damn it, Scrap," he said, hopping about on one foot. "What the hell did you do?"

Night had fallen like a black curtain by the time he reached Ash Fork. He'd gotten there only by tracking the white line down the center of the highway.

He stopped at the intersection on the outskirts of town and rubbed the kink out of his back. Maybe he'd kill Scrap West, put his body in the gorge. Nobody would ever find it, except maybe some archaeologist a million years hence. Even so, he'd probably assume they were the remains of the missing link, which wasn't far from the truth.

Just as he started to turn toward Linda Sue's trailer, lights pulled up behind him. The door opened, and a man got out. When he stepped into his own headlights, Hook recognized him as Ben Hoffer. Ben walked to Hook's door and leaned in. He smelled of booze and swayed a little as he peered at Hook.

"Runyon," he said. "And all by hisself. You afraid to turn on your lights?"

"What do you want, Ben? I'm in kind of a rush."

"Guess you would be," he said. "What with no woman to hide behind."

"Look, Ben, I'm sorry about all this misunderstanding. Let's you and me call a truce."

"Our business ain't finished, Runyon. You got an ass kicking coming."

"I'd be happy to accommodate you some other time, Ben. Thing is, I need to get somewhere, and I have this busted toe. It just isn't a good time for me to whip your ass, again."

Ben hissed, and spittle blew from between his teeth. "Hook's toe hurt?" he said.

"Yeah," Hook said. "You'd be surprised. Now, why don't you move on? You and me can dance some other day."

"Climb on out of there, Runyon," he said. "Nobody clips me and gets by with it."

Hook lit a cigarette and looked at Ben.

"Some other time," he said, shifting into low and pulling over Ben's foot.

Ben threw his hands in the air, his mouth agape. Hook shoved the jeep into reverse and backed over it again. Ben fell to the ground and began squealing. Hook flipped his cigarette onto the road.

"Hurts, doesn't it?" he said.

HOOK PARKED IN the trees outside Linda Sue's trailer. Unable to see the window from there, he climbed the old elm that sprawled over the driveway. Once up, he leaned back to catch his breath. As a kid, tree climbing had been his specialty, but it had turned into a tough job.

Linda Sue's yard had grown into a tangle, and no lights could be seen in the trailer. But from the tree, he could make out the back door and the window in question. He reached for a cigarette, only to discover he'd left them in the seat of the jeep.

"Damn it," he said.

Within the hour, a sound emanated from the darkness. Hook held his breath and listened. It came again, a whishing sound like footsteps in the grass.

A figure appeared in the darkness, little more than

a shadow slinking along the side of the trailer. The shadow moved, paused, moved again. At the window, it lifted the screen and disappeared into Linda Sue's trailer without a sound.

Hook drew his sidearm and started down the tree. Suddenly, he lost his grip, dropped the gun, and slid down the tree trunk. Desperate to stop the descent, he grabbed at a passing limb.

The momentum propelled him outward and onto the limb, and he dangled by one arm like an orangutan. He struggled in vain to pull himself up. Sweat ran into his eyes as he calculated the consequences of letting go. Long ago he'd established a rock-hard policy against unimpeded falls and saw no reason to abandon it now. But his arm burned with fatigue, and all feeling in his fingers had disappeared.

Reaching up, he swung his prosthesis hook over the limb above him. With luck, maybe it would hold him long enough so that he could managed a new grip.

But the second he let go, he knew that he'd made a big mistake. The shoulder harness tore away first, followed by his shirtsleeve, and he shot downward through the darkness like a rogue meteorite.

He landed on his back, and it knocked the wind out of him. He gasped for air. Above him, the first stars of night winked through the tree leaves. He could smell damp earth, and a cricket sawed from the bushes.

He had no idea where his P.38 had dropped or if he'd been heard falling from the tree. But when he rolled over, his hand dropped onto his P.38. He took a deep breath and shoved it into its holster, a bit of luck that had come in mighty small doses lately.

He figured that the window accessed the sleeping

area of the trailer, but he couldn't be certain. His visit to Linda Sue's house had been brief, and he hadn't paid that much attention.

On top of that, without his prosthesis, climbing through the window turned out to be especially difficult, but once he'd gotten a leg in, he managed to struggle through.

He squatted in the darkness and oriented himself. A faint light bled through the beaded curtain at the end of the hall, and he could hear a tune being played on Linda Sue's record player.

He slipped out his sidearm and edged along the hallway until he could see into the kitchen. Corporal William Thibodeaux stood at the stove.

"What's for dinner, Corporal?" Hook asked through the curtain.

Thibodeaux spun around with the skillet in his hand. His shirt hung loose about his neck, and his beard had grown dark and scraggly.

"What the hell," he said.

"Wouldn't move if I were you," Hook said.

"Who are you, mister?" he asked.

"Mind telling me what you're doing in here, Corporal?"

"Linda Sue said I could stay here while she was gone."

"That right? Where'd she go?"

"I, uh…her mother's. She went home to see her mother."

"I heard she'd gone to jail," he said. "I heard some bastard blacked both her eyes and left her behind to fare for herself."

"I didn't think she'd mind if I used the trailer," he said.

"Right," Hook said. "Why would she mind you making yourself at home while she's sitting in the county jail?"

"Can we talk about this?"

Hook stepped out from behind the curtain. "Sure," he said. "We can talk. Let's start with why you killed Erikson."

"Hook Runyon," he said.

"I'd say you killed him over Linda Sue and that you set him up by changing the train schedule and then made the whole thing look like an accident."

He waited as Thibodeaux gathered himself up. "I didn't kill him," he said.

"You're out there walking the tunnel while Erikson's in town playing house with your girlfriend. On top of that he derails your promotion. Sure would make me mad."

Thibodeaux shook his head. "I admit that the more I got to know Erikson, the more I hated him. But I didn't kill him."

"Some man steals your girl *and* your promotion. Enough to make a fellow fighting mad, I'd say."

"I didn't," Thibodeaux said, pausing. "I wanted to, but I didn't have the grit for killing a man."

"You had the grit to cash his check, to go AWOL, to commit armed robbery, and then to let your girl take the heat for it. Things just don't wash, Thibodeaux."

"She never shut up," Thibodeaux said. "She was at me every second. How I ruined everything and how she'd be on the run the rest of her life because of me."

"So you smacked her around and left her in the john. And when you ran out of money and a hiding place, you came back to steal what she had left. You're a goddang prince, Thibodeaux."

"I've been sitting on that tunnel out there ever since the war started," he said. "This country owes me something."

"I could see how you might think that way, given the sacrifices you made."

"Yeah," he said.

Hook patted his pocket. "You wouldn't have a smoke?"

"Pall Malls," he said.

"Left mine in the jeep. Mind lighting it for me? My arm's swinging from a tree at the moment."

Thibodeaux lit a cigarette and held it out to him, but when Hook reached for it, Thibodeaux lunged, knocking him off balance. Hook recovered and reared back just as the skillet whizzed by his head.

He leveled the sidearm and took aim, only to discover that he hadn't cocked it. Cocking a gun one-handed had limitations even *with* a prosthesis. Without one, it bordered on the impossible.

The corporal hesitated just long enough for Hook to stick him under the rib cage with the gun barrel. Thibodeaux honked and snorted and gasped for air. Hook wrenched the skillet away and backhanded it across Thibodeaux's nose. Thibodeaux's legs wobbled, and he tumbled onto the floor.

"They tell me cold steak will help those eyes in the morning," Hook said.

He searched out the cigarette from under Thibodeaux's leg and puffed it back. Pall Malls were not his favorite, but then that's the kind of day it had been.

TWENTY-EIGHT

HOOK PICKED UP Linda Sue's phone and checked the dial tone. He called the operator and asked for Sheriff Mueller's office. The deputy on duty answered and said that the sheriff had been called out on something but that he'd radio him.

Hook hung up and called Eddie Preston, collect.

"This call is coming out of your pay, Runyon," Eddie said.

"What pay?" Hook said.

"So what's so important that you have to call collect?"

"Corporal Thibodeaux's lying here on the floor. Just thought you might like to know."

"Dead?"

"No, he isn't dead, Eddie."

"Where are you?"

"Linda Sue's house."

"Linda Sue who?"

"His girlfriend, Eddie, the one Blue Boy called you about."

"Oh, her. You didn't break in, did you?"

"The corporal invited me in for coffee."

"So, what do you want from me?"

"A transfer."

"Like I told you before, I need you out there."

"Look, Eddie, I caught the copper thieves. Linda

Sue's in county. Corporal Thibodeaux's taking a nap right here at my feet, and there isn't a criminal within a hundred miles of this place."

"That tunnel is critical to the war effort. I want you to keep an eye on things."

"I don't have reliable transportation, Eddie. How about getting a decent popcar over here?"

"So you can leave it on the main line," he said.

"Copper thieves, Eddie. What's a man to do?"

"You've already wrecked more equipment than the Germans, Runyon."

"I can't take care of security afoot, you know."

"There's a popcar sitting on the siding over to Bellemont. She's a little on the old side, but she runs well. I'll have the riptrack crew drop it by. They're pulling ties up there. Try not to kill anyone with it. In the meantime, hitch a ride if you have to. You've had lots of experience at it."

"They got the whole army guarding the tunnel now, Eddie, and the war's over. Send one of those Baldwin Felts graduates out here. It would be damn good experience."

"Have you thought about another line of work, Runyon? 'Cause you're about one second away from losing this one."

"What I've thought about this work could send me to prison, Eddie," he said, hanging up.

He checked his watch and poked Thibodeaux in the ribs with his foot. Thibodeaux moaned and turned his head.

Hook opened the refrigerator. Thibodeaux had stocked it with bread, milk, and hard salami. By the looks of it, he'd been checking in at the Linda Sue Hotel for a while now. A pint of Hill and Hill bourbon sat next to the sink. He poured himself a shot in a water glass and downed it.

Just then car lights flashed through the window. Hook looked at his watch. Sheriff Mueller and a three-toed sloth would clock about the same response time.

He clicked on the porch light and opened the door. "Glad you could make it, Sheriff," he said.

Mueller's shirt gaped about his neck, and the hair on his ears shined in the light.

"An accident out at the intersection," he said, rolling his shoulders. "Had to make a run to the hospital."

"What happened?"

"Ben Hoffer ran over his own feet. I ain't figured yet how he managed that."

"Ben's peculiar that way," Hook said.

"I says, 'Ben, how can a man run over his own feet with his own car?' And he says, 'Did I break the law, Sheriff?' And I says, 'Not so's I can tell. If you'd broke the law, I'd be arresting you, Ben, 'cause the law's applied equal around here.' And he says, 'Then it ain't none of your damn business, is it?' So I says, 'I hope they cut both of them feet off at the ankles, Ben, you son of a bitch.' And he says, 'I do, too, Sheriff, 'cause I'm going to mail them to you in a box for Christmas.'"

"Ben can be unreasonable," Hook said.

"So where's this corporal, Hook?"

"Taking a nap in there on the floor."

Mueller went in and turned Thibodeaux on his side. "Looks like he came up on a sudden stop."

"Think you could give him room and board while I get the charges gathered up, Sheriff?"

"I got a vacancy, I guess. Jim Holstead's old lady bailed him this morning."

Mueller cuffed Thibodeaux and led him out to the patrol car. When he came back in, he said, "I hear you landed those copper thieves, Hook."

"It's like fishing," Hook said. "Sometimes they bite. Sometimes they don't."

"I don't suppose the railroad could help with the groceries on this fellow?"

"Been my experience, the railroad doesn't do much helping with anything, Sheriff. Might try the army."

"Uh-huh," he said.

"I figure he'll be on his way to Leavenworth before he gets his breakfast finished anyway," Hook said. "The army's plenty worked up over this guy's disappearance."

"I better get back, Hook. That deputy cries like a newborn if he pulls overtime. Maybe you could lock up around here?"

"Listen, Sheriff, I hate to ask, but suppose you could get my arm before you go?"

Mueller ran his finger around his collar. "I been wondering what happened to it but didn't want to ask."

"Come with me," Hook said. "I'll show you."

Hook stood at the bottom of the elm and shined the light onto the prosthesis that still hung from the limb. It swung a little in the breeze, like a man waving goodbye.

"I'd go get it myself, but I can't climb with one arm," he said.

Mueller took out his chewing tobacco and loaded his jaw. "How did it get up there in the first place?"

"Danged if I know," Hook said.

The sheriff rolled his cud and spit. "It's kind of like

running over your own feet, ain't it? Some things can't be explained."

"Yes, sir," Hook said. "It can be done, but it's not easy."

Mueller paused. "Just hold the light, and I'll climb up. That way I don't have to listen to no more lies tonight."

Hook waited until the sheriff's lights had disappeared down the drive before going into the trailer. Standing in front of Linda Sue's mirror, he put his prosthesis back on. He rubbed the ache from his neck and combed back his hair. Maybe Eddie had been right. Maybe he should think about a different line of work. Chasing thieves and climbing trees had lost some of its excitement. But then what could he do? Last time he'd checked, the demand for one-armed hoboes was pretty limited.

He poured himself another drink of Hill and Hill from Thibodeaux's bottle. He wished he had a little of Runt Wallace's shine instead. It had a way of healing a man from the inside out.

Thibodeaux had collected the newspapers off the porch and tossed them in a pile at the end of the couch. Picking up the latest, Hook scanned the ads. The town had scheduled a rummage sale to help the struggling hospital. Though books were often scarce at rummage sales, they could be a real bargain if found. Maybe, if things ever settled down, he'd find time to go.

He lit up a Pall Mall from a pack on the table, sat down on the couch, and stared at the phone. Sooner or later the lieutenant would have to be called about Thibodeaux. He didn't mind involving the army so much, and he certainly didn't mind the lieutenant's company. But he didn't want to be the only one sharing information in this deal.

On top of all that, it *was* late, and he'd have to call collect. Of course he could just put it on Linda Sue's bill. Nobody said he couldn't pay her later.

He squashed his cigarette out and dialed the number the lieutenant had given him.

A man answered. "Private Johnson," he said.

"Is this the Department of Transportation?" Hook asked.

"No, sir. This is the OSS building."

"Maybe you could help me," Hook said.

"I'm just cleaning the office, sir," he said. "I don't know nothing."

"Cleaning?"

"Got drunk and set my bunk afire."

"Is there a Lieutenant Capron there?"

"Ain't no one here but me, sir."

"Do you know Lieutenant Capron?"

"No, sir. I never heard of him."

"Her," Hook said. "Lieutenant Allison Capron."

"Her either, sir."

"Thanks, Private. Take my advice and lay off the hooch. I can tell you from experience that it's a hard road."

Hanging up, Hook lay back on the couch. Maybe the lieutenant had lied to him about her duty assignment as well. But why?

The night had cooled, and a gentle breeze came through the door of the trailer. He yawned and tucked the couch pillow under his head. The last few days had been tough and his sleep disturbed. Stretching out, he basked in the silence, in the absence of pusher engines and cranes and hogs. Maybe he'd take a little rest, close his eyes a bit before heading back to the yard.

WHEN HE AWAKENED, he sat straight up and checked his watch. He'd been asleep for hours. He locked up, climbed into the jeep, and clicked on the lights.

"Damn you, Scrap," he said, pulling onto the road in the darkness.

At the intersection, he turned onto the highway and had West's Salvage in sight when emergency lights lit up in his rearview mirror. He pulled onto the shoulder and waited.

Sheriff Mueller got out and came up to his door. "Hook," he said. "You don't have your lights on."

"I know, Sheriff. I don't have any. Scrap West took them."

"It's against the law to drive without lights, Hook."

"It's not my jeep, Sheriff. I told you it's Scrap West's jeep."

"But you're responsible for the vehicle you're driving, Hook. You might kill somebody or run over their feet."

"Look, Sheriff, I've been kind of pressed for time tonight. You might recall me capturing a felon earlier."

"Sure, I remember," he said, reaching for his pad.

"What the hell you doing, Mueller?"

"Writing a ticket."

"You're writing a ticket?"

"Jesus, Hook, you ought to get your hearing checked."

"You're going to give me a ticket, Mueller, you jerk?"

"Don't take it personal, Hook. The law's the law," he said, tearing off the ticket and handing it to him. "You go straight on home, hear. I could have you towed but seeing as how you're a yard dog, I'll let it go this time."

WHEN HOOK ARRIVED at the salvage yard, Scrap had just turned on the office lights. He looked up and rearranged a few strands of hair over his bald head.

"You want some coffee, Hook? You don't look so good."

"I've been sitting on the highway getting a ticket, Scrap."

"You're too old to be out drinking all night, Hook."

"Some idiot stole the lights off the jeep."

Scrap poured water into the coffeepot and took up his chair. He searched out his pipe.

"I came up short on headlights when I was building that generator plant for my good friend, Hook Runyon."

"Well, it cost me a ticket and dang near my life," Hook said. Scrap got up and poured two coffees. He handed one to Hook.

"It's a hard man what borrows and bitches," he said.

Hook took a sip and set the cup on Scrap's desk. "Anyway, the sheriff said that ticket's your responsibility. He said you're damn lucky he didn't come here and arrest you on the spot."

"And how does he figure that, I wonder?"

"Because it's your jeep and that makes you responsible." Scrap filled the bowl of his pipe and stuck it in the corner of his mouth.

"I might not look so smart to you, Hook, but I'm not dumb enough to pay your fine."

Hook pushed the last of his coffee aside and stood.

"Well, I figured anyone who buys his own copper back might just go for it."

Hook took a shower and changed clothes. He fed Mixer and let him out. He lay down in the bunk and listened to the pusher thump away on the siding. Maybe he'd make a run out soon as the new popcar arrived. He'd promised Blue that he'd talk to the crews, and he figured to start with that survey bunch. And maybe he'd have a chance to nose around a little, talk to the guard again. For the life of him, he couldn't understand all the fuss over that damn tunnel.

TWENTY-NINE

HOOK WALKED AROUND the old popcar and shook his head. Oil dripped from the motor, and the windshield was broken. A roll of toilet paper had been shoved under the seat, and a broken pick handle lay on the floor. Blue smoke boiled into the air when Hook cranked her over. Mixer marked all four wheels before jumping into the car.

"All right," Hook said. "But no side trips."

Mixer peaked his brows this way and that. Hook lit a cigarette, goosed the popcar, and they clacked off down the track. This one ran worse than the other, if such was possible.

As they moved into the countryside, Hook took in the extent of the upgrade. The rails had been lined and leveled, and many of the ties replaced. Old crossings had been removed and the right-of-ways cleared. But the 3 percent grade had not been lessened, and with the engine compression nearly gone, they soon slowed to walking speed as they labored into the ascent.

Hook propped his foot up and looked at Mixer. "Why didn't they go north with a new line?" he said. "They could have bypassed the tunnel, cut the grade, and at half the cost."

Instead of answering, Mixer curled into a ball and went back to sleep.

Hook braked the popcar as they rolled out onto the

trestle. The clack of the wheels turned hollow, and the earth opened beneath them. Ahead, the tunnel penetrated the solid basalt like a rifle bore.

Despite Hook's warning, Mixer bounded away to hunt and was soon out of sight. Hook climbed the path toward the guardhouse. He stopped to catch his breath and take in the landscape. From there, a man could see the canyon stretching into the desert. Only the power of nature could have rendered such an open slash.

He found Corporal Severe waiting for him at the top, his binoculars around his neck, his rifle leaned against the porch.

"Mr. Runyon," he said, standing. "Thought that was you."

Hook held up his prosthesis. "Kind of hard to mistake, I guess."

"Something I could help you with, or are you just out for a ride?"

Hook lit a cigarette. "Checking out the line," he said. "You boys had any trouble out here?"

Corporal Severe took the binoculars from around his neck. "Had to scrape a coyote off the trestle this morning," he said. "Monday, damn near got snakebit walking patrol."

"Sounds normal to me," Hook said.

"But there's been a decided lack of sabotage ever since I got here. Guess the Germans figure there's no reason to blow up what God nor man doesn't want."

"You don't know where that survey crew is by now, do you?" Hook asked.

Corporal Severe pulled at his chin. "A work train came through here the other day. Said they were just east of Kingman."

"Thanks," Hook said. "Anything you boys need, let me know."

"A transfer to the Bahamas would be nice."

"You're talking to a man who can't get himself out of a junkyard," Hook said.

"I guess there's always someone worse off than yourself," he said, smiling.

Hook nodded. "By the way, we rounded up that Corporal Thibodeaux."

"Oh?"

"He's in Sheriff Mueller's jail. I tried to get hold of Lieutenant Capron but wound up with the wrong department. Wonder if you could get in touch with her for me? Tell her Corporal Thibodeaux is on ice in Ash Fork."

"I'll give her a call."

"Thanks," Hook said. "I'll let you know if anything comes up on the Bahamas deal."

WHEN HE COULDN'T call Mixer in, he left him in the canyon, figuring he'd be hunted out and hungry by the time he came back through.

It took nearly an hour to reach the work crews on the outskirts of Kingman. A flatcar, cluttered with tools and supplies, sat on the siding. The survey crew had gathered around the watercooler.

Hook approached one of the men. "I'm looking for the foreman," he said.

The man drank from the dipper and wiped his chin. "Rudy Edgeworth? He ain't here."

"Know where I could find him?"

"And who would be looking for him?"

"I'm the railroad bull."

"You going to put him in jail?" he said.

"Not planning on it."

"Too bad," he said. "Kingman depot, be my guess. He had to make calls."

"Thanks," Hook said.

When he turned to go, he noticed a stack of chain links on the end of the flatcar.

"What are those?" he asked.

"Links from a three-ring Gunter's chain," the man said.

"What you use them for?"

"For surveying, but a Gunter's chain don't make a bit of sense."

"How's that?"

"It's exactly sixty-six feet long, made up of links precisely 7.92 inches in length. The rings on the ends of each link are one-half inch in diameter."

"Why those particular measurements?"

"'Cause if they weren't that, they'd be something else," he said.

"Sounds like something Scrap West would build."

"Excuse me."

"What's with these here?"

"Wore out," he said. "Those rings stretch with use and give bad readings. Without replacing them once in a while, this railroad could wind up going in a circle."

"Maybe you should change them more often," Hook said, climbing up on the popcar.

HE FOUND RUDY EDGEWORTH sitting in the lobby of the depot drinking a cola. When Edgeworth saw Hook's prosthesis, he stood.

"Mr. Edgeworth?" Hook said.

"That's right."

"I'm Hook Runyon, railroad bull. You might remember me?" Edgeworth drained his cola and set the empty bottle on the windowsill.

"I remember. What is it you want?" he said.

"Blue's Café asked if I'd talk to you."

Edgeworth pushed his hat back with fingers thick as rail spikes.

"So, talk."

"It's the general policy of the railroad to spread their eating around," Hook said. "Makes for good relations with the community and all that."

"I'm a contractor, Runyon."

"I understand," Hook said. "It's just that Blue could use the business, and the food's good. Thought you might consider it."

"I got a job to do here, and I have to cut a profit in the process. Shuttling my crew back and forth to Ash Fork doesn't do it. I guess Blue's Café is just going to have to live with that."

"There's no law says you have to," Hook said. "I told Blue I'd ask, and I did."

"Anything else you want to ask? I've got calls."

"No," Hook said. "Well, maybe just one thing."

"And that would be?"

"You did say your company's headquartered in Kansas City?"

"That's right."

Hook lit a cigarette at the door. "Didn't happen to know a Joseph Erikson there, did you?"

"Kansas City's a big town," he said.

"Right," Hook said. "Damn big town."

EVENING FELL AS Hook made his way back to Ash Fork. He donned his coat against the cool and watched the moon climb skyward.

The trip had been fruitless, and he should have known that it would be. Edgeworth could only be described as a son of a bitch. Scratch the surface of a son of a bitch, and there's another one just like him underneath.

Hook listened to the clack of the wheels. The sound soothed him, as it always did, and cleared his mind. For him, nothing came as close to freedom and contentment as clicking down the rails.

When he spotted the surveyors' flatcar on the siding, he idled back. The supplies and tools had been secured for the night, and the men were gone. Hook brought her down and shut off the engine.

He walked over to the flatcar and relieved himself. Bats darted through the night sky in search of prey, and the smell of creosote hung thick in the air. He lit a cigarette, his match illuminating the stack of links from the Gunter's chain. He picked up a link, turned it in his hand, and dropped it into his coat pocket.

EVEN THOUGH HE'D double-checked clearance at Seligman, Hook tensed a little as he rolled into the Johnson Canyon Tunnel. No one entered the tunnel without some anxiety, the sounds, the absence of light, the lack of recourse in the event of trouble.

When he exited, he brought the popcar to a stop. The lantern light flickered from the guardhouse window. He whistled for Mixer, who came bounding up the canyon path. Mixer, panting, his tongue lolling from his mouth like a wet rag, leapt onto the car and thumped his tail.

As they rolled onto the trestle, Hook looked back at the guardhouse. It stood stark and lonely on the mountainside, its light glowing in the window.

When they reached West's Salvage, he parked the popcar on the far siding and went to the caboose. After feeding Mixer, Hook dropped into his bunk.

The day had been unproductive, and he knew no more now than when it began. But there *was* Corporal Thibodeaux, and he knew exactly where to find him.

THIRTY

SCRAP WEST STOOD in the doorway of the caboose, pipe stuck in his mouth.

"You going to sleep all day, Hook?"

Hook sat on the side of his bunk. "You woke me up to ask me that?" Hook pushed the hair from his eyes and searched for a cigarette. "Okay, Scrap. What's going on?"

"Just doing my duty as railroad secretary and personal messenger."

"And?"

"That female lieutenant called. Said she'd got the message from that guard about Thibodeaux, and she'd pick you up here in a couple-three hours. Said you'd know what she was talking about."

"Lieutenant Capron?"

"How many female lieutenants do you know?"

"Do you always answer a question *with* a question? Jesus."

"What's wrong with that? Well, I better get to work. Someone's got to around here."

AFTER SHOWERING AND shaving and eating, Hook headed for the front gate of the salvage yard to meet the lieutenant. Scrap's crane roared and clanked from the junk pile. Mixer trailed behind Hook.

At Scrap's office, Hook opened the door and whistled Mixer inside.

"No," he said. "You can't go along. Stay." He took Scrap's coat from behind the door and tossed it on the floor. "And don't sleep on it," he said.

WHEN THE LIEUTENANT pulled in, she set her briefcase on the backseat and unlocked the door. He slid in. Her hair, the exact color of a new penny, curled out from under her army hat.

"How was the trip?" he asked.

"Early start," she said, pulling out for Ash Fork. "Corporal Severe said you've arrested Thibodeaux?"

"He's in Mueller's jail. He'd taken up residence in Linda Sue's trailer."

"This is excellent news," she said.

As they drove up to the sheriff's office, the old man who had helped push Hook's jeep sat on the bench outside. Hook came around and opened the lieutenant's door.

The old man looked them over. "You under arrest?" he asked.

"No," Hook said.

"That your wife?"

"No," Hook said. "She's in the army."

He looked up at the lieutenant. "Can you push?" he asked.

"Push?"

"I can't get my own shoes on," he said. "Bad back."

"Sorry to hear it," the lieutenant said, looking at Hook. Hook guided her inside.

The lieutenant hung her purse over her shoulder. "What was that about?"

Hook shrugged. "Every town has one, you know. I'll have them bring the corporal out."

THE DEPUTY BROUGHT Thibodeaux into the office handcuffed. "You can take them off," Hook said.

Thibodeaux sat down and rubbed at his wrists. Both eyes were black.

"You have a smoke?" he asked.

"I owe you one," Hook said. "Drink, too, though that will have to wait."

The lieutenant took a notepad from her purse. "Corporal," she said. "The army will be filing formal charges. You'll be transferred to the base and tried under army regulations. Do you understand?"

Hook lit Thibodeaux's cigarette. "Yes, ma'am," he said.

"You'll be charged with armed robbery, desertion, and the murder of Sergeant Joseph Erikson."

"Murder! But I didn't kill no one, ma'am. Maybe I did some of those other things you said, but I didn't kill the sergeant."

The lieutenant said, "I admit to misjudging this case. But I can no longer believe that Sergeant Erikson's death was accidental. Evidence to the contrary is now convincing; I might say overwhelming."

"No, ma'am," he said. "I didn't kill him. I swear it."

The lieutenant leaned in. "Sergeant Erikson was involved with Linda Sue, your girlfriend. He held up your promotion. You had the motive and the means, and you've since proven yourself to be capable of criminal behavior. Somehow you managed to get Erikson in that tunnel, knowing the whole time that train was coming."

Thibodeaux drew on his cigarette. "I hated Erikson,

I admit. He didn't care about no one, see, and after spending all that time together at that tunnel. A man can listen to only so much, you know. I'm glad he's dead. I wished him dead a thousand times. I wished I'd been there when that train ended the bastard's life. But I wasn't there, and I didn't kill him."

The lieutenant jotted something in her notebook. "You'd save yourself and the army a great deal of trouble if you'd confess, Corporal. Get this burden off your shoulders.

"Mr. Runyon," she said, turning to Hook. "If you have anything to ask, do so now. The corporal will no longer be under civilian jurisdiction."

"A couple of questions," Hook said. "Were you going to make a career out of the army, Corporal?"

Thibodeaux snorted. "I'd as soon pick cotton."

"Were you in love with Linda Sue?"

Thibodeaux paused before answering. "Lap cats can be real cozy. But in the end, they don't give a damn whose lap they're sitting in."

"No more questions," Hook said.

The lieutenant stood. "I'll arrange for the transfer, Corporal, and for a defense attorney. You'll be hearing back from me soon."

When they came out of the sheriff's office, the old man had gone.

"I need to talk to Blue," Hook said. "Would you care for a cup of coffee?"

"All right," she said.

"Let's walk," he said. "It isn't far."

The lieutenant's heels clipped on the concrete as they walked to Blue's Café. Blue himself poured their coffees and set the pot on the table.

"This is Lieutenant Allison Capron," Hook said.

Blue nodded. "Lieutenant."

"I talked to that survey crew foreman, Blue," Hook said. "He didn't strike me as the sharing kind."

Blue scraped at the spot on his apron. "Appreciate you trying, anyway, Hook."

"Maybe things will pick up," Hook said. "Looks like a pretty good crowd here now."

Blue shrugged. "Oh, it's a crowd, all right. Same crowd's been in here all morning telling lies and getting free refills. Come lunch, they'll all disappear without so much as a tip.

"I heard you caught that corporal breaking into Linda Sue's trailer."

"We caught him. Thanks to you," Hook said. "You ain't heard from Linda Sue, I guess?"

"I don't figure they'll be too hard on her. She didn't hurt anyone but herself."

When Blue had gone, Hook sipped at his coffee. He looked up to find the lieutenant watching him from across the table.

"What?" he said.

She set her cup down. "Now that things are wrapping up, I guess you'll be moving on?"

"Not so long as Eddie's unhappy."

She dropped her spoon into her coffee. "That's not really why, is it?"

"What do you mean?" he said.

"You've contended all along that Sergeant Erikson's death was suspicious. Now that we have the culprit, and with blood on his hands, you aren't convinced?"

"I'm not saying this guy is an upstanding citizen.

Any man who hits a woman shouldn't be on her take-home list. I'm just not certain he's our killer."

The lieutenant poured sugar into her coffee and stirred it. "So why the skepticism?"

"When I arrested Thibodeaux, he had the advantage on me for a brief moment. He could have taken my head off."

"And?"

"He hesitated."

"And you think that exonerates him?"

"Not necessarily."

"Then why the change of mind about him and Erikson?" He thought about her question.

"There are too many parts missing," he said. "And I'm not sure he's capable of murder."

"He's the only one who had a motive," she said.

"I don't know what I don't know yet," he said.

"You do know you can be exasperating?"

"So I've heard," he said. "Look, there's a town-wide rummage sale. Want to go?"

"Books?"

"With luck."

"No, thank you." She ran her fingers through her hair. "There's a great deal left to do. I'm afraid Corporal Thibodeaux has complicated the situation."

"In the scheme of things, maybe it's not so much," he said.

"I've arrangements to make."

"Sometimes it's best to back off a problem," he said. "Stop trying for a while. Let the world go on its own."

She shrugged. "I'm afraid the army doesn't work that way, but good luck with your rummage sale."

Hook walked around town until locating a promising

sale. Boxes were stacked about everywhere, and tables overflowed with items dug from closets and attics and garages. Two women sitting at a card table manned the cashbox. Pickers were already busy gleaning bargains from the piles of junk.

Soon, he discovered a trunk that had been shoved under one of the display tables. When he opened it, the smell of old books rose up. A set of *Encyclopedia Britannica* lay on top.

Hook stacked them to the side. Everybody bought encyclopedias, being convinced they would keep their kids from growing up stupid. Didn't work; besides, there was almost always at least one volume missing.

Digging deeper, he found a 1932 first edition of *Battle: The Life Story of the Rt. Hon. Winston S. Churchill*. He didn't read everything he collected, but Churchill was a pretty interesting subject. A book could be rare and unreadable. It could be readable and not rare. The relationship between the two things was pretty weak. Churchill was a man among men and a drinker of fine whiskey. How could he not be interesting?

From there, he worked his way into the garage, looking through piles of old planters, kitchen utensils, kids' clothes, and tools with broken handles. He spotted a box full of old books, fifty cents for the lot.

He paid his money and sat on the curb to examine his purchase. A spider skittered over his hand and disappeared into the grass.

Finding nothing of value, he lit a cigarette and checked his watch. He'd completely forgotten that he had no transportation back to the caboose. He'd just have to walk. Taking the box of books back to the garage, he slipped the Churchill book under his belt and headed down the road.

Scrap sat at his desk going through his weekly figures. He dropped his glasses to the end of his nose and looked at Hook.

"How'd that dang dog get in my office?" he said. "I found him in here sleeping on my coat."

"I knew him to be smart," Hook said, "but didn't know he could open doors."

"If I ain't mistaken, you might of had something to do with it."

"That's mighty small of you, Scrap."

"Maybe you'll want to use my jeep again, or maybe you'll need some secretarial work for the railroad."

Hook walked to the door. "Like to stay and chat, but I've got to go find my dog. He's likely been hurt or shot up by a crazy man."

"Well, he ain't, but that don't mean he don't have it coming."

"Good night, Scrap."

"Night," he said. "And you can tell that sheriff I ain't paying no fine."

HOOK FIXED MIXER's food and sat it on the floor. "From now on, stay out of Scrap's office," he said. "His sense of humor isn't what it should be."

He fixed himself a shot of whiskey, neat, and then doubled it for luck. He took another look at his purchase. The Churchill had been a good find and made the long walk back worthwhile.

In the distance, the whistle of a westbound rose and fell. The caboose trembled and creaked as an old steam engine rumbled by with a short haul. Little more than a car or two long, it ticked off into the night.

He fixed himself another drink and slipped off his shoes. He thought about the lieutenant, about her account of things, about the inconsistencies in her details. He wondered why she was so anxious to get the corporal out of his reach? But then he had only one Eddie Preston to answer to. The lieutenant, being in the army, probably had a dozen just like him. Such could account for her odd behavior at times.

In any event, he was determined to concentrate on the facts before him. In the detective business a person could get in trouble following his emotions instead of his head.

THIRTY-ONE

HOOK FOUND SCRAP fueling up his crane. "How about borrowing the jeep for a bit?" Hook said.

"Maybe you'd like to borrow my wife, take her for a spin and then back to your caboose like them other poor girls."

"You don't have a wife."

"And now you know why," he said.

Hook kicked his foot up on the platform. "Well?"

"Well, what?"

Hook scratched his head. "Can I borrow the jeep or not? I want to go talk to Sheriff Mueller."

"I guess you won't be drinking and getting tickets and such?"

"I hadn't planned on it, Scrap."

"And you might put a little gas in her while you're at it," he said, handing him the keys.

"Did you get those headlights fixed?" Hook asked.

Scrap knocked his pipe against the heel of his shoe before blowing it out.

"I take care of my equipment, Hook."

"Where did you get them?"

"That old school bus back by the fence."

"Jeez, Scrap. A school bus?"

"'Course, you could always drive railroad vehicles, I suppose."

Hook picked up the keys and walked to the door. "I'll be back before dark," he said.

SHERIFF MUELLER CAME out of the men's room zipping up his pants. "Making love by yourself?" Hook asked.

"Beats board games," he said, grinning.

Pulling up a chair, Hook waited for Mueller to sit down.

"I've been trying to wrap this tunnel thing up, Sheriff, but I've still got a few loose ends."

"You wanting to talk to that corporal again, Hook, you better hurry up. That Lieutenant Capron called. She's coming in to finish up the paperwork. They can't wait to get him in the brig. Didn't know the army could work that fast."

"I don't need to talk to Thibodeaux," Hook said. "But I am needing to run a check on someone. Think you could help me out?"

"Possible," he said. "What's the name?"

"Rudy Edgeworth."

Sheriff Mueller took off his hat and tossed it on the desk. "Never heard of him."

"He's the foreman on the surveying crew, the one who's working the track upgrade."

"What you needing to know, Hook?"

"Just a standard check, criminal record, that sort of thing. He's out of Kansas City, I think."

"Anything I should know?"

"Just routine. Someone's been picking up a few Santa Fe tools, thinking they own them."

"All right, Hook, I can make a call and get back to you."

"I'm in a bit of a rush on this, Sheriff."

Mueller checked his watch. "I reckon I could do it now. Give me a minute," he said.

Hook sat on the bench outside. The sun cut through the morning, and a slight breeze blew in. He could hear Mueller through the window, though he couldn't make out the conversation.

He lit a cigarette and looked down the street. A car had parked next to the filling station, and an elbow protruded from the window. The sun moved behind a cloud, and Hook could see a man behind the wheel of the car. He wore a fedora and was smoking a cigarette.

Sheriff Mueller opened the door behind him. "Hook?"

Hook stood. "Yeah?"

"No record."

"No criminal record?"

"No record, period."

"I don't understand."

"Well, there was a Rudy Edgeworth, all right. The only thing is, he's been dead for five years."

"That's a bit peculiar, Sheriff. Well, thanks for checking."

The sheriff straightened his gun belt. "About that traffic ticket, Hook?"

"You tearing it up, Sheriff? I'd sure do the same for you had it been on railroad property."

"It's overdue. A man don't pay his traffic ticket could wind up in big trouble."

"Scrap said he'd pay it, given it was his fault in the first place."

"The driver's what owes the ticket, Hook, though I don't care who pays it, long as it's paid."

"I'll check on it and get back to you, Sheriff."

"And you might want to keep an eye out for Hoffer.

He's been hobbling around town saying as how he's going to give you an upbringing."

"Thanks, Sheriff. I'll keep an eye out."

BLUE SLID INTO the booth across from Hook.

"Sure you wouldn't like something, Hook? You look a little peaked."

"It's from living with Scrap West," he said, pouring a sugar into his coffee. "Open up his head, and all you'd find would be frayed wires and junked cars."

"He tried to sell me a cement mixer once," Blue said. "Claimed I could make a hundred pounds of pancake batter in half an hour. I said, 'What the hell would I do with a hundred pounds of pancake batter, Scrap? This ain't the army, you know.' 'Freeze what you don't use and sell it on the open market. You'd be a millionaire in no time, once you got the bugs worked out. 'Course, I wouldn't require a cent more for giving you the idea,' he said."

Blue pulled at his chin. "So I says, 'Does it run?' And he says, 'All it needs is a new motor, and she'll be good as new.'"

"You didn't buy it, did you?" Hook asked.

Blue laughed. "I ain't stupid, 'cept on special occasions, but I admit to thinking it over. Scrap has a way of making everything seem possible."

"Dealing with Scrap is like sitting in a boat with a hole in the bottom. Sooner or later you know you're going to drown."

Blue turned to check the cash register. When he turned back, he said, "I heard from Linda Sue."

"Oh? How is she?"

"She thinks she might get prohibition."

"You mean probation?"

"That's what I said. Jesus, Hook, you've been living with Scrap West too long."

"You got that right," Hook said.

"Since she's never been in trouble before, they think they might cut her some slack."

"Well, I've run into worse criminals in my time," Hook said. Blue got the coffeepot and brought it back to the table to top off Hook's cup.

"The truth is, I've been thinking about asking Linda Sue to marry me," he said. "She cornered me in the kitchen one time, and the steam whistled out my ears so loud folks thought the *Super Chief* had come in early."

"Why, Blue, that sounds like a hell of an idea to me."

"And I wouldn't have to pay no waitress, either."

"Wages can come in many forms, Blue. But I can see you making a hell of a couple."

"Well, a man my age gets to thinking," he said.

Hook stirred another sugar into his coffee. "You haven't seen any strangers in town lately, have you?"

Blue leaned in on an elbow and thought it over. "A man was in here earlier and ordered eggs Benedict. I says, 'We got eggs been raw and eggs been scrambled but no eggs Benedict.' The son of a bitch didn't crack a smile."

"Maybe he was a railroad official," Hook said. "They've been known to be uppity."

"I don't think so. He had clean fingernails and wore a fedora."

WHEN HOOK APPROACHED the jeep, he paused and looked over at the car. The man was gone. He opened the jeep door and glanced in the side mirror as he slid in. Someone ducked into the alley behind the pool hall.

"Enough of this," Hook said to himself, climbing back out. When he stepped into the alley, he could see the Dumpster and the stacks of empty beer cartons. The jukebox thumped from the pool hall, and the smell of cigar smoke wafted from out the back door. Snooker balls clattered in the distance, and men laughed.

He edged along the wall, keeping in close. When he reached the Dumpster, he squatted down in the shadows to wait. There were two ways out of the alley, through Harry's kitchen or by him.

Several minutes passed and then half an hour. Hook shifted his weight and double-checked the safety on his sidearm. Just as he had about given up, he heard movement.

When the man stepped out, Hook snared his cuff with his prosthesis and dumped him facedown onto the ground. The man moaned, and his fedora flew off. Hook placed his knee on the back of his neck and jabbed his P.38 under his jaw.

"I don't know who you are or what you want," he said. "But I don't abide a tail. You got something to ask, you got about five seconds to do it."

The man struggled to turn over, but Hook leaned in with his knee and cocked the P.38.

"Time's expired," he said.

"Let me up," the man said.

The blow caught Hook across the back and shoulders, and he pitched forward into the alley. He struggled to fill his emptied lungs and to orient himself against his assailant. But his nose took the brunt of the next punch. Blood oozed into the corners of his mouth, and his eyes watered. He shook his head to clear it and could just make out Ben Hoffer standing over him. Hoffer hesitated for a moment to revel in his conquest.

"Fancy meeting you here, Runyon," he said.

Hook had learned the hard way that a man interested in living should never squander an opportunity. He lunged forward, catching Hoffer's ankle tendon with his prosthesis, snapping it like a rubber band. Hoffer howled and danced about on one leg. Hook jumped up and clipped him with an uppercut. His head popped back, and he slid to the concrete.

Hook spun about, prepared to take on the tail next, but only his fedora remained behind.

Hook bent down and lifted up Hoffer's head. "This time you're going to jail, Ben," he said.

Hoffer muttered something unintelligible. Hook leaned over. "Say what?"

"Lousy yard dog," he said.

Hook dropped his head onto the concrete. "Thought that's what you said."

THIRTY-TWO

Hook poured a cup of Scrap's coffee and dialed the operator.

"Give me Value Survey Inc. in Kansas City, please." He lit a cigarette as he waited for the connection.

"Value Survey," a woman said. "How may I help you?"

"This is contracts, Santa Fe Railroad out of Topeka," he said. "You have one of the survey agreements on our upgrade out of Ash Fork, Arizona. We have a mix-up somehow on your contract. What is the name of your foreman there, please?"

"One moment," she said.

Hook stubbed out his cigarette and rubbed his shoulder. Hoffer had caught him with a solid blow. He was likely to sport a nice bruise by morning.

"Sir," she said, coming back on the line. "Our foreman out there is a Mr. Rudy Edgeworth."

"I see," he said. "We're having a little trouble bringing these forms up to date. Perhaps you could fill in some details for us?"

"Normally that wouldn't be a problem," she said. "But Mr. Edgeworth is a new employee here at Value. We're still waiting on his paperwork."

"You hired him without recommendations?"

"Men with his skills are hard to find, what with the war," she said.

"Yes," he said. "Of course. Do you not have any information, then?"

"Well, we have a contact number from the interview if that would be of help?"

"Yes," he said. "They're kicking about the records around here. It's a real pain trying to please the brass, you know."

"Do I ever," she said. "One moment. I'll get it for you."

AFTER TAKING THE number, Hook dialed and waited through four rings.

"Hello," a woman said.

"Hello. This is the Kansas Highway Department. We were needing to hire some men for our new road project, and it's my understanding that someone at this number might be interested in a surveying position."

"My ex-boyfriend is a survey engineer, but he's gone."

"I see. We did have one application, but I don't recall his name. Perhaps you could describe him."

"His name is Alex Gregor," she said. "From Canada. Big, two forty, maybe bigger. Wears glasses and has hands like catchers' mitts. Chews tobacco. Disgusting, actually."

"Nope. Different guy, but thanks."

"If you see the bastard, let me know, will you? The only thing he didn't take with him were his bills."

Hook hung up the phone. Picked it up again and called Eddie Preston.

"Security," Eddie said.

"I didn't disturb you, did I, Eddie?" Hook asked.

"A lawyer in Ash Fork took care of that."

"What do you mean?"

"He's claiming the local yard dog beat up his client, a Ben Hoffer. Said he's got a concussion, and he's not walking so good."

"The son of a bitch jumped me, Eddie. What was I supposed to do?"

"I see a lawsuit coming, Runyon, and it's your baby."

"I was on duty. The railroad is going to pay for this one, Eddie."

"In an alley behind the pool hall? Christ, Runyon, you can't go around beating up people and expect the railroad to pay for it."

"My expectations are pretty low."

"Well, expect a Brownie."

"Look, Eddie, I've got a tail. What the hell is going on?"

"How should I know?"

"I don't like to be tailed."

"Have you been stealing books from the library again?"

"That was a black lie, Eddie. I just forgot to take it back; besides, they don't tail you for late books."

"They said it was a rare first edition."

"Coincidence, the bastards."

"Exactly why did you call, Runyon?"

"We've got a contractor working under a dead man's name."

"And how would you know that?"

"It came in a vision, Eddie. How do you think? I'm pretty sure this guy's name is Alex Gregor instead of Rudy Edgeworth."

Hook could see Scrap coming across the yard. He'd developed a slight limp over the years and swung his arm out from his body to balance himself. The limp worsened after Scrap had put in a day on the crane.

Eddie said, "Check it out before you go stirring things up, Runyon. There are lots of guys out there beating the draft, and engineers are damn hard to come by, you know."

"Right," Hook said. "Look, I need another popcar out here. I can't check on things without reliable transportation."

"I just got you one."

"I need one that runs. That's what reliable means."

"Another Brownie and you're dead, Runyon. There won't be a thing I can do."

"That's just it, Eddie. I want to be dead."

"So long as it isn't on railroad property," he said, hanging up.

Hook watched from the window as the sun dropped. The crane, silent for the night, squatted like a giant bird against the sunset. He could wait until tomorrow to track down this Edgeworth thing. Riding that popcar into the desert at night didn't rank high on his want-to list. But this didn't smell right, and in this business, a few hours mattered. Unattended, things could fall apart in a hurry.

He retrieved the jeep keys from his pocket and jangled them on his finger. Maybe he'd just take the jeep instead of the popcar, fill it up with gas; after all, nothing pleased Scrap more than getting something for nothing.

He shut the office door behind him, climbed into the jeep, and turned on the lights. Nothing happened. He tried the lights again. Nothing. Only then did he notice the headlight beams had lit the top of the crane like a streetlight. He dropped his head against the steering wheel.

AFTER CHECKING THE board for clearance, Hook laid his coat across the seat and cranked up the popcar. She coughed and sputtered, and blue smoke boiled up around him. Mixer clambered aboard and dropped down in the seat. He looked up at Hook, his eyes sad and innocent.

"No hunting," Hook said, "or being put down's going to take on a whole new meaning."

Hook checked his watch. He just might make the Kingman siding before the survey crew went to bed. This time, one way or another, he intended to get to the bottom of things.

The popcar groaned and wheezed as Hook throttled up and onto the main line. The desert sky erupted with stars, and the temperature dropped in the arid night. He lit a cigarette and considered what lay ahead. No one took a dead man's name unless he had something to hide. So what did Edgeworth or Gregor or whatever his name was have to hide?

When they dropped into Johnson Canyon, the lantern in the guardhouse window winked like a yellow eye in the night. The popcar gathered up fumes as she coasted toward the trestle, backfired once, and choked down to a crawl. Mixer, seizing the moment, bailed off and within seconds had disappeared into the depths of the canyon.

"Damn it, Mixer," Hook said, goosing the engine back to life. The popcar clacked out onto the trestle, the sound of its wheels turning hollow and insubstantial beneath him. Cool air lifted up from the depths like an open grave. And as the popcar moved into the tunnel, Hook took a last look back for Mixer. He'd have to be left, picked up on the way home, and he swore never to bring him along again.

The noise of the engine, magnified within the confines of boilerplate and solid rock, pierced his ears like shards of glass. The air stank of creosote and grease, and the night stars blinked away. As he hit the curve, he smelled blood and carnage, and Sergeant Erikson's crumpled remains flashed before his eyes like a photograph. Hook's skin tightened, and he wished for an end of the tunnel.

When at last he rolled into the night, he pulled his collar up, lit a cigarette, and, with full throttle, headed on toward the Kingman siding.

MEN HUNG AROUND the bunker cars, smoking and talking. The cook, an older man with eyebrows like steel brushes, came out of the cook's car and tossed his dishwater into the ditch. He looked up at Hook.

"You want something to eat, go around back," he said. "I got a few beans left; otherwise, move on down line."

"I'm the yard dog," Hook said, pulling his badge.

"Damn my eyes," the cook said. "Who would've thought."

"I'm looking for the survey crew."

"Survey's gone," he said. "These men here are leveling track, when they ain't lying or bragging, which don't leave much time for leveling track."

Hook worked a sandbur out of the cuff of his pants. "Do you know where survey is?"

"Don't know where *I* am most of the time," he said. "Best that way, I figure."

"Do you know who *would* know?"

"Martinez, the foreman, might."

"Thanks," Hook said.

"I never met no one-armed yard dog before," the cook said.

Hook scratched his chin with his prosthesis. "Me neither. Maybe I'll take you up on those beans before I leave."

HOOK KNOCKED TWICE on the foreman's car before it opened.

Martinez buttoned his shirt over an ample belly. "Yeah," he said, "I'm the foreman."

Hook flashed his badge. "Yard dog out of Ash Fork."

"I told these bastards no drinking in town. 'You get popped,' I said, 'don't come to me for bail.'"

"It's not that," Hook said. "I'm looking for the survey crew."

"They finished up. We're wrapped, too. There ain't a bump no bigger than a gnat's ass between here and Flagstaff."

"Survey go home?"

"Don't take but a day or two to piss away a paycheck," he said, rubbing the back of his neck.

"Give me a call if someone shows up, will you?"

"We're moving out," he said. "Survey ain't my problem."

"Right," Hook said. "Thanks."

Hook stopped at the cook's car and had a bowl of pinto beans with fatback, corn bread, a green jalapeño, and a glass of buttermilk.

"Mighty fine eating. You ought to be a chef for the *Super Chief*," he said, pushing back.

"I'm sticking here," he said. "These bastards will eat the silverware and call it good.

"You find out what you needed from Martinez?"

"He wasn't much forthcoming," Hook said.

"He's a little sore's all. The bull over in Tucumcari found a bottle of tequila in his truck. Cost him a Brownie."

"They say liquor can ruin a man," Hook said. "Though it hasn't been entirely proven."

"You might try Frick's bar in Kingman," the cook said. "Survey spent their weekends there."

"Thanks," Hook said.

The cook scrubbed out a pot and set it in the cupboard. "Those boys been stealing from Uncle John?"

"Sure," Hook said. "Who hasn't? But I'm looking for their foreman, Edgeworth."

"Rudy Edgeworth?"

"Yeah."

He dried his hands on a dish towel. "You won't find him in Kingman."

"What do you mean?"

"Edgeworth disappeared. I figured his men cut his throat and dumped him in a coal hopper, but Gonzales spotted him walking down the tracks with his suitcase. They had to bring in a new foreman to finish the job."

HOOK CRANKED OVER the popcar and waited as she struggled to life. He checked his watch. With Edgeworth gone, he saw no point in going on to Kingman, and he had plenty of clearance time to make it back to Ash Fork if he left now.

As he headed into the desert, the night turned crystal, and the moon eased above the horizon. Martinez had been right, he'd never known a track to be as straight and flawless as this one. The heat from the popcar engine drifted up, warming his feet, and he tucked his hands into his coat pockets.

The drone of the engine had nearly lulled him to sleep when suddenly it bumped, caught, and then regained its speed. Hook's pulse thumped.

Suddenly, the engine rolled over, a dry and metallic thump, and died. The popcar coasted to a stop, and the night fell quiet as death. Hook tried cranking the engine, but it wouldn't budge. He checked the fuel tank.

"Damn it. Empty," he said, looking down the track.

He couldn't be certain where he was, but he remembered passing the Yampai siding not far back. A short haul had been sided there. Maybe he could push the popcar back and get it off the main track.

It took nearly an hour and all his strength to push the popcar to the siding. Once there, he dropped into the seat and wiped the sweat from his face. The moon rose high overhead, and his shadow stretched out into the right-of-way.

The cars were old with sagging frames and weathered paint. He rolled a door back on one and found it loaded with sacks of sand. He shook his head. No figuring the railroad. He'd just have to walk, though he'd probably starve or freeze stiff as a drawbar before he got back.

At that moment, he wished a slow and deliberate death for Eddie Preston. He wished him standing in the Johnson Canyon Tunnel when the *Super Chief* came through. He wished him handcuffed to Scrap West's crane or, better yet, to Scrap West himself.

After buttoning his coat, he headed down the track. He hadn't gone far when he smelled camp smoke. He paused and searched the darkness. When he spotted the flicker of firelight down line, he crouched and pulled his sidearm. Coming upon a camp at night could be dangerous. But it was on railroad property and his job to check it out.

THIRTY-THREE

UNABLE TO SEE, he slipped in closer. A single man hunkered over the fire, his hat clamped down and his collar up. He might be no more than a runaway boy or a father looking for work, but he might be a murderer with a straight razor in his sock. Given the unpredictability of the situation, Hook moved with caution.

The man, large, with sloped shoulders, pulled his makin's and sprinkled tobacco into a paper. He slid his tongue along the paper's edge, rolled it over, twisted the ends, and hung it in the corner of his mouth. He lit the cigarette with a stick from the fire, and red embers raced up into the blackness. A bottle sat on a stump next to him.

When Hook stepped into the light, the man stood.

"Take it easy, mister," Hook said. "Thought you might share your camp. I'm froze up."

The man drew on his cigarette, and its end glowed in the darkness.

"You alone?"

"Yeah," he said. "Missed the eastbound. Can't run like I used to."

"Redballers," he said. "Sons of bitches don't slow for nothing." He walked around the fire, peering into the darkness behind Hook. He turned and sat down on the stump. His fingers, yellowed with nicotine, were as knurled and weathered as tree limbs.

"You riding the rails?" Hook asked.

"It's against the law," he said. "Where you headed?"

"I'm traveling east," Hook said.

"The Salvation Army's dried up in Flagstaff," he said. "Takes an hour's preaching for a hard bunk and chicken soup."

"I've logged enough preaching hours for a free pass to heaven," Hook said. "Can't say it took."

The man rose and tossed a stick onto the fire. His shadow danced in the firelight. He chewed at a nail as he looked Hook over.

"Traveling men have to take what comes down the track," he said.

"Not many care about a man one way or the other," Hook said, searching for his smokes.

"Especially no law," he said. "Saw a cop beat a man to death with a coupler hose back in Amarillo.

"Have a drink," he said.

"I don't want to be drinking up your whiskey."

"Wouldn't ask otherwise," he said, handing the bottle to Hook.

Hook took a pull. "That's top rung," he said.

"Cream of Kentucky," he said. "Have another? A man what drinks alone is prone to tremors and black thoughts. You'd be doing me a favor."

Hook took another draught and handed the bottle back. "It's your life I'm saving then," Hook said.

"Likewise," he said, tipping up the bottle.

He tossed on another stick of wood, and the fire blazed up. Sparklers scattered into the darkness. Hook moved back from the heat.

"See these hands?" the bo said, holding them in the firelight. "Twenty-five years laying brick. Didn't ask for a goddamn thing 'cept the chance at work. Twenty-five years, one brick after another, and then came the day I looked at that hawk and trowel and I couldn't do it no more. I couldn't set another brick if hell opened up and swallowed me."

He held the bottle up to check its level. "Have another go," he said.

Hook took a drink and closed an eye. "A man does what he has to do," he said. "No shame in that."

"Left the wife on her momma's porch," he said. "Caught a coal car headed north and never looked back."

Hook nodded and rubbed his face, which had fallen numb from being too close to the fire. He started to stand but decided that to leave too soon might offend his host.

"One for the monkey," the man said.

"And to the demise of black thoughts and tremors," Hook said.

The man gathered up more firewood and tossed it on the fire. The circle of light danced and pushed back the darkness. He sat down and took out his makin's again. After lighting up, he looked straight at Hook.

"What happened to your arm?" he asked.

Hook rubbed his shoulder. "Shriveling fever," he said.

"I've heard of that," he said.

"Some say it's been detected as far north as the Rockies," Hook said.

"How'd it come about?"

"While I was taking a bath."

"Maybe the bath's what set it off."

"When the fever topped a hundred and ten, the arm fell off."

"Did it hurt?"

"No more than an elephant standing on your balls."

His mouth twisted. "Is it catchy?"

"No appendage is immune to its devastating effects, if you know what I mean."

The fire roared and crackled, and the man studied Hook through the flames.

"I believe I'd as soon lose an arm such as yourself," he said.

"Things could have been worse," Hook said. "I'd advise against unnecessary bathing, that's sure."

"Ain't that the goddangest lie ever told?" he said.

"Yes, it is," Hook said.

A train whistle lifted up in the distance, and the man fell silent. He rose, picked up a stick of firewood, and hiked it onto his shoulder. Firelight gathered up in his eyes and in the blackness of his beard. Hook threw up his elbow to ward off the blow, but the stick of firewood dropped him headfirst into the dirt.

HOOK AWAKENED TO the churn of the engine gathering up steam. He shook his head and rubbed at the knot that had blossomed on the side of his head. His mouth tasted of ash, and his bones ached. Smoke roped up from the fire. He reached for his wallet to find it intact, and his sidearm as well. What the hell kind of bo left money behind? He checked the clip to make certain it was still loaded because he intended to use it on the son of a bitch if he ever caught up with him.

Down line the steam engine chugged and wheezed as she nursed the cars off the Yampai siding. She pulled back onto the main line. Steam shot from her sides and rose into the glimmer light. Hook headed for the tracks to catch her.

The ground trembled, and black smoke boiled skyward as she gained momentum. Hook scrambled up the embankment, waving the whole time. But the engineer paid no mind, throttling up, his whistle screaming. The engine thundered toward him.

Hook ran down track to keep from being yanked out of his shoes when he snared the ladder. At the last moment, he grabbed on and pulled himself up. The driver wheels churned below him, and the boiler heat scorched his face.

Just as he reached the top of the ladder, a foot came out and began kicking at his head. Hook swung out on the ladder to escape the pummeling. The ground raced beneath him, and the wind sucked at his body.

"Security!" he yelled. "Stop!"

Someone stuck their head out the cab door. "What the hell?"

"Yard dog," he yelled through the clamor of the engine. "Haul me up, you bastard."

Once in, he rolled onto his back to catch his breath. Frenchy leaned over him, his cigar clenched between his teeth. The bakehead stood at his back with his hammer at the ready.

Frenchy said, "Hook, is that you?"

"You damn near killed me, Frenchy."

"We thought you was a robber," he said.

"Do I look like a robber?"

Frenchy lit his cigar and glanced over at the bakehead. "Maybe you don't want to know what you look like, Hook. That goose egg on your head ain't all that inviting."

Hook touched his temple. "I got a little distracted and let a bo slip up on me."

"Distracted by busthead liquor by the smell of it," Frenchy said.

Hook smelled his sleeve. "That's expensive cologne and likely unfamiliar to engineers."

Frenchy checked his pressure gauge. "Only a yard dog could find whiskey in the middle of the desert."

The bakehead grinned. "Yard dogs can sniff out about anything long as it isn't a thief or a bo."

Hook warmed himself at the boiler. "You boys couldn't tell a thief from a yard dog with his badge nailed to his forehead."

"It's like telling twins apart," Frenchy said, winking at the bakehead.

"Well, a man ought check before he starts kicking people off a moving train," Hook said.

"Didn't expect no yard dog in the middle of the desert," Frenchy said.

"My popcar broke down. Anyway, yard dogs show up where least expected and in surprising ways," he said. "That's why we're the law. Maybe you should keep that in mind.

"What you doing out here, Frenchy, other than kicking people off trains?"

"Called out to move these cars to the Johnson Canyon siding," he said.

"In the middle of the night?"

"Appears so."

"Why didn't they wait for a scheduled run?"

"I don't get paid for thinking, Hook."

"You can be thankful for that," Hook said.

Twenty minutes later, they'd barely made speed. As

they hit the grade, the steamer bore down, beating and thumping like a giant heart.

"Hell," Hook said. "I could walk faster than this old hog."

"Just have at it," Frenchy said, puffing on his cigar. "Them cars are heavy sons of bitches. Anyway, this ole bullgine ain't made for speed."

"Who would have thought," Hook said. "What does this tinga-ling weigh?"

"Half a million, more with a full tinder. These old calliopes can squash a penny flat as a fireman's head."

An hour later, as they approached Johnson Canyon, Frenchy lay in on the whistle. He pulled through the tunnel and over the trestle. He backed the boxcars onto the siding. Hook uncoupled and set the brakes.

"Frenchy," he said. "Mixer jumped out on me coming out from Ash Fork. Give me a minute to see if I can call him in."

Frenchy wallowed his cigar over and shook his head. "Dang it, Hook, my cab stank for days last time that critter climbed aboard."

"Was probably the fireman you smelled, Frenchy. Bakeheads been known to go all winter without touching water."

The fireman pushed his hat up and rubbed his face. Frenchy hit his whistle a couple times and waited as Hook called for Mixer. "I can't be waiting all night," Frenchy said. "They're shutting down the line until further notice."

Hook looked over his shoulder. "Shutting the line? What for?"

"Usually the big boys ask me before they make a decision, Hook. I guess this time they just forgot. Said

I was to come back soon as the line opened and haul those cars back to Kingman."

"They wouldn't close this line for a baby carriage stranded on a crossing, Frenchy."

"No, but they might for something important," he said, grinning. "Reckon that dog is going to have to get back best he can."

"His life is on your conscience, Frenchy."

Frenchy turned his head to the side and lit his cigar stub. He looked at Hook and nodded.

"Some things a man just has to live with," he said.

"Well, wake me when we get there, if I haven't died of old age yet."

"That's the one thing you ain't going to die from, Hook. I guarantee it."

Even though Hook's head throbbed, and the old engine pounded and groaned, he soon fell asleep. When Frenchy announced the wigwag crossing outside of town, Hook yawned and lit a cigarette. The lights of Ash Fork glowed in the distance. The boiler fire flickered in the cab. Hook moved to the door.

Frenchy eased the bullgine to a stop. Air shot from the brakes, and the smell of smoke settled in around them. Hook swung out on the ladder and worked his way down a few rungs. He looked up at Frenchy, who leaned out the cab window.

"Hold on a minute," Hook said.

He dropped off the ladder, retrieved the link from the Gunter's chain he'd taken from the surveyors' flatcar, and slipped it beneath the driver wheel of the bullgine. He waved Frenchy off. Frenchy rolled his eyes and pulled away.

When he'd gone, Hook searched for the link, finding

it half buried in the cinder. The engine had squashed the link away, leaving only the flattened end ring. He took the ring that he'd found beneath Sergeant Erikson's body that day and laid it on the track next to the flattened Gunter's ring. They were identical.

In the distance Frenchy's whistle wailed at the crossing east of town. Hook walked toward the caboose. He paused, lit a cigarette, and looked back toward Johnson Canyon Tunnel. Someone from that survey crew had been there the night Sergeant Erikson died, and he had a fair idea who. What he didn't know was why. And now they were closing the corridor. Short of a catastrophe, that just didn't happen.

THIRTY-FOUR

Hook pulled off his shoes and rubbed his feet. Times like this, he envied those soft-handed men with office jobs, though he doubted he would last long behind a desk.

He shuffled through the stack of books sitting next to the table, picking out a 1938 first edition of *The Yearling* by Rawlings. He'd perused it earlier and had a notion that someday it would be of value. But it needed a closer look.

Right now the sack called out to him. He crawled beneath the covers just as Scrap's crane roared into life. Exhausted, he put the pillow over his head and fell asleep despite the noise.

But at some point, he stirred, dreaming of missing dogs and of a baby carriage sitting on a crossing. When black smoke boiled onto the horizon, he ran to the rescue. His heart hammered in his chest, his ears rang, and just as he reached the carriage, the steamer roared onto the crossing. In that last dying moment, he looked into the carriage to see the lieutenant staring up at him.

He sat up and dropped his legs over the side of the bunk. Sweat trickled down his cheeks, and his heart thumped out of control. He rubbed his face to make certain he'd awakened. Rarely did he dream, and never something as vivid as this. He could sleep anywhere, in a boxcar, on the rods, or in a culvert under the tracks.

Perhaps the Cream of Kentucky had caught up with

him, or perhaps his subconscious had awakened him. The years had taught him not to ignore it, to pay attention, because it often spoke truth.

Maybe the lieutenant had more to do with all this than he'd admitted to himself. Maybe he'd failed to look hard enough because he didn't want to know.

He lit a cigarette and thought about the lieutenant's eyes staring up at him from out of the carriage. He rose and looked out the window at the main line. Darkness had fallen. He'd slept longer than he thought.

The note he found in her brief had said to deliver J.B. on the seventh at 0100 hours and to secure all points. The only J.B. he could think of was John Ballard, the name she'd scribbled on the hotel notepad. But this was the sixth, not the seventh. He squashed out his cigarette in the ashtray. 0100 hours, military time, would put it an hour after midnight, which would make it the seventh.

Who was this John Ballard, and why would the lieutenant deliver him anywhere? In the end, only she had the answers, and he delayed far too long in getting them.

Hook took his coat and walked through the darkness to Scrap's office, pausing at the copper cars long enough to check his watch. If he could wrangle transportation out of Scrap, he should have plenty of time to locate the lieutenant if she was in town.

When Hook walked in, Scrap was sitting behind his desk working on his books.

"It's late, Scrap. You counting your money?"

"What the hell happened to your head?" he asked, looking up.

Hook touched his temple. "Fell out of bed."

"If you'd drink buttermilk instead of blue john, that wouldn't happen, Hook."

"I didn't come for advice from a junk dealer on how to live my life."

"You can stop living it altogether far as I'm concerned."

"Look, I need to borrow your jeep. I only need it for a while. It's urgent."

Scrap took out his pipe, pulled the stem off, and blew through it.

"Well, I don't know," he said, putting it back together. "There's a little matter of gas. I got demands on my funds."

"Like what?"

"Like buying milk for the babies," he said.

"You don't have babies."

He filled his pipe. "That may be true, strictly speaking. But if I *was* to have babies, there'd be no milk, would there?"

"I'll put gas in the jeep."

He pulled the jeep keys from his pocket. "I guess I can make the sacrifice this once."

"What about the lights?"

"I ain't had time for fine-tuning no lights, Hook."

"Lord help me," Hook said, taking the keys.

WHEN HOOK PULLED onto the road, the power lines and the tops of the trees lit up like daylight, but the road ahead disappeared into the darkness.

When at last he made it to the motel, he took a look around the parking lot. A number of cars had pulled in, but no signs of the lieutenant.

He decided to check with the manager and found him

sitting behind the desk listening to the radio. He turned it down and looked at Hook through dusty glasses.

"We don't give out information on our customers," he said.

Hook showed him his badge. "Railroad security," he said.

"This ain't the railroad," he said.

"Track crews *used* to stay here," Hook said. "They're not likely to again."

"A female lieutenant, you say?"

"That's right. Drives a staff car."

"Yeah," he said. "She left not long ago."

"Did she say where she was going?"

"She didn't say nothing. Paid her bill and left."

"Thanks," Hook said.

"Pretty, though," he said.

"Right."

"Wasn't alone either. Had a man with her. Probably nothing to worry about, though. She paid for separate rooms."

HOOK SAT IN the jeep, rocking the steering wheel. He could think of only one other place she might be. He pulled off for the Johnson Canyon Tunnel.

The night had turned clear as ice, and his headlights shot off into space as he navigated the road next to the tracks. The moonlight raced along the rails, and the smell of juniper filled the night air.

A good distance from the tunnel, he coasted to a stop, far enough away so as not to be spotted. From there, he could see the lantern in the guardhouse window and the lieutenant's staff car parked at the bottom of the steps.

He moved in closer just as the door opened, and the lieutenant came out on the porch. A man followed her, and they talked for several moments. The man went back in the guardhouse, and she made her way down the steps.

Hook slipped in closer to the car and waited. When she opened the car door, he stepped out and clamped his hand over her mouth. She struggled, but he held tight, all the while pulling her back into the shadows.

When safely out of sight, he said, "Lieutenant, it's me, Hook." She squirmed under his hold, and her heart thumped against his wrist. "Take it easy. I'm not going to hurt you. We have to talk. I'm going to let you go now, but you must stay quiet."

The lieutenant nodded, and he released his hand. She turned and faced him.

"What are you doing here?"

"Looking for answers," he said.

"There's a lot you don't understand. Go now. I can't explain."

He took her arm. "I've been running in circles, Lieutenant, and each time the tracks lead back to you."

"Please, go. Time is short."

"Then you better get started, hadn't you?"

"What is it you want to know?" she asked.

"You've been lying to me. I want to know the truth."

The lieutenant looked up at the guardhouse. "There are things I can't discuss. Can't you just trust me on this?"

"I have an unexplained death on railroad property. I can't let that go. And I have enough information to turn things upside down around here if I have to."

She looked up at the guardhouse again and then back at him. "All right," she said. "You don't leave me much choice, do you?"

THIRTY-FIVE

"First, who is it you really work for?" Hook asked.

"I did work for Transportation like I told you, but a few months ago, they assigned me to OSS."

"OSS?"

"Office of Strategic Services. Army intelligence."

"Jesus, you're a spy?"

"No. It's kind of an operation."

He took her arm. "Lieutenant, I'm already in this up to my eyeballs. This railroad is my jurisdiction, and I can raise more different kinds of hell with an operation than you can imagine."

The lieutenant pushed her hair back from her eyes. "You could get me into real trouble."

"Exactly."

"A nuclear locomotive," she said.

Hook stepped back and looked at her. "What did you say?"

"A nuclear locomotive. The Naval Research Laboratory has developed a small reactor that's cooled by helium. It has been put in a locomotive. It's a steam-driven turbine and can generate up to six thousand horsepower. They believe it has the potential to run thirty thousand miles without refueling.

"If this thing works, the technology could then be adapted to all manner of transportation, even airplanes. Just think of it. The world will never be the same."

Hook said, "I know these folks are pretty smart, but even an old cinder dick like me knows better than to strap a bomb on wheels and roll it down the track."

The lieutenant said, "I'm in the army, Hook. It's my duty to carry out orders, and our future may well depend on us developing nuclear-powered transportation."

Hook walked over to the staff car then back. "They're going to do a test run, aren't they? That's why the line upgrade and why the corridor is closed?"

"A tow engine is deadheading the prototype from Kingman Army Airfield tonight and is due to be here at 0100 hours. There will be a passenger car attached for the technical crew. The nuclear engine will be coupled onto those loaded boxcars down there on the tunnel siding to get a traction analysis."

"Has Division been in the know all along?"

"Only that it's a military operation. They were eager enough to receive funds for the upgrade."

"I don't know much about this nuclear stuff," Hook said. "But anything that could slug a locomotive thirty thousand miles without taking a breath has to come with some risks."

The lieutenant turned her face into the moonlight. "That's why all the precautions. Contained, its power is immense and productive. Uncontained, as you know, it can blow up a continent."

"That's just crazy," Hook said. He ran his fingers through his hair. "I admit to not being the smartest guy around, but I've been riding the rails in one fashion or another for some time now. I have a fair idea how fast a gully washer can take out a bridge, how a hotfooter, half asleep or drunk, can straighten out a curve, how a cinder cruncher, thinking about quitting time, can

throw the wrong switch and send a freighter screaming up the wrong track.

"Given these things happen in spite of the railroad's
best efforts, how does it make sense to take the guts out
of an atomic bomb, put it inside a locomotive, and fire
it down the track? Knowing all the while that there's
no way of preventing bums, saboteurs, and local mo-
rons from throwing the switch or changing the signal.
Add that to the possibility of a leaky boiler, which happens with some regularity, and you're running the risk
of killing every breathing creature from here to Albuquerque. I don't get the odds."

The lieutenant said, "All I know is that nuclear
power is too important to be denied. The United States
knows it and so does the enemy. It's too late to pretend
it doesn't exist, so we can only hope to make it our own.
The process has to start somewhere. The potential is
simply too great to ignore."

"For Christ's sake, Lieutenant, this is something
Scrap West would dream up."

"There are concerns," she said. "That's why all the
secrecy involved in this project. We're not the only ones
in the game either. If we don't do it, someone else will.
Germany and Japan have been working on this for a
while, even Russia has been scrambling to harness nuclear power since the dropping of the bomb. We're further along, and they know it. There's nothing they'd like
better than to delay our progress."

Hook pulled his cigarettes out of his pocket and then
put them back.

"But why here? Why in this place?" he asked.

The lieutenant rubbed her arms against the chill.

"The line is remote, and it has the steepest grade in

the United States. If that engine can make this run with deadweight, it can go anywhere. After the test, the engine will be towed back to Kingman Army Airfield. By daylight, we should know the answers."

"And who is this John Ballard?"

"You know about him, too?"

"Your note in the hotel," he said.

"Careless of me," she said. "He's the nuclear physicist who designed the prototype, the brains behind the project. It has been his baby from the beginning. We brought him in from Schenectady for the test run, keeping him as low profile as possible. I've been charged with his security. Without Ballard, there would be no prototype, and he's up there in the guardhouse right now."

"And so you are the one who had me tailed?"

"After Sergeant Erikson's death, we couldn't take any chances with anyone involved. That included you. By the way, you nearly scared the life out of our agent in that alley."

"Did Sergeant Erikson know about this test?" he asked.

"The decision had been made to keep both him and Thibodeaux on as guards throughout the process. Even though they probably knew something was going on, they had already been cleared by security to guard the tunnel. Our plan was to reassign them and bring in our own people at the last minute. We figured the less attention we brought to this matter the better. Unfortunately, it hasn't worked out that way."

"You never thought that Erikson died from an accident, did you?"

"At first I thought just that. You were the one who convinced me that something else might be going on."

"And Thibodeaux?"

"He's being interrogated as we speak. A petty thief, we believe, but he's caused us plenty of worry. Although we thought his information was minimal, we couldn't be certain. I must say, you were helpful with Thibodeaux as well."

"I'm a helpful kind of guy," he said. "Especially when I don't know what the hell is going on."

"I can understand you being upset, but we had no choice. We had to keep as few people in the know as possible."

"And those two replacement guards?"

"Folsom is Navy Intelligence," she said. "Severe is regular military police."

"That would be *Captain* Folsom, I assume?"

"How did you know?"

"Found his insignia bars in the bottom of his brief-case," he said.

"Is there anything you've missed?"

"A nuclear locomotive," he said. "I missed that."

"I've got to get back. They'll be looking for me."

He took her arm. "Erikson had money under his bunk. It's likely he'd been recruited. A guard on the wrong side of this thing could do a lot of damage."

"We don't know anything for sure," she said. "Erikson's death may have been no more than the result of a love triangle as you suggested."

Hook checked his watch. Midnight. He could see the light in the window of the guardhouse and someone moving about.

Taking the rings from his pocket, he dropped them

into the lieutenant's hand. "I'm pretty sure Erikson was murdered by someone else," he said. "I found one of these under his body in the tunnel. The other one came from a surveyor's Gunter's chain. It's been run over by Frenchy's steam engine."

The lieutenant studied the rings. "I don't understand."

"They're identical. Both came from a surveyor's chain, and they were both run over by a train."

"But who?" she asked.

"My guess is Rudy Edgefield, a contract surveyor for the railroad. I think he chained Erikson to the track to make it look like an accident, leaving him there to die. Afterward, he came back and removed the chain."

The lieutenant handed the rings back to Hook. "And Erikson dropped his flashlight outside in the process?"

"Exactly. Look, I've found out that Edgeworth and Erikson are both from Kansas City. Quite a coincidence, isn't it? And someone who fits Edgeworth's description made contact with Erikson at his home there. To top it off, Edgeworth has been working under a false name. His real name as far as I can determine is Alex Gregor. He claims to be from Canada, but he's left a mighty small trail."

"You think he's a saboteur?"

"My guess is that money exchanged hands between him and Erikson, but the deal turned sour. Until this moment, I didn't have a motive for murder, not much beyond a couple of guys fighting over a girl. But I have one now, and it's a whopper."

"We made a mistake leaving you in the dark on this," she said.

"And now Edgeworth's disappeared," he said. "Gone without a trace."

The lieutenant covered her mouth with her hand. She walked to the staff car and looked out over the darkness of the canyon.

She said, "Then he could be out there somewhere. He could be out there waiting for us this very minute."

THIRTY-SIX

WHEN HOOK AND the lieutenant came in the guardhouse door, Folsom reached for his rifle. Severe circled to the side of the room. John Ballard, who had been working with pad and pencil, rose from the kitchen table. The fear in his eyes, magnified behind his thick glasses, could not be concealed. He wore dress slacks, loafers, and a short-sleeve shirt that exposed the loose flesh beneath his arms.

"It's okay," the lieutenant said. "Mr. Ballard, this is Hook Runyon, railroad security. He knows everything."

For the next few minutes, the lieutenant filled them in on what Hook had told her about Edgeworth. Folsom paced the room, and a trickle of sweat raced down from behind his ear.

"We've checked out every inch of this place a hundred times," he said. "There's no evidence of anyone having been snooping about or tampering with anything. This is no more than speculation."

Hook's eyes narrowed. "That canyon isn't so long as canyons go, but it's as rugged as they come, Captain. Edgeworth could be standing ten feet from you, and you'd never know it. You can't afford to dismiss anything as speculation, and time is running out. The consequences of a mistake are just too damn grave."

Ballard stood and removed his glasses, his eyes

shrinking to dots. He held the glasses against the light before wiping them clean on his shirttail.

"He's correct," he said. "There's no room for error. If that reactor should be derailed…" He turned to Folsom. "We're dealing with an unknown quantity here, and we would be smack in the middle of it if things should go awry."

Folsom's face hardened. "We should have turned this place into a fortress instead of trying to hide everything. I told them that."

The lieutenant said, "A saboteur could strike anywhere along the entire run. A moving train simply couldn't be protected every step of the way. The operation had to be covert. In any case, we don't have time to rehash operational decisions."

"Now it's neither covert *nor* secure," Folsom said.

"Any kind of sabotage would most likely be executed here," Hook said. "Both the tunnel and the trestle make the train vulnerable to attack; besides, why go to the trouble to recruit a tunnel guard if he's not to be used?"

Hook looked over at Folsom. "I'm assuming you have security plans in place?"

"I'll be guarding the tunnel. Corporal Severe is taking the trestle. Once the engine leaves the siding, onboard security takes over. We have two armed guards in the engine cabin, another in the passenger car. When the test is completed, I'll escort the lieutenant and Mr. Ballard back. Corporal Severe will return with the passenger car and test engine to Kingman Army Airfield."

"And who's left to guard the tunnel?"

"After tonight, the guard detail ends."

"Only seconds would be needed to set a charge off

that could cripple your test, not to mention shutting down our entire corridor."

Folsom's eyes bore down on Hook. "That's why we are here, sir."

Hook walked to the table. Pages of calculations were strewn about where Ballard had been working.

"The problem is that there's a midtunnel curve, a blind spot," Hook said. "What kind of communication is in place?"

"We've a communications blackout," Folsom said. "Nothing is secure."

Hook said, "There needs to be some sort of signal system in case there is trouble."

"What kind of signal system would you suggest?"

"The railroad keeps fusees available in high-risk places like this. There should be some around here somewhere."

"What's a fusee?" the lieutenant asked.

"A flare. It looks like a stick of dynamite, but it's made of nitrates and fuel. Once struck, the flare's red glow can be seen for miles at night. The railroad uses them for signaling and for keeping trains apart. These particular flares have a steel spike on the end for setting into ties. Most are timed for a ten-minute burn, and it's against railroad rules for a train to pass over one until it's spent."

"I wondered what those were," Severe said, pointing to a wooden box next to the door. "I saw some in there."

Hook opened it and found a bundle of flares. He took one to demonstrate. "Remove the outside cap, take out the striker, and scratch it across the igniter. She'll burn hot, so be careful.

"I suggest that Corporal Severe guard the west

entrance and Captain Folsom the east. If either of you spots trouble, ignite your fusee. With luck, it will alert everyone and bring the train to a stop.

"I'll take the trestle. I will be high enough for a good view of the canyon. The moon's full, and once the engine exits the tunnel, her glimmer should light things up pretty well."

"You expect us to be inside that tunnel when this thing comes through?" the captain asked.

"Sergeant Erikson already tried that," Hook said. "A flare might give us a little time, and as of now, it's the only way we can stop that engine."

"This whole thing is off plan. The general will have us all shot for breaching security," Folsom said.

"This happens to be *my* railroad, Captain, and I'm not letting anyone blow it up." Hook slipped a fusee into his coat pocket. "Once the engine gets through the tunnel, I'll make for the passenger car."

Captain Folsom clenched his jaw. "You can't board that train."

Hook checked the clip on his sidearm. "No one knows this run better than me, and it would be a big mistake to get in my way, Captain. This is one train ride I don't intend to miss."

"Hook," the lieutenant said.

He looked over at her. "Just keep your head down when you get on that car, Lieutenant. You're as safe there as anywhere. We don't have many men, but then neither do they."

"Be careful," she said.

HOOK WAITED UNTIL Folsom and Severe had assumed their positions before taking the trail to the bottom of the trestle. He checked his watch, twenty 'til one. He had enough time to make a pass from end to end before starting the climb.

Along the way, he searched for fresh tracks and broken branches, finding neither. At five minutes 'til, he hoisted up onto the first trestle span. By securing his hook onto an overhead timber, he could balance long enough to reach up with his good arm and climb up to the next. But the absence of touch in the prosthesis increased both the effort and the anxiety, and sweat soon ran into his eyes.

Halfway up, he paused. From there he could see the tunnel opening through the trestle and the depths of Johnson Canyon spreading out below him. At the bottom of crevices, the carcasses of wrecked boxcars reflected back the moonlight.

Hook figured that he wouldn't be able to do much more than strike a flare in the event of trouble, but another set of eyes couldn't hurt.

He felt it first, a tremble that passed through the rock and rails and gathered in the beams of the trestle. In practice, engineers lay in on the whistle before entering a tunnel, but tonight only the quivering timbers beneath him announced the arrival of Ballard's locomotive. Leaning out, he searched the area for any signs of movement or light.

Hook watched the tunnel mouth for the revealing red glow of a flare but saw nothing. The rumble of the engine grew in the canyon, riding in from the rock heart of the mountain. It gathered in the core of his body, and the trestle heaved and creaked in anticipation.

And when the engine rounded the tunnel curve, her glimmer lit the canyon into daylight. Hook looked into the crevices and rubble for any movement. But when the engine rolled onto the trestle above him, his concentration faltered, and he stared upward into the belly of the largest engine he'd ever seen.

Ballard's bullet-shaped prototype, big as a dirigible, with its glass-bubble cab and curved door, slid silently behind the tow engine. Her driver wheels, a dozen sets and a dozen feet high, screeched in alarm at the slightest deviation of the track.

Her converted tinder with leaded shield shut away the moonlight and dwarfed the darkened passenger car behind it. Now Hook understood why the timbers had been replaced with boilerplate. There couldn't have been an inch to spare between the engine and the tunnel walls.

The timbers groaned under the weight, and debris spilled down on Hook's head as the engine passed over the trestle.

Captain Folsom signaled from the tunnel with his flashlight and swept the area from side to side as he walked toward the trestle. Hook had been wrong about everything and was damn glad of it. Satisfied that things were under control, he started his descent, working his way through the timbers as fast as possible.

Dropping off, he sprinted back to the trail. In the distance, the tow engine drew down as she maneuvered Ballard's engine onto the siding.

Just as Hook started up the trail, he heard something coming from behind. He stopped, listened, and then moved into the shadows at the edge of the trail.

He pulled his sidearm and clicked off the safety. These were likely not copper thieves or hoboes but trained foreign agents, those who had vodka and yard dogs for breakfast.

He stilled his breath. Crickets chirped from out of the rocks, and down the canyon, coyotes gave chase to some misbegotten creature.

The sound came again, but this time closer, and the hair prickled on his neck. With luck, he might nail one of the bastards and distract them long enough for Ballard's engine to pull out.

Something rushed up the trail, fast and hot and without caution. Hook cocked his sidearm and brought it up just as a shadow leapt skyward, arching against the moonlight. It knocked him backward into the blackness. When he stopped rolling, he lay flat on his back, and Mixer stood on his chest with both front feet.

"Damn it, Mixer," Hook said. "You know how close you came to a bullet?"

Mixer circled him a couple of times, sniffing out possible transgressions, before bounding off into the darkness once more.

At the top of the trail, Hook met Folsom and Severe coming down track.

"Anything?" Hook asked, brushing off his knees.

"Clear," Folsom said. "You?"

"Nothing human," Hook said.

Severe said, "When that engine came in, I froze. I've never seen anything like it."

Hook could hear the tow engine coupling Ballard's engine into the cars on the siding.

"Got to run," he said. "There's a dog on the loose around here. Don't shoot him. I intend to do it myself later."

Hook swung up on the grab iron of the passenger car just as the tow engine took out the slack to uncouple. The report traveled the length of the cars and trailed away.

When he opened the door, a half-dozen officers sat in the dark looking up at him. The guard in the back of the car lifted his rifle. When he spotted Hook's arm, he lowered the rifle. The lieutenant and Ballard sat near the front. Hook slipped into the seat next to her. The car bumped again before settling back. The lieutenant turned to him, her brief clutched in her lap.

"Are we going to make it?" she asked.

"I'll feel better once we are on the move," he said.

"I've explained your presence to the guard."

"I gathered," he said.

The tow engine pulled out onto the main line. When it chugged past the window of the passenger car, Hook could see the engineer's elbow protruding from the cab window. Steam rose up and into the night.

Hook turned to Ballard. "What happens now?" he asked.

Ballard looked at him over the tops of his glasses. "Now for the run," he said. "Now for the test."

THIRTY-SEVEN

WHEN SOMEONE KNOCKED on the car door, the men all moved forward and into the modified tinder car. The lieutenant pulled a notebook from her briefcase before setting it at her feet. She handed the notepad to Ballard, who entered something and then laid it on his lap. A hum, like swarming bees, emanated from out of the tinder.

"What's going on?" Hook asked.

"They're bringing the reactor up," Ballard said. "The fuel rods will generate heat, which in turn produces steam."

Hook glanced out the window. "What steam?"

"The system is closed," he said. "Steam propels a turbine connected directly to the drive wheels. The water is then condensed and reused. The hammer blow of a piston-driven steam engine is eliminated, and much higher speeds can be obtained."

"And the problems?" Hook asked.

"No reverse," he said.

"Been there," Hook said.

"A smaller reverse turbine has been installed to fix that problem."

Ballard looked at his watch, picked up the notebook, and made another entry.

"There is one other thing," he said.

"Oh?"

"Meltdown. If the cooling system should fail, there'd be no controlling the reactor, and it would release radiation. The consequences would be catastrophic."

Hook glanced over at the lieutenant and then back at Ballard. "But you've solved this little issue, right?"

Ballard pushed his glasses up. "We've developed a helium cooling system," he said. "With that, we've been able to minimize the weight and size of the reactor. In effect, it's what made this engine possible."

"But it's safe, this helium system?"

The moonlight struck through the window and ignited Ballard's black eyes.

"The system performed perfectly," he said, pausing. "In the lab."

"And what about in the field?"

"That's what this run is all about, isn't it, Mr. Runyon? Now, if you'll excuse me, I must go forward."

Hook waited as Ballard entered the tinder car. The lieutenant clasped her arms about her.

Hook said, "You've known about this meltdown thing all the while?"

"My job was to get Ballard here and get him home. Beyond that, I don't know much more about the specifics than you. It's all immensely complicated."

The hum of the reactor from the tinder had grown low and resonant, a sound springing up from the earth's core, a sound alien to Hook's ears.

The car edged forward, the hum merging into a liquid acceleration. Gone were the thumping and grinding of gears, the hammer of pistons, the steam and smoke and pounding drivers. Gone were the sweat and toil of firemen and the stink of Frenchy's cigars.

The car continued to accelerate, its speed twisting in

Hook's stomach as a trillion flashes of light propelled them down track.

And when they hit the ascent, that grade defeating steamers and diesels alike, the velocity only increased, slamming them against their seats as they drove forward. Wind rushed outside the car, scrambling their thoughts.

When they hit the curve halfway up the ascent, wheels screeched, and the smell of iron and heat filled the car. The lieutenant clung to him, her fingers icy on his arm as they shot up the mountainside.

Hook leaned over and looked out for a full view of the cars as they rounded the bend. He stood, his pulse ticking up. The door of the end boxcar had opened. He could see the sacks of sand, some of them emptied and flapping in the wind. Surely they wouldn't have left the door ajar.

The thought that came to him next caused his skin to crawl. But for someone to exit out the side door of a moving boxcar at these speeds required skill and backbone. They'd have to climb out onto the door, cling to the bracing long enough to pull up onto the roof, all while the car bucked and bobbed down the track like a bronco. He'd done it himself on one occasion, but not at these speeds, and not so much from bravery as from fear, the car having been on fire at the time.

"I'll be back," he said.

The lieutenant grabbed his arm. "Where are you going?"

"There might be a problem," he said. "I'm going to go check."

"You can't go out there," she said. "It's too dangerous."

"Don't worry," he said. "This is *my* territory."

The guard stepped into the aisle to stop him, but the lieutenant waved him off. Hook opened the door and moved out onto the platform. The ties raced below in a blur, and the wind whipped around the sides of the boxcar. He stepped onto the knuckle coupler, which danced under his feet. Grabbing the brake rod, he pulled himself over.

Straddling the rod, he worked his way up by digging his toes into the siding grooves. He peeked over the edge of the roof before pulling up. The wind blasted into his face and set his eyes to watering. The cars pitched and rolled ahead as the power of Ballard's engine propelled them up the grade.

He could see no one on top of the cars. Perhaps the whole thing had been no more than an open door, his imagination running wild. It had been that kind of twenty-four hours. Or perhaps someone hid between the cars with sabotage in mind. Riding the rails had taught him plenty about rounding up hoboes, a hell of a lot less about foreign agents.

Either way, it was go or quit, and quit had never paid the bills.

HOOK INCHED ALONG on his stomach. The wind screamed in his ears and tugged at his body. The car lurched and rolled under him like a ship in a storm. By the time he made it to the last car, his legs trembled with exhaustion.

He hoisted up and crawled his way back. The only place for someone to hide would have been between the cars, and he'd cleared them all. Soon enough they'd be at the top of the grade. At this point, the run couldn't be over fast enough for him.

When he reached the end, he paused. His shirt flapped in the wind and stung his ears and face. The track raced away behind the car. He'd been wrong. The door must have not been secured and just slid open on its own. He took a final look over the end.

The blow came from below, from out of nowhere, and caught him square on the nose. Hook pitched back, his eyes watering, black spots swarming in the blue above him. The wind sucked him sideways, his feet swinging out into space.

At the last second, he caught his hook on a deck bolt and pulled back onto the roof. He lay on his back, blood dripping from his nose and into the pocket of his throat. A dull pain settled in under his jaw.

When he started to get up, a voice said, "Only room for one passenger up here, friend."

Hook could make out only bits and pieces of a face, like a puzzle. He shook his head. When the pieces slid together, he recognized the figure as the bo from the Yampai siding. His sidearm was pointed at Hook's head.

"You," Hook said.

"I should have finished you when I had the chance," he said. "No matter. I can do it now."

"You've been in that boxcar since Yampai?" Hook said. "You rode in on Frenchy's short haul?"

"So long, yard dog," he said.

Ballard's engine accelerated yet more, and the car lurched forward. The bo fell back on his haunches. His eyes widened as he teetered against the pitching of the car. His weapon dropped onto the roof and slid away.

Hook tried to clear his own sidearm, but by then the bo had recovered and threw a punch from the shoulder, catching Hook on the chin. Hook's teeth loosened in their sockets. The bo glared at Hook from under thick brows. The wind whipped his hair, and spittle gathered in the corners of his mouth.

When he came closer, Hook grabbed him around the middle and clinched him up close. The bo roared, not words, but a howl, like an animal in distress. Hook buried his head in the bo's chest, knowing that another blow might be his end. He smelled of onions and sweat, and his muscles quivered under Hook's hold. The boxcar swayed and rolled beneath them, and the clack of the wheels beat like an iron heart.

Hook brought his head up, catching the bo under the chin. The bo's neck cracked back, and his eyes rolled white. Hook took him again, a short blow to the throat, and he gurgled like a ruptured brake gut. Snorting and sucking for wind, he dropped onto the roof.

The wind swept him to the edge of the car, and for a moment, he hung there as if suspended by some invisible force. A sound issued from his throat, a primal shriek filled with hatred and fear, as he disappeared over the side.

THIRTY-EIGHT

ONCE BACK AT the tunnel, Ballard's engine eased onto the siding, and the whine of the reverse turbine trailed off. The engine decelerated and came to a stop. Hook's ears rang in the silence, and he dabbed at the perspiration on his forehead. The lieutenant sat still, her eyes locked on the door.

Hook searched for a cigarette as the first light of dawn broke on the horizon.

"It was a ride to remember," he said, turning to the lieutenant. "But there's something I don't understand."

She picked up her briefcase and set it on her lap. "What would that be?"

"I don't understand what that bo was up to."

She turned in her seat. "Sabotage," she said. "What else? Anyway, how do you know he was a hobo?"

"The way he put together a jungle for one thing, and the way he worked that car. It wasn't the first time for him, I can tell you that. In any case, there were no explosives, no way of destroying the train.

"It was one bo with a pistol against armed guards. Why send a hobo out to commit sabotage in the first place?" He paused. "Unless it was for a diversion."

The passenger car bumped back as the tow engine coupled in. Captain Folsom opened the door.

"Success," he said. "A perfect run."

Hook stood. "It's possible this thing isn't over,

Captain. I'm going out to make sure the trestle is safe.
Lieutenant, check with the guards, will you? In the
meantime, Captain, you might want to get Ballard out
of here."

Folsom nodded. "I'll take him to the guardhouse,"
he said. "Lieutenant, get up there as quickly as possible.
The sooner he's home safe, the better."

"Yes," she said. "The moment the engine has cleared."

WHILE THE LIEUTENANT alerted the guards, Hook walked
the trestle, checking the bracings for explosives. Afterward, they stood at the switch point and watched in
silence as the engine pulled onto the main line. And
when it had disappeared into the tunnel, they both took
a deep breath.

"Come on," Hook said. "I'll feel better when Ballard is on his way."

As they approached the guardhouse, they could see
Captain Folsom sitting in the old rocker that had been
placed on the porch by the guards. He sat facing the
door as if waiting for someone to come out.

Not a creature stirred in the morning hush, and the
smell of smoke still hung in the valley.

At the landing, Hook called up so as not to surprise
Folsom.

When he didn't move, something cold edged down
Hook's spine.

He turned to the lieutenant. "Wait," he said.

He looked back, checking the terrain to make certain no one came. The canyon trekked off into the desert behind him. Sunlight reflected from the tops of the
boxcars below, and the trestle, having only moments

before borne the immensity of Ballard's locomotive, stood like a fragile skeleton over the gorge.

"Something's wrong," he said, pulling his sidearm. "Keep low." At the top, he scanned the area. "Captain," he said.

Folsom didn't move. Reaching out, Hook touched his shoulder, and the chair turned on its base. A garrote made from phone line twisted into the soft flesh of the captain's neck. Blood pooled in his chin, a black mass, and his eyes, bulbous, ruptured orbs, stared into some other world. Saliva strung from his lips in silver threads, and his chest swelled in search of the breath that never came. His rifle lay at his feet.

The lieutenant stiffened and grasped Hook's arm. Hook put his finger to his lips and guided her to the guardhouse wall.

Pressed against the coolness of the rock, he took a moment to steady his hand and his mind before kicking open the door.

THIRTY-NINE

HE WENT IN low, alert to any movement. Light struck through the window, an oblong beam illuminating the far corner of the guardhouse. The table had been tipped over, papers scattered about. One of the bunks lay on its side.

The lieutenant stepped in behind him. "My God, what's happened?"

"They've taken Ballard," he said.

She glanced at the door. "And murdered Captain Folsom. But who?"

"Edgeworth," Hook said.

"We've got to find them," she said. "Ballard's critical to the operation. Without him, the whole program is compromised."

"We could get the law," he said.

She shook her head. "No. We have to keep this quiet." The lieutenant rubbed her temples. "But where would they go? How would they get out of here?"

"Maybe he's taken one of the vehicles," Hook said. "Made for parts unknown."

"I took the keys out of both cars," she said.

"Good thinking, and the jeep is parked a fair distance away. Edgeworth has no idea it's even there. That means they're afoot, probably in the canyon, and they can't be that far ahead."

When they stepped out onto the porch, a breeze

swept through. Folsom's chair creaked, and his head bobbed as if in agreement with their assessment.

"Edgeworth outsmarted us all," Hook said. "My guess is he suckered the bo onto the train to use him as a diversion. It didn't matter to Edgeworth if the bo succeeded or failed because all along he planned to grab Ballard after the test run, after our guard was down. And he's had plenty of time to prepare for his escape. He likely has a cache of supplies waiting somewhere out there in the canyon, enough to get him through."

"But with Ballard along? Even if they managed to get through the desert, how would he ever get him out of the country?" the lieutenant asked.

Hook lit a cigarette. "Maybe he has no intentions of trying. He'll get whatever information he can from Ballard and then kill him." He drew on his cigarette, dropped it on the ground, and squashed it out with his foot. "I'm going after them," he said.

"Then I'm going with you," she said.

"I don't think that's a good idea."

She clenched her jaw. "Ballard's safety is my responsibility."

He pointed to her shoes. "Wearing those? Hardly made for that canyon."

The lieutenant looked down at her shoes and then lifted her chin. "I'll manage," she said.

At the bottom of the trail, Hook waited for the lieutenant to climb down.

"So which way?" she asked.

Hook looked up and down the canyon, but before he could answer, Mixer bound from out of the rocks, dirt stacked on the end of his nose. He put both feet up on Hook's chest and licked him on the cheek.

"All right, Mixer," Hook said. "Let's go find a skunk."

Mixer marked the trail and then struck off up canyon. Now and again he'd stop, his tongue lolling, and look back at them. They struggled to keep up as Mixer bounded through the jumble of rocks, sometimes disappearing, only to reappear farther up the way.

When he reported with a sharp bark, Hook said, "He's hit a trail."

Within the hour, the sun broke over the canyon rim, and the temperature mounted. Hook tied his jacket around his waist. Soon, the air fell still, and the heat rose in ribbons from out of the rocks. Sweat ran into his eyes and dripped off the end of his nose.

The lieutenant's hair clung to her neck in wet curls. In despite of her shoes, she followed close behind and without complaint. They had no water or food. And in a place like Johnson Canyon, those things could make the difference between life and death.

They stopped to check for tracks. The lieutenant's hands trembled, and she hid them under her arms. He lit a cigarette.

"We could stop for a rest," he said.

"No," she said. "All's lost if Edgeworth gets away."

The sun bore down, and the rocks scalded their feet and hands. Each time their confidence waned, Mixer would fire up somewhere in the distance, assuring them that what they sought lay just beyond.

Without the horizon, Hook's sense of direction faltered, and he lost his feel for distance in the monotony of the canyon. On top of that, the rocks rendered his prosthesis useless, and fatigue twisted deep into his back.

When they rounded a bend, Mixer had stopped at a

small spring that gathered at the base of a rock over-hang. The earth smelled damp, and moss thrived from the cracks and crannies around the spring. An old juniper twisted from the rocks.

The lieutenant bent to drink from the spring. Scratches marked her arms, and her socks sagged with burrs and dirt. She dabbed the water from her chin with the back of her hand.

Mixer nosed here and there. Suddenly, he barked, his tail wagging.

"What is it, boy?" Hook asked.

The lieutenant moved over to where the water trickled into the sand. "Look, over here," she said.

A footprint had been left in the soft earth and, next to it, a heel print from a smaller shoe.

"Two of them," Hook said. "We're headed in the right direction."

Mixer took off and within moments yelped somewhere up canyon.

The lieutenant ran her fingers through her hair to straighten out the tangles.

"We better get moving," she said. "Before that dog makes the Canadian border."

When Hook came around a sharp turn, he pulled up. The canyon wall, having given way at the top, had slid to the bottom of the canyon and clogged the passage with tons of rubble.

The lieutenant shaded her eyes and looked at the slide. "Now what do we do?" she asked.

"That's been there a long time by the looks of it," he said.

She searched out a place to sit. Taking off her shoe, she pulled her sock away to reveal a blister on her heel.

"We'll stop awhile," Hook said.

She slipped her shoe back on. "It's nothing," she said. "I'm ready to go."

Hook scanned the mass of rock that blocked the passage. Over the years, crevices and cracks had opened up, some several feet wide.

"The thing is, there's some pretty tough climbing up there."

The lieutenant worked her cuff down and stood. "I know how to climb," she said.

He rubbed at his shoulder. "It's not you I'm concerned about." Hook walked down the canyon a distance. He lit a cigarette and considered the path they'd have to take. Even if he managed the climb, there were no guarantees that it would pay off.

At best, it would be a scramble for them to catch up with Edgeworth. But the rocks provided a perfect place for a cache, and he figured that was where Edgeworth had headed.

Mixer barked again, a hot yelp from somewhere above. Hook returned to where the lieutenant stood, her hands on her hips.

"Well?" she said.

"Okay. We go up, but you might regret this."

THE SUN BORE down on their backs as they climbed their way up the slide. Their lips cracked with the heat, and their throats turned to dust. Again and again the lieutenant dug her heels in, reached out, and pulled him over. Her jaw set, she bore ahead, her fatigue masked with determination.

Sweat stung Hook's eyes as he struggled to keep up. Even with the lieutenant's help, his lack of grip and balance soon caused fatigue to gather in his core like a hot iron.

A rock shelf, large and flat enough for a rest, presented itself. Hook dropped down and leaned back. He rubbed at the tension in his shoulder. The rocks around them had cracked into fissures, the result of frigid nights and torrid days.

A lizard sunned in the boulders above and watched with shuttered eyes. Locusts hummed from the canyon below, and buzzards circled like kites in the sky. Even Mixer had grown quiet as the temperature soared.

The lieutenant removed her shoe and rolled her sock down. The blister had broken and refilled with blood.

"You okay?" he asked.

She pulled her sock up. "I haven't heard Mixer for a long time now," she said.

Hook stretched out in the shade. "He's not big on overtime. Comes from hanging out with railroaders."

He looked up to see the lieutenant's face paled. And when a dry rattle issued from out of the crevice behind him, he froze. A snake, fat as a man's wrist, its jaw unhinged and its fangs cocked, fixed its black eyes on him. Sunlight lit the pink of its mouth and the yellow of its engorged venom sacks. Adrenaline dumped into Hook's veins, and his ears rang like engine bells.

He lurched to the side just as the snake struck, its length propelling from out of its den with the force and speed of an arrow. The fangs sank into his arm.

He rolled away, tearing at the snake's writhing body, flinging it into the rocks. His heart shriveled in anticipation of the poison rushing toward it.

"Oh, my God!" the lieutenant screamed.

Hook fell back and looked skyward. Soon his body would swell, and his lungs would fill with body fluids. He'd die a slow and suffocating death.

The lieutenant, her hands trembling, searched for the wound. She sat back on her haunches.

"This one?" she asked.

"Yes," he said. "It's gone dead as a post."

"For heaven's sake, that's your prosthesis."

Hook sat up and looked at his arm. "I knew that," he said.

For the next hour, they clambered over the rockslide. The lieutenant's foot worsened, her limp more pronounced as they worked their way along. When the sun had lowered and the shadows had lengthened, Hook stopped.

"Let me take a look at that foot," he said.

"It's all right."

"If you don't mind."

She crossed her leg over her knee and slipped off her shoe. The blister had eroded deep into her heel.

"It isn't good, Lieutenant, and it will be dark soon."

She rubbed her foot. "Why would Edgeworth come up here in the first place?"

"Only one reason," he said. "A supply cache."

"We couldn't follow him into the desert without our own supplies?"

"No," he said.

He stood and studied the canyon face. At first he

thought it was Mixer waiting for them to come, but when he looked again, he could see the top of a man's head.

He slid down next to her. "I think there's someone up there."

"Edgeworth?"

"I need a closer look."

They crept up to higher ground. Hook eased his head up and then dropped down next to her again.

"It's a man all right," he said. "I'm going in."

"Be careful," she said. "He might have heard Mixer. He could be waiting."

Hook pulled his P.38 and worked his way in closer. He stood and leveled the sidearm.

"Lift 'em," he said. The man neither moved nor acknowledged Hook's command. "You've about two seconds before I empty this clip, mister," he said.

He circled to the side. John Ballard sat on the ground, his legs stretched out in front of him. A forked stick had been jammed under his chin and staked into the ground between his legs to hold him erect. His hands were secured to his ankles with strips from his shirt, and his torso had been wrenched forward until the forks penetrated the glands under his ears. His tongue, having been bitten through, bled down his front.

A garrote made from a belt still hung about his neck, and his eyes were now sunken and indifferent. Hook's stomach tightened. He spat in the dirt and then untied him. John Ballard, still warm in death, slumped over onto the ground.

"Oh, no," the lieutenant said from behind him. "Edgeworth's killed him. He's killed Ballard."

Hook turned. "Yes," he said. "And not the easy way.

Like you said, he knew we were coming, and he didn't want us to hear a gunshot."

She knelt, touching Ballard's shoulder. "He's been tortured," she said.

"Edgeworth knows his business," Hook said. "Whatever he wanted from Ballard, he probably got."

Hook dug out a cigarette, lit it, and threw the empty pack away. "He left in a hurry," he said. "I think we're close. If we push ahead, we might just catch him."

She leaned back. Dirt covered her uniform and her hands. She pulled back the hair that had fallen across her face.

"You better go on without me."

"What?"

"My foot," she said. "I'm slowing you down."

"Come on, you can make it. I'll help."

"I'll be okay here. You can come back for me."

"But I can't leave you alone."

"All I know is that we must not let Edgeworth get away. There's too much at stake, and I can't keep up any longer."

Hook chewed at his lip. "I don't think so. He could circle back. He might even be watching us at this minute."

"This is not your decision," she said. "Edgeworth has one thing on his mind right now, escape, and he might have gotten information from Ballard that could cost us dearly."

He handed her the sidearm. "Then you take this. Use it if you have to."

"Edgeworth is armed," she said. "You might need it; besides, you know what kind of shot I am."

"It's this way," Hook said. "You keep the weapon or I don't go."

She looked at him, weariness in her eyes. "Okay," she said, taking the gun. "Now get out of here before it's too late."

FORTY

HOOK STRUGGLED ON, but without the lieutenant's help, the going turned slow. Mixer fell silent as the moon lifted into the sky.

At first Hook thought it only a moon shadow in the rocks. He crouched and waited as the moonlight edged into what appeared to be the opening of a small cave.

He approached with caution. Edgeworth could be anywhere. When satisfied that the cave was empty, he moved in. Containers of water, crackers, and packets of jerky had been stacked next to the wall. A rolled sleeping bag lay near the entrance.

It had to be Edgeworth's cache, and he had abandoned it all in his rush to escape them. Without supplies, no sane man would attempt to make it through the desert. Edgeworth was ruthless but not stupid. He knew that his only hope for escape now would be to double back.

Hook checked his watch. By taking the high ground, he could bypass the slide and make up some time. With a little luck, he just might get there before the next train came through.

HOOK PAUSED AT the trestle to catch his breath. In the moonlight, it looked like a giant centipede stretching across the canyon. On the far side, the boxcars waited to be towed back to Kingman. On the nearside, the tunnel entrance opened into the mountain as a black hole.

As he worked his way toward the tunnel, he considered his strategy. He'd check the guardhouse first. Then he'd cross over the trestle and clear the boxcars. They presented a damn good hiding place for Edgeworth to wait for the next train.

The clean smell of the desert night rolled in. He crouched in the darkness and checked for any signs of movement. Turning his ear into the night, he gauged the sounds. Somewhere in the distance, a screech owl hooted.

He paused at the tunnel entrance, where a cool draft swept out from the mountain. From this vantage, he could see the guardhouse and Folsom's outline in the rocking chair on the porch. The guardhouse windows lit in the moonlight, shining like the eyes of a giant cat.

Suddenly, a flashlight clicked on from the darkness of the tunnel. Hook turned and stared into its glare.

"Been expecting you," a voice said from behind the light.

"Edgeworth," Hook said. "Or should I say Alex Gregor?"

"The name Edgeworth has served me well enough," he said.

He stepped forward with his weapon pulled. "I'll have that gun of yours, Runyon. Butt first."

"I'm unarmed," Hook said, showing him the empty holster.

"The car keys," he said.

"The army has a thing about giving civilians the keys to their vehicles. You might try Captain Folsom."

"He didn't have them. Unfortunate, because in this business you need a reason to keep on living."

"And what business would that be, spying for the Ruskies?"

Edgeworth smiled. "It might surprise you to know that the Russians already have their nuclear engine, except for one small detail."

"The cooling system," Hook said.

"Without that, all else fails," he said.

"So that's the information you extracted from Ballard?"

"What's a secret or two shared between allies?" Edgeworth said. "A few minutes more, and I'd been on my way. There's a contact with a departure plan all set to get me out of the country. You have caused me considerable trouble, Runyon."

"You killed Erikson and set that bo up?" Hook said.

"Erikson made his contribution, though his information was limited. And then he turned greedy."

"And the bo?"

"Caught him stealing supplies from the cook car. Offered him a deal to stay out of jail and some spending money on the side. All he had to do was catch a train and stir up a little trouble."

"Sabotage had never been the plan," Hook said. "You needed Ballard. You needed the cooling system."

"You're smart for a yard dog, Runyon," he said, cocking his sidearm.

Mixer barked from the canyon trailhead, and Edgeworth whirled about. Hook ducked into the darkness of the tunnel, moving into its depths as fast as he dared. His only hope was to make the exit before Edgeworth could reach him.

He'd gone only a few yards when the first volley whizzed by his ear. Heat rushed through his veins. He scrambled back, the blackness enveloping him.

The second shot rang out, slamming into the rock face and spraying chips into his neck. He spun about. Pain from the cuts seared its way into his stomach. He dropped into the cinder bed and lay still.

But then came Edgeworth's footsteps running through the tunnel, his flashlight swinging to and fro.

Hook struggled to his feet and edged farther back into the darkness. He could see Edgeworth's light getting closer and closer, bobbing in the darkness behind him. Now and again the light would pause and pan the area.

Hook stumbled on in the darkness, but Edgeworth continued to gain on him. Hook could hear his breathing and the crunch of his footsteps in the cinders. He had nearly reached the curve when Edgeworth's light picked him up.

Hook leapt forward and scrambled just beyond the curve. Something sharp gouged into his side, and he remembered the spiked fusee flare still in the pocket of his coat. He worked to free the flare, but Edgeworth's light found him yet again.

"There now," Edgeworth said.

Hook stared into the muzzle of Edgeworth's sidearm and clenched his jaw against what awaited. But when the shot rang out, it came not from Edgeworth's gun but from somewhere behind Edgeworth. The bullet ricocheted through the tunnel like an angry wasp. Edgeworth cursed and dropped his light, plunging the tunnel into darkness.

Hook dug the flare from his pocket. He could hear Edgeworth's breathing as he searched for his light.

Hook struggled to hold the flare with his prosthesis in order to twist the cap off with his good hand. Sweat ran into his eyes, and the flare slipped from his grip. He swept the ground, searching for it, his heart pounding in his ears.

Finding it only inches from his feet, he clenched the flare between his calf and thigh, bore down with all his weight, twisted off the cap, and ignited the flare. The tunnel exploded in a shower of sparks. Edgeworth fired into the light, but the bullet whined away.

Hook drove forward and plunged the flare spike deep into Edgeworth's chest. Edgeworth clutched it with both hands, his face illuminated in the crimson glow. Air whistled from his lung. He looked up at Hook, sighed, and fell back as the flare sputtered and hissed in a fiery tribute to his end.

Hook knelt and picked up Edgeworth's weapon. "We all run out of reasons to live sooner or later," he said.

The lieutenant stepped from the darkness, her P.38 in her hand. Mixer stood at her side. The red glow of the flare danced in her hair and in her eyes.

"Later is better," she said.

Hook stood. "But I thought…"

"I decided to push on," she said. "I found the cache and figured you had come back. Mixer was waiting at the tunnel entrance. Sorry about being such a lousy marksman."

"Lieutenant," he said, "as far as I'm concerned, there's no better shot alive."

FORTY-ONE

Hook sat back in Scrap's chair and dialed Eddie Preston.

"Division," Eddie said.

"Hook here. Why didn't you tell me the line was to be shut down, Eddie?"

"It was a military thing, Runyon. Even I don't know the details."

"I'm security, for Christ's sake. I should have been told. I could have been killed."

"Right," he said. "Look, I'm transferring you to Albuquerque. Frenchy will be picking up the caboose."

"What for?"

"Call me when you get there."

"That old popcar is sitting on Yampai siding. You need to send someone."

"What's the matter with it?"

"Out of fuel," Hook said.

"There's a work train coming through. Catch it out. Next time, remember to gas up before driving out on the main line."

"Thanks for the help, Eddie."

"And, just so you know, the board's decided you had no business giving away railroad property without permission. It will be coming out of your paycheck."

"What the hell was I supposed to do, Eddie?"

"And that yodel out of Ash Fork dropped his assault case against you."

"Hoffer?"

"He couldn't get his lawyer paid. Just be thankful you didn't get another Brownie out of this, Runyon. Hadn't been for me, you'd be sleeping under a bridge."

WITH GAS CAN in hand, Hook swung off the work train at Yampai siding. He waved it off and walked over to the popcar. The desert morning crackled with sunshine, and the smell of creosote rose up from the steeping ties. The cuts on his neck tightened when he lifted the gas can, and the sounds of Edgeworth running into that tunnel came rushing back to him.

He set the cap and cranked over the engine. Blue smoke drifted off as she choked down. He cranked again, and she struggled back to life.

After pushing the car out onto the main line, he secured the switch and climbed aboard. He'd checked for clearance and had plenty of time before the *Super Chief* came through on its run west.

Mixer had taken off yet again that night, and Hook hoped to call him in at the trestle. Leaning back, he watched the scenery slide by. Riding a popcar into the desert came as close to freedom as a man could expect in this life.

When the tunnel opened up in front of him, he idled back. The clack of his wheels resounded in the darkness as he moved into the mountain. As he rounded the mid-tunnel curve, his scalp crawled. In that place, he'd come as close to death as he cared to remember.

The sun fell warm on his face as he emerged from the tunnel and brought the popcar to a stop just short of the trestle. From there he could see a staff car parked at the bottom of the guardhouse steps.

Lieutenant Capron came to the door. Her copper hair lit in the sunlight, and her smile broadened when she recognized him.

"Hook," she said. "Come in. I'm in the process of closing out the guardhouse."

Hook stepped in past the lieutenant, her perfume lingering after him.

"Thought it might be you," he said.

"I'm sorry I didn't get to talk that night," she said. "There were calls and things that had to be done, as you can imagine."

Hook sat down at the table. "What happens now?" he asked. "I'm being transferred to Command," she said.

"So, it's the army for you, is it?"

She shrugged. "It fits me, you know, and things will be changing, for women I mean. I'd like to be part of that."

Hook ran his hand through his hair. "How's the foot?"

"Oh," she said, turning her ankle. "Better."

"About Ballard's engine?"

"The program has been suspended," she said.

"Because of the risks?"

"No. Something about the weight and tractive-force ratio not working. I don't really understand."

"And what about Edgeworth, Ballard, Captain Folsom?" Allison walked to the window and looked down on the canyon.

"Captain Folsom died in the line of duty like so many others have. Ballard, according to the coroner, suffered heart failure back in Schenectady. And, as you know, Edgeworth is just a name stolen from a dead man."

Hook rose from the table. He studied the lieutenant against the morning light. "And the bo?" he asked.

"He couldn't be identified," she said. "Then none of this ever happened?"

She turned. "No. It never happened. And what about you? Where do you go from here?"

Hook lit a cigarette. "I've a dog to chase down and then Eddie has something doing in Albuquerque."

She came across the room. "Maybe someday I'll take you up on one of those book hunts."

"I know just the place," he said.

Hook sounded off his best whistle, and it wasn't long before Mixer came bounding out of the canyon.

"I ought to make you walk," Hook said.

Mixer wagged his tail, piled onto the popcar, and flopped down for the ride.

Hook cranked up and moved out onto the trestle. He looked back to see the lieutenant standing on the guardhouse porch watching him.

He throttled up for the run home. There were lots of things in his life he would like to pretend never happened. This wasn't one.

* * * * *